FINDING
Focus

JIFFY KATE

Finding Focus

ISBN: 978-0-692-57369-3

This book is a work of fiction. Names, characters, places, and incidents either are products of the author's imagination or are used fictitiously. Any resemblance to actual persons, living or dead, events, or locales is entirely coincidental.

Editor:
Indie Solutions
www.murphyrae.net

Cover Designer:
Jada D'Lee Designs
www.jadadleedesigns.com

Interior Design and Formatting:
Christine Borgford, Perfectly Publishable
www.perfectlypublishable.com

CHAPTER *One*

Sheridan

"WHAT DO YOU MEAN YOU'RE leaving?"

"Dani, it's no big deal. I'm just taking a little vacation—a little *me* time."

"But it *is* a big deal," I tell him, squaring my shoulders. Graham, my boyfriend of four years, is leaving the country without me—for a *week*—and he doesn't see the significance of this decision. "It's not like this is a spur-of-the-moment decision to have a vacation without me. It's obviously something you've been planning."

He can say whatever he wants, but we both know what this is: a vacation *from me*.

"You're overreacting," he groans, rubbing his face with his hands and letting out a frustrated sigh. Did he think I'd be okay with this?

I bite my lip to keep from saying something I'll regret. This has the potential to be one of the biggest fights in the history of our relationship, but I don't want him leaving the country with our last words spoken in anger. So, I ignore the overreacting statement. "Are you going alone?" I finally ask, changing the subject.

"What kind of question is that?" he asks.

"A legitimate one." I hate having to ask, but why else would he be running off like this? He's either traveling *with* someone or planning on hooking up once he's there. I've never had any reason to accuse him of cheating before, but what am I supposed to think? I mean, our relationship isn't perfect—who's is?—but I can't seem to wrap my brain around his urgent need to leave like this.

Well, that's not entirely true.

If I'm being completely honest, I can admit I've had thoughts of escaping, too. Escaping the city, my job, and yes, even the dull relationship I have with Graham. The difference is I'd never actually *do* it. I certainly have my selfish desires, but I'd never fully be able to enjoy myself. I'm supposed to *want* to be with him, and he's supposed to *want* to be with me.

"Don't be stupid, Dani," he says after staring at the floor for what feels like forever. The way he can't make eye contact with me makes my suspicions grow. When he finally looks up and grabs his suit jacket from the back of the couch, there's nothing but annoyance. No remorse or sadness or second-thought. I'm more than certain he won't even miss me. And it hurts.

"I'll see you in a week," he says, shutting the door behind him. And just like that he's gone. No *I love yous*. No *take care of yourself*. Nothing.

What an asshole.

I can't believe I wasted my time faking an orgasm with him last night.

I dump my soggy, uneaten cereal into the kitchen sink before shuffling down the hall and unceremoniously plopping onto my bed. Letting out a frustrated groan, I throw my arm over my face to block out the sun and the world, allowing my soft down comforter to wrap around my body like a fluffy cocoon—a safe place—where negativity and shitty boyfriends can't get to me. A place where only good thoughts and happy memories flow. While my mind drifts to blue skies and warm sunny days of a life I hardly remember, I begin to fall asleep.

Moments, or possibly hours, later, the sound of a rapper declaring his love of huge asses stirs me awake. I blink my bleary eyes, trying to gain my bearings before I realize what's happening.

Piper.

My arms flail wildly as I untangle my body from my comforter, just barely reaching my cell before the call goes to my voicemail.

"Hey, Pipe."

"Sheridan Reed, are you still in bed?" she asks, letting out an over-exaggerated breath. "I've about had enough of your little pity party. Don't make me fly all the way up there to kick your ass!"

Piper Grey has been my best friend since the first day of our freshmen year in college. She's spunky, artsy-fartsy, and has a tendency to take on a mothering role with me, hence her full-naming and threatening me all in one breath. I know she means well, and because I haven't been mothered in a really long time, it's nice to feel cared for.

"It's not just the job thing," I sigh, suddenly trying to keep tears at bay. "Graham is going on vacation . . . without me," I whine. "A vacation I could really use, but he didn't ask me to go, and it feels shady. I mean, who goes on vacation alone?"

"Whoa. That's a douche-move—even for him. Are you okay?"

"Yeah, I guess." I let out a deep breath and try to decide what I am. Mad? A little. Hurt? A lot. "I think I'm more shocked than anything. I mean, it takes huge balls to do that, right?"

Piper guffaws into the phone. "You know better than anyone how not-huge his balls really are, so whose balls did he steal? That's the real question here!" Her snort-laugh in my ear works its magic, and I'm laughing so hard, I can barely catch my breath. It's no secret my best friend doesn't think very highly of my boyfriend. They tolerate each other. And while I should probably defend Graham and his balls, I just need my best friend's comedic relief.

I sit up in bed and wipe my eyes, letting out a deep sigh. "Thanks, Pipe. I needed that."

"Don't thank me yet. I'm not done with you." I can hear the smile in her voice.

"What are you talking about?" I ask, a mixture of apprehension and curiosity bubbling up inside me.

"I'm talking about the fact that I just got your recently-fired ass a job with *Southern Style*. As of tomorrow, you'll be freelancing for me in the great state of Louisiana for a whole week. Think of it as your very own solo vacation. I mean, it'll be work, but at least it'll get you out of the city for a few days."

Being out of the city and away from reality sounds perfect, but her mentioning me being fired causes doubt to creep into my mind. What if I can't do this? What if she's putting too much trust in me? I start thinking of all the reasons I should say no:

I've never worked on my own before.

Did I mention I've never worked on my own before?

And last, but not least, I'm scared shitless.

"Piper, I appreciate the offer, but I can't just pack up and leave the city."

"The hell you can't. What else do you have going on? You were just fired from your job, and your boyfriend is leaving the country. Sounds like this is perfect timing and exactly what you need. Plus, you'll get to see me!"

She's right. Of course, she's right.

"So, tell me about this assignment," I sigh into the phone, already mentally packing.

The shrill sound of Piper celebrating my acceptance pushes me out of bed to pack for real.

Aside from the normal clothes and toiletries, I throw in some sunscreen, bug spray, my laptop, camera, and my two trusty notebooks. One of the notebooks has a plethora of information I've been collecting since college: helpful tips and tricks, shortcuts for my camera, and notes from every job I've done since I finished school. The other notebook is probably my most-valued possession. It has all of my granny's recipes in it and the beginnings of something I started a long time ago . . . something that's been calling to me lately. I decide to bring it along, just in case inspiration strikes.

CHAPTER Two

Sheridan

ONCE I BOARD THE PLANE, I relax back into my seat and settle in for the flight. Surprisingly, it's peaceful—almost too quiet. There's not one baby crying or one coughing passenger. So, I lean back, pull out my book, and try to enjoy the flight, but that only lasts so long. I shut my book after staring at the same page for twenty minutes. Everything seems to be cascading down all at once, and my mind won't shut up. Thoughts about losing my job, Graham, the way he dismisses me so easily, the way it all makes me feel, crowd in, tearing away any excitement for this trip I was feeling.

My thoughts inevitably drift back to last week when my boss called me into his office. Just thinking of it makes the disappointment fresh. I can't say I've never failed at anything, but I sure as hell have never been fired. I felt like I had let everyone down, including Graham.

Was I devastated? Yes. Surprised? Not really.

I'd lost my creative mojo, my muse . . . my desire to do just about anything, months ago. I guess I should've been surprised I wasn't fired sooner. Everything I'd put out lately had been shit. I knew it. My boss knew it. Graham certainly knew it—he wouldn't let me forget it. He's always so worried my performance will reflect on him. Heaven forbid his pristine reputation be tarnished.

Graham has always held himself at a higher standard than everyone else. He was born into this industry. With his dad being a well-known newspaper editor in New York, he really has nothing to fear. His name alone could get him a job practically anywhere. There was a time when Graham's work ethic appealed to me. He's always been so take-charge. In the past, that quality made me feel safe, but in the last year or so, his motivated attitude morphed into controlling and pretentious.

I bet he didn't even fight for me. He'd said it was out of his control, but I've heard him use that excuse before when someone was fired or an account he wasn't in favor of was dropped. It's his politically correct way of saying he couldn't care less.

It's not like I wasn't trying; I was trying harder than I ever had in my entire life. I knew my job was at stake and unlike Graham and most of my friends, I don't have anyone to fall back on—no family to catch me if I fall face first. But taking pictures of the local social scene in New York just wasn't doing it for me anymore. It seemed like the harder I tried, the worse I did. And more than that, there was no challenge. It was too easy. Add in the disappointment in my relationship with Graham and the fact that my best friend moved to Birmingham, Alabama almost four months ago, and you have my very own recipe for disaster.

Damn, can you have a mid-life crisis at twenty-five?

I've always been one to keep my shit together. Ambitious to the core, I went above and beyond to ensure my work was done to the best of my ability, my friends were happy, and my boyfriend was taken care of. Somewhere along the way, though, I started losing my footing, and now that everything seems to be crumbling, I'm not sure how to get it back. It's like my compass is broken and I can't seem to find direction.

Once Piper left, I didn't have her there to distract me from how bored I was with my job or the fact that I'm not in love with Graham anymore. Actually, this might be the first time I've even admitted that to myself. I don't know when it happened, and I don't know how to feel about it, but my heart hurts. Maybe for what once was, or maybe be-cause I've been defined by his presence for so long, I'm not sure who I am without him. Whatever the reason, it hurts.

Thirty-thousand feet in the air and halfway to Baton Rouge, I begin to wonder how the hell I'm going to pull this off. This could be the most epic of my failures yet. Disappointing Piper would be the straw that breaks this camel's back. But the fact that she has enough trust and faith in me to offer me this job in the first place helps a little with my lack of confidence. I mean, if she's willing to put her neck on the line for me, I'm willing to put forth the hard work and effort to show her how much I appreciate this fresh start. Besides, what have I got to lose?

A week taking pictures of the Landry Plantation, along with the family who owns it, and the small community surrounding it, sounds amazing. Add in the opportunity to eat some delicious Cajun food, hang out with Piper, and refuel my desire to be a photojournalist, and you have a happy Dani Reed.

Thinking of being in the south, getting out of the city, is enough to put me in a better mood. I've always wanted to travel, immerse myself in a new location, and tell its story through my lens. With that thought, I can't stop the excited smile that covers my face—stupid boyfriends and pink slips be damned.

The airport in Baton Rouge is surprisingly busy, even for a Friday, and I'm thankful I thought ahead and reserved a car online last night. Once my luggage and equipment are loaded into the rental and I set the GPS to my destination, I pull onto the highway, heading toward I-10.

Even with the typical road construction and idiot drivers, I don't mind the drive through Baton Rouge. It's amazing what a little change in scenery can do for your mood. When I take Exit 166 leading me from the hustle and bustle of the city into the quiet comfort of country life, I relax back into the seat and enjoy the view.

The nearest hotel to French Settlement is over twenty minutes away in a neighboring town, so I settle for a quaint, locally owned, roadside motel. If I'm going to get a good grasp on who these people are and portray them in the most honest light while writing the article, I figure I need to have a first-hand experience, so Willow Oak Motel it is.

I pull into the gravel drive, humored that my rental is the only car in the parking lot. From first sight, I would assume they're closed, but the man on the phone last night assured me a room would be available and I wouldn't need a reservation.

When I walk through the glass door, the old bell above it chimes. A pretty blonde about my age with tall, big hair and a bright smile, greets me in a thick southern twang. "What can I do for ya?" Her face lights up and her eyes sparkle when she looks at me. For a moment, I'm afraid I've stepped into an episode of *The Twilight Zone*. The wood paneling on the walls has to be from the seventies, and the decrepit green sofa obviously came with it. Actually, the entire room must have been a packaged deal. I focus back on the woman, trying not to let my overactive imagination run wild with cliché horror movie scenarios.

"You must be the girl from New York City," she says with a slow drawl when I don't respond.

Funny, I'm pretty sure I spoke with a man last night.

"Um . . . yeah, Dani Reed. I spoke to a gentleman last night about a room."

"My daddy told me to be watching for you. Said you were worried we wouldn't have a vacancy for you," she explains with a giggle.

"Well, you never know when a hotel will be booked. I like to be prepared."

The girl throws her head back and laughs like I just told the funniest joke ever. I furrow my brows in confusion, obviously not getting the joke. As she continues to hoot and holler, lost in her own hysterics, my expression morphs to incredulous. I just want my room.

"Honey, make no mistake, this is a *mo*-tel, not a hotel, and the only time it's ever full is on prom night." She winks. "You're adorable, though. The guys here are just gonna go crazy over you."

"Any room you have available will be fine, I'm sure. And I'm only here for business. Besides, I have a boyfriend back home."

Why did I just say that?

She ignores my room request again. "But," she says, drawing out the word, "have you ever been with a southern boy?" She leans over the counter, positioning herself closer to me as her voice drops an octave. I shake my head in answer, slightly shocked by her forwardness. She shakes her head in return, pity in her eyes. "Girl, you are missing out!

Especially the crazy Cajun guys we have around here," she continues as she walks to the wall behind the counter and peruses a row of keys. "They're very . . . *passionate*, I guess you could say." She winks at me over her shoulder and her knowing smile tells me she has personal *experience* in this matter—probably a lot of it.

"Uh, well, thanks?" I say, but it comes out more of a question than a statement. I'm not sure what I'm thanking her for, but I don't know how else to respond to her or her claims to the ways of the south. I'll just have to take her word for it. "So, um, I'm guessing I'm the third door down?" I ask, looking at the number on the extra-large key she hands me. A real, honest-to-goodness key. I didn't even know hotels—*motels*, rather—still had these.

"Yes, ma'am. Third door down. And if there is anything we can get you to make your stay more comfortable, please let us know!"

Her chipper voice carries through the open door as I make my way back out to my rental car to retrieve my belongings.

When I turn the key and step into the room, I'm relieved to find it's not as creepy as I thought it might be. It's sparsely decorated, but after a thorough inspection, it seems clean enough. The most important thing is it's quiet, just like the rest of the town. Actually, I'm not even sure you would consider this place a town. I think I counted one stop light and a handful of stop signs. There's a neon sign lit up down the street that looked like an eating establishment and a gas station across the street from the motel, but other than that, I hadn't seen much industry or retail on the drive in.

The feeling of adventure slowly creeps through my veins. It's a feeling I haven't had in a long time. The irony of finding adventure in a place like French Settlement, Louisiana doesn't escape me, but I find myself really looking forward to exploring.

After I unpack and feel somewhat settled, it's almost four o'clock in the afternoon, which gives me plenty of time to find my way out to the Landry Plantation for my five o'clock meeting with Annie Landry.

I haven't seen this many different shades of green in years. The window to my car is down, and as I drive farther into the country, I'm flooded with memories from my childhood—tall oaks, shaded dirt roads, and the quietness that comes from being miles from a city. The sights, sounds, and even the smells take me back to a time when life was much simpler, easy . . . fun.

Not one to wallow, especially right before meeting a client, I clear my throat and push the memories down, focusing on the road ahead of me. As I get closer to my destination, the landscape changes to a narrow two-lane road with thick mossy trees on either side, the foliage only breaking occasionally for a sizeable house or two and the bright blue sky.

Spotting a modest sign boasting *Landry Plantation ~ Established 1932*, I slam on my brakes. The trees lining the long driveway are some of the tallest I've ever seen. They curve and bend while the limbs sway in the gentle breeze, creating an archway over the road leading all the way up to the house.

The Landry Plantation is everything you'd imagine a plantation to be. It's substantial, statuesque, and looks as though it could tell a million stories better than any history book. The term "house" does *not* do this place justice. It's only two stories, but there are windows as far as you can see.

Lilac bushes in full bloom line each side of the stairs leading up to the front door. The grand wrap-around porch is lined with white wicker chairs and small tables, perfect for sitting and having conversation—the picture of southern hospitality. This house has great curb appeal.

Well, if it were near a main road . . . and had a curb.

I can definitely understand why *Southern Style* would want to do a piece on this place. It's hard to believe the magazine hasn't done one before. I can practically hear my camera calling my name; the photographic possibilities are endless.

"Just wait 'til you see out back. Ms. Annie has quite the green thumb. If you think the front is pretty, you're gonna love the gardens."

I let out a yelp and quickly turn around, clutching my chest. "Who's there?"

"Whoa, whoa, whoa. I didn't mean to startle you." A young guy with muddy brown hair and tanned skin walks up to me, holding his hands up in surrender. "My name is Travis. I work here, I promise."

I look him over, noting his t-shirt and jeans covered in soil and a dirty shovel in his hands. His friendly smile makes me relax, so I intro-duce myself.

"Hi, I'm Sheridan Reed. I'm supposed to be meeting with Mrs. Landry about a magazine article I'm doing on the plantation."

"Oh, yeah! Ms. Annie will be thrilled you're here. She's been talking non-stop about meeting you all week."

"That's sweet. I'm excited about meeting her and getting to work on the article. This place really is gorgeous." I take another look around, shielding my eyes from the sun.

"Sure is," he says, joining me in my appreciation. "Let me walk you in and introduce you." He motions toward the front steps.

"I appreciate that. Thanks."

I shoot Travis a genuine smile, feeling at ease in his presence.

"How long have you worked for the Landrys?" I ask as we walk up to the front doors.

"Oh, for about five years. I've known them all my life, though. My mama and Mrs. Annie have been friends since they were knee high to a grasshopper," he says, smiling back at me.

He stomps the dirt off his boots on the welcome mat before walk-ing in the front door without knocking.

As we step into the foyer, a very loud, somewhat angry voice comes from another room close by. It sounds as though the woman is speaking in another language. Now, *this* is more like home.

"What do you mean you only have a sixty-five pound pig for me? I have a hundred people comin' over next weekend for Micah's birthday, including *your family*, Owen Miller, so you know damn well we're gonna need a ninety pounder at least! What kind of *cochon de lait* do you think I'm gonna have? Certainly not a half-assed one, I assure you!"

My eyes grow wide as I take in the beautiful woman screaming non-sense into the phone while Travis just shakes his head and laughs.

The woman continues. "Mmm-hmm. Yes, well, I guess we'll just have to have *two* pigs to roast to make sure we have enough." She pauses. "Yes, Owen, two sixty-five pound pigs should be fine. Be sure to tell your daddy I said thank you for finding another pig for us on such short no-tice." She rolls her eyes even though the man on the other end of the line can't see her. I giggle at her sarcasm.

Hanging up with a huff, she turns to Travis. "I swear, that Miller family gives me the *choux rouge!*"

I give Travis a confused look, not understanding what just came out of this woman's mouth. "Oh, um, Mrs. Annie is just a little upset right now."

"Travis LeBlanc, I am *not* 'a little upset'. I'm *pissed off!*" The fiery Cajun woman finally turns completely around to find me standing in the doorway.

"Oh, good Lord! Where are my manners? I'm usually not so rude. Please, forgive me."

Travis tries to stifle a laugh, but the woman hears him and swats at his arm. "Shut up, Travis. I mean, I'm not usually so rude when I have guests all the way from New York in my house." She smiles sweetly as she makes her way around the center island to greet me. "I try to wait until I know them a little better before I let them see me get too fired up." She laughs, pulling me into a hug tighter than I thought possible from such a tiny woman.

"You must be Ms. Reed. My name is Anne-Marie Landry, and I'm simply thrilled you're here!" she exclaims, her eyes lighting up like I hung the moon or something.

After I recover from her bone-crushing hug, I formally introduce myself.

"Hello, Mrs. Landry. I'm Sheridan Reed, but you can call me Dani."

"Well, in that case, you need to call me Annie. My husband's mama was Mrs. Landry, and she's been dead for ten years now! Travis, would you please fetch Dani's things and bring them inside?"

Wait. What?

"Oh, no, Mrs. Landry . . . I mean, Annie, I have a room at the motel in town. My things are already there."

"Wilbur Young's place? Mercy, that man squeezes a quarter so tight the eagle screams. Why on earth are you stayin' at that dump? We have plenty of room here," she says earnestly. I know I can't accept her hospitality, but damn if I don't want to. Staying inside this magnificent home would be a dream.

"That's a very generous offer, but I can't accept. I really do appreciate it, though."

Annie places her hands on her hips while the pout on her mouth shows just how unhappy she is with my refusal. I assume no one tells Annie Landry no and she's trying to go easy on me. I can already tell working with her is going to be interesting, to say the least.

"Well, fine, but if you change your mind, just say the word and we'll get you set up here lickety-split."

Her sweet southern drawl and interesting choice of vernacular makes me nostalgic. After thanking Mrs. Landry for her invitation and making plans to be back out here early tomorrow morning, she walks me to the porch and I take one more look at the house before hopping in my car.

On my drive back to the motel, I can't stop the grin that covers my face. Taking pictures of the Landry Plantation is going to be an amazing experience. I can feel it. However, I also feel the pressure. If I do a good job on this, it could lead to other jobs—something I desperately need and want. I want to prove to myself, and even to Graham, that I can do this.

With the thought of Graham comes the memory of what he said to me the day I was fired.

"How could you get fired, Dani? All you do is take pictures and write a few captions. How hard can that be? Do you have any idea how this makes me look?"

Second to dating him for so long, working for the same magazine was the biggest mistake of my life. Graham never supported me, and he never encouraged or defended me. He'd always say he was harder on me than other employees so I'd "toughen up" and grow the "backbone" needed to succeed in the publishing world. He'd know best, of course.

When I pull back into the gravel lot at the motel, I force myself to put the self-loathing on the backburner for a while. I park in front of my room that faces the parking lot. Right next to me is a large obnoxious truck taking up more than its fair share of the parking lot. Rolling my eyes at the stereotypical southern-boy display, I quickly grab my purse and walk to my room.

I've seen *Varsity Blues*. I know what guys who drive big souped-up pick-up trucks are like.

Just as I'm about to unlock my door, I hear a banging sound, followed by a loud crash. I freeze and hold my breath, trying hard to hear what else is going on in the room next to mine. Someone may need help. My eyes sweep the area around me. Not seeing anyone else outside, I relax enough to unlock my door and push it open.

As I step inside my room, two more loud bangs shake the wall I share with the room next door and then the bangs morph into steady thumping. The moans that follow confirm two things: someone's getting *busy* and they're getting busy right next door.

Awesome.

Relieved someone's life isn't in danger and a tad bit embarrassed I'm hearing an obviously passionate couple have sex, I enter my room and slam the door, hoping they'll hear it and realize they're not alone.

As the minutes pass, it becomes obvious my door-slam didn't faze the amorous duo. I grab the remote, turn on the TV, and tick the volume up to ear splitting, but thumps, grunts, and passionate screams are all I hear.

I fall back onto the bed and let out a snort. As irritating as it is to be an unwilling third party to their fuck fest, I'm also incredibly jealous. No one has ever made those kinds of sounds leave my mouth, not even my trusty battery-powered toy. Disappointment flows through me, officially putting an end to the mild arousal I was beginning to feel.

Assuming they'll be finished soon, I give up on watching TV and decide to get some work done instead. My shoulders slump as I realize my bag containing both of my notebooks, my camera, and my earbuds are still in my rental car. I slap myself in the forehead a few times before accepting the fact that I have to go outside again. I won't be able to sleep until I make notes for tomorrow's shoot. Plus, there's no way I'm leaving my camera outside; I don't care if this town is smaller than Mayberry. I don't bother putting my bra back on or slipping on my shoes. I just grab my keys and walk out the door.

"Yes, Micah! That's it! Fuck me bowlegged!"

Well, I've never heard that one before.

The woman keeps screaming his name while the guy continues to screw her into the sheetrock until, after one last bang; I hear them both sigh in relief, signaling the end of their sexy times.

Fucking finally!

Figuring I have no reason to rush, I stroll to my car, looking at the mostly-empty parking lot. Even though the majority of the rooms here are empty, it's just my luck to get the one right next to the horny humpers. It makes me wonder if this Micah is a soldier about to go on a tour of duty, or maybe he just got home. I guess it's possible that they could be on their honeymoon. My mind continues to wander, brewing up possibilities of a newly released prisoner or a politician having an illicit affair, when I hear a man's voice call out behind me. "See ya later, Val."

The sound of him shutting the door to the room causes me to panic a little and I hit my head on the roof of the car. Turning around I see the guy leaning against the outside of the motel while he pulls a boot onto his foot.

Micah, I presume.

He twists the cap off a water bottle and I shake my head, willing myself to keep moving, but the sight of his disheveled hair and defined abs peeking through his unbuttoned white button-down keep me in place.

My mouth goes dry as my eyes continue to linger, honing in on his toned stomach and the way his jeans sit low on his hips.

Even though we're a few feet apart and the sun is beginning to set, his light blue eyes are noticeable and full of mischief. I always thought when people said someone's eyes twinkle, they were full of shit, but his do. And the way the edges of his eyes crinkle when he smirks makes my insides twist.

His eyes stay on mine for a moment before traveling down my body and back up, lingering on my breasts, no doubt due to the fact my nipples are trying to break through the cotton of my tank top. I know I should be offended by him so blatantly ogling me after just having sex with someone else, but I can't help but be mesmerized by this man.

Finally, he puts the bottle of water up to his mouth, downing its contents in one long drink. A few drips trickle down his chin and he swipes them away. Giving me a wink, he simply says, "Hey," before grinning and strutting off toward the pimped-out truck parked next to my car. Of course it would be his. I'd say he was overcompensating for something, but I'm pretty sure *Val* would disagree.

Before I close the door to my room, I watch Micah roll down his window. He cranks his radio up and slaps the side of his truck as he peels out of the parking lot. I can't help but shake my head and giggle at his display, but at the same time, I wish I could live like that: free and full of life.

CHAPTER *Three*

Sheridan

WHEN THE ANTIQUATED ALARM CLOCK beeps uncontrollably, I fumble around until I'm able to slap the top of it. For a brief second, I'm disoriented. The cinder block I'm sleeping on is not my bed, but it takes a moment for me to register where I am.

Keeping one eye closed, I glance around the room. A sliver of light shines through the thick curtains, and the clock reads 6:00 A.M. Wanting to get an early start on the day, I roll out of bed, forcing myself to get up. I shuffle toward the bathroom for a quick shower and get dressed. Since the plan is to make headway on the property, getting a nice overview of the land and exterior, I throw on a light t-shirt and slather on deodorant and sunscreen.

After I grab my camera bag and make sure I have everything I need for the day, I head out the door and pause. The morning sun is breathtaking. The way the rays paint the sky pink, orange, and blue reminds me once again of my life in Mississippi. Seeing the sunrise in the morning always gives me an extra burst of energy. The thought that this is a new day and it's mine to take gives me renewed ambition.

But first, coffee.

"Good mornin'," the chipper girl behind the counter sings, her high ponytail swinging as she moves.

"Good morning," I mumble, making a beeline to the coffee pot in the corner. Conversations do not happen this early without coffee.

"Sleep good?" she asks, watching me grab a Styrofoam cup off the counter.

I pour myself a cup and add in two packets of creamer. "Uh, it was okay." I want to tell her it sucked—that their beds *suck*—but I turn and give her a smile. When I look back down at my coffee, it's still black. Okay, maybe not *black*, but it's definitely not the creamy tan I was going for. Opening three more packets of creamer, I pour them in and pray to God this doesn't taste like road tar.

"So, where ya headed this mornin'?"

"Oh, I'm going to the Landry Plantation. Have you heard of it?"

She laughs, exactly the same way she laughed at me yesterday for referring to this *quaint* establishment as a hotel.

"I'm guessing that's a yes?"

"Oh, honey," she starts, waving her hand toward me, *"everyone* knows the Landrys."

"Well, they seem like lovely people."

"So, you've met them?" she asks, quirking an eyebrow at me. *"All of* them?"

"I met Mrs. Landry yesterday. Oh, and Travis, although I guess he's not related, but he was really nice. He was working in the flower beds while I was there."

"Just wait," she says, her smile turning big and wide. I think her cheeks might even blush a bit. "Maybe you'll have the *pleasure* of meeting the rest of the clan today."

I nod, taking a step toward the door, needing to get going if I'm going to make it to the house before seven.

"Valerie," an older man says as he walks from the room behind the counter.

Valerie?

"Hey, Dad. This is Dani Reed from New York City," she says, nodding in my direction.

Hold the phone. Like, Val Valerie?

"Good mornin', Ms. Reed. I hope your stay has been good so far."

"Yes, it's been good." I nod, a hand glued to the door handle and the other holding on to my coffee.

Like . . . that Val? The Val who got fucked into next week? That Val? How many Vals are *there in French Settlement?*

"Well, you be sure to let us know if we can get you anything." He smiles and his eyes crinkle. "Val, me and your mama gotta run into Red Stick today, so you'll have to hold down the fort."

Yeah, she'll hold down the fort . . . with her back pressed to the door. I almost laugh out loud before I catch myself.

"I've got it covered, Daddy," she says, offering up a cheek for him to kiss. "No worries."

"Have a good day, Ms. Reed." He nods in my direction, and I wave with my coffee cup. His face is kind, and he has really pretty gray hair. It's the perfect color of light gray and combed just so. His hair says, "I have a business meeting", but his overalls and plaid shirt say, "Where's my tractor".

"Well," I sigh, realizing I've spent a lot longer here than I'd intended, "I've gotta run."

"See ya later." She smiles and waves.

"Yeah, see ya later."

On my drive back out to the plantation, I choke down my road-tar coffee and inhale a granola bar. When I was planning my day, I hadn't considered there not being local fast food establishments nearby. I make a mental note to find somewhere to stock up on granola bars and, if I'm lucky, some bottled Starbucks . . . or a coffee pot for my room. There's no way in hell I'm drinking that shit Val and her dad call coffee again.

I hope the inspiration I was feeling yesterday will still be there and I'll get some good shots, something I can send over to Piper tonight . . . something that will make her proud and not regret offering me this job. I called her last night after my encounter with the fuck god and she said something came up and she probably won't be able to visit as we originally planned.

During the quick drive, I roll my windows down and soak in the morning sun and fresh air. The warm breeze wraps around me, caus-ing my heart to stutter, and suddenly I'm missing my granny so bad, my chest physically hurts. It's funny how it just hits me out of nowhere sometimes. It's been seven years since she passed away and seven years since I've been this far south of the Mason-Dixon Line. Being here makes me miss her more, but it's also like a soothing balm, water in a des-ert . . . exactly what my soul needs. Letting out a deep breath, I try to let go of the sadness while keeping her memory with me. I could use a little granny magic today.

I can picture her at her kitchen stove, her back turned to me. When she would hear me come in the door, she'd call out my full name, telling me to get myself in there. Then she'd hug me tightly, tell me I'm too skinny, and make me sit at her table while she cooked for me. Her kitch-en always smelled like sugar and fresh baked bread. The second I would walk in, I knew I was home. I haven't felt that way in a long time. What I wouldn't give to be able to drive this car to Mississippi to see her.

I pull up in front of the large white house and step out of the car, taking a deep breath of fresh air. Tilting my face to the sun, I let the warmth wash over. The yellow and gold of the morning illuminates the tops of the trees, making them glow. The drops of water on the grass from the sprinklers glisten like diamonds as the freshness of pine and lilac fill my nose. It smells like home and family and happiness.

As my feet touch the first step, the front door swings open and a radiant Annie Landry steps through, looking like the epitome of a southern lady. Her pale blue linen pants flow in the breeze, as does her loose-fitting blouse. "Good mornin', Dani Reed," she calls, waving from the top of the steps. "You're sure out here early."

"Early bird catches the worm, right?" I smile, making my way up to her.

"That, it does, darlin'. That, it does." She takes my arm and links hers around mine, pulling me into the house. "I was hoping you'd stop by early enough for some breakfast. Everyone needs a good meal to start the day." Her cheerful voice is like a song. I could stay and listen to her for hours, but I really need to get to work.

"Well, actually, I had a granola bar on the way out here this morning, and I'm running a little later than I had planned."

"Oh, shoo." She waves me off. "You have a few minutes to sit down and have a croissant. I just pulled them out of the oven."

The smell of baked pastries and fresh-brewed coffee hits my nose and my mouth begins to salivate. "I'm sure a few more minutes wouldn't hurt anything." That's my stomach talking.

Annie's brilliant smile tells me I've made her very happy. "Good," she says. "Now, sit. Let me fix you a plate."

A moment later, she sets a plate full of fresh fruit and a warm croissant in front of me. "Juice, coffee, or both?"

"Coffee, please." I practically moan in appreciation. I really did need this. "The coffee at the motel this morning left a lot to be desired," I explain, trying to be polite. "And the last meal I had was yesterday before I left New York."

"Well, that just won't do." I look up to see her expression take a serious turn. "We can't have our guest starving. I mean, what will you write about us?"

We both laugh lightly. "I promise it will be all good," I tell her.

"Maw!" a boisterous voice calls out from the foyer and a door slams shut, cutting me off from saying more.

"Kitchen, Deacon. And please, use your manners. We have company." Annie rolls her eyes as a tall, buff man walks into the kitchen. He gives me a wide smile that matches his mother's, and two large dimples dip into his cheeks. He's cute, in a ruggedly handsome kind of way. Actually, he looks like the kind of person who would be offended by the word "cute".

He immediately scoops Annie up in a hug, covering her small frame with his large one, and she squeals, demanding him to stop. "You've gotta watch this one, Dani." She smirks, nudging Deacon with her elbow. "This one's *canaille*." She winks, swatting him with the dishtowel in her hand.

Having no idea what she's talking about, I quirk an eyebrow in question.

She laughs. "He's got mischief oozing out of him." She reaches up and pinches his cheeks. "Can't you see it?"

I laugh with them. "I can."

Deacon looks at me with all that mischief his mother spoke of moments before.

"Dani Reed," I tell him, offering my hand across the counter.

"Hello," he says, dipping his head and taking my hand. "Deacon Landry, ma'am." His sly smile and syrupy-sweet voice lets me know he's pouring on the manners to suit his mother, and it makes me laugh. "So, you're the city-slicker photographer who's come to take our pictures?"

"Yes. I'm here to do an article on the plantation and all of you."

"Well, this oughta be fun." He slaps his hands together, and I can't help but agree.

"Annie, thank you so much for the delicious breakfast." I wipe my mouth on a napkin and stand to take my dishes to the sink before she can stop me. "Deacon," I say, turning to the mammoth beside me, "it was lovely meeting you."

"Likewise, Ms. Reed."

I shake my head. If his mother weren't around, I doubt he'd be this formal. From the smile on her face, she knows it, too.

It's cute. They're cute. Their ease and playfulness is contagious and kind of addictive, but I excuse myself and hurry outside, knowing I have a lot of work to do and hanging around with them would not be conducive to that.

I quickly pull my camera from the car, adjust the settings, and get to work, not wanting to waste these last few moments of precious morning sun. As I make my way around the property, the story begins to unfold in my mind.

The grand porches set perfectly for slowing down and listening to a friend.

The open doors.

Open windows.

White curtains dancing in the breeze.

Lush green against stark white.

Rolling fields that have stood the test of time.

Tall oak trees whispering quiet strength and confidence.

Inspiration comes easy. It's just a matter of portraying what I'm seeing onto the glossy pages of a magazine.

Occasionally, I find a soft spot to sit, pull my small notepad from my pocket, and jot down specific shot locations and areas I'd like to revisit with different lighting.

The overhead sun beating down on me lets me know it's probably noon. A small pond catches my eye and I stroll over, shooting a few mid-day shots. There isn't a lot I can accomplish with the sun so harsh, but I make the best of my time.

A few hours later, I find myself under a welcoming shade tree and sit down to rest my feet. A bead of sweat drips down my face and I wipe it away as I pull a bottle of water and another granola bar out of my backpack. It'll have to suffice for lunch. Thank goodness Annie insisted I eat some of her delicious croissants and fruit this morning, or I'd be famished.

Once I finish my snack, I stuff the trash back into my backpack and look up to see the house in the distance. I didn't realize just how far I'd walked. Not ready to make the trek back just yet, I pull my shoes and socks off, and sink my toes into the coolness of the grass. Leaning back against the tree, I begin looking through the shots on my camera, immediately seeing a few I know are going to be keepers. I can't wait to get them onto my laptop so I can see them on a bigger screen.

Placing my camera in my lap, I lean my head back and close my eyes. The breeze cools my hot skin, and I let my mind relax as it plays back beautiful images of the day.

Green grass.

Green trees.

Vast blue skies.

Dirt roads.

Slow pace.

Open embraces.

Warmth.

"Hey." Something nudges my foot, and when I don't open my eyes, it nudges my leg. "Rise and shine."

A smile plays on my lips, but I still don't open my eyes. "Hey, Deacon."

"You've been out here awhile, city-slicker. Mama sent me to look for you. You can't just disappear and not check in. She'll have an all-out search and rescue party putting an APB on your ass."

I open my eyes, realizing the sun is far into the western sky, which means I must have fallen asleep. "I'm sorry," I tell him, trying to stand. His large hands grip my arms and pull me the rest of the way up.

"No big deal." He smiles a big, toothy grin. "I wasn't worried. You'll have to apologize to Mama, though."

I laugh lightly, not knowing whether he's joking or not. "I guess I lost track of time," I tell him.

"Sleepin' on the job is more like it."

The hint of a smile on his face tells me he's just giving me a hard time.

"You gonna tell my boss?"

"I might. Is this a common habit?"

"Only when I'm working in the seventh layer of hell on a June day and slept like crap the night before."

"So, Willow Oak Motel doesn't have Sleep Number beds yet?"

I laugh loudly. "No. Willow Oak is lacking in several areas of hospitality . . . well, unless you're a *special* guest."

He frowns at me, not following.

"Never mind," I tell him, waving him off. I've only been here a day. I think it's a little too soon for me to join in on the town gossip.

"You hungry?" he asks, walking beside me as we make our way back up to the house.

"I could eat."

"Good, because my mama made it my job to make sure you get fed, but first, we've gotta stop in the house and show her you're still alive and kickin'." He winks my way and the way he smiles lets me know there's a little truth behind his claim.

"She seems really concerned about people eating."

"She is. She makes it her job, and she takes it very seriously."

"I can see that." I nod.

"Maybe it's a southern mama thing. It doesn't matter if you're her kid, neighbor, or a stranger, she's going to make sure you always have something to eat."

I smile, knowing exactly what he's talking about. He just described my granny. She was always cooking for someone: me, church, someone sick, a new mom, her neighbors.

When we get to the house, we walk through the large French doors leading into the dining room.

"Deacon!" Annie calls from the kitchen. "Please tell me you have that pretty girl with you."

I smile and shake my head.

"See? What'd I tell ya?" Deacon snickers from my side.

Following Annie's voice, we walk into the kitchen. She's facing away from us, her shoulder length hair now twisted up in a bun and she isn't wearing the flowy casual clothes from earlier. She has on an understated black dress with capped sleeves. The thin black line down the back of her stockings adds a touch of sexiness, and from the manly hands on her backside, I'm obviously not the only one who thinks so.

"Maw! Dad! Shit," Deacon groans, covering his eyes.

"Oh, seriously, Deacon Samuel, there was only one immaculate conception, and I hate to burst your bubble, but it wasn't you." Annie shakes her head as she rights herself, turning around to face us. "Dani, I'm relieved to see you're alive and well." She gives me a look I assume she reserves for when her children are out of line, and I actually shrink a little. I'm not used to checking in with anyone. If I were out on a job in any other location, I'd be completely on my own. No one would care if I ate lunch or checked in, but it occurs to me Annie considers anyone in or around her home her responsibility.

"I-I'm sorry. I didn't realize—"

"I'm Sam Landry, and you must be Sheridan Reed," the very handsome, distinguished man standing behind Annie says, cutting me off. He steps around her and offers his hand.

"Dani," I tell him, shaking his hand, only to be practically swooned right out of my shoes as he winks at me before kissing the back of my hand. "It's a pleasure to meet you, Mr. Landry," I say, managing to gather my wits and speak coherently, avoiding embarrassment.

"The pleasure is mine, Dani. It's so good to have you here, doing an article on our little piece of happiness."

"Don't let him charm you, Dani," Annie interrupts. "Remember what I told you about this one?" she asks, pointing at Deacon. "Well, he learned from the best."

Deacon and Sam both laugh, and something about them seems familiar, but I can't quite put my finger on it.

"Sam, we need to go or we're going to be late." Annie grabs her clutch off the island and Sam begins leading her out of the kitchen. "Deacon, be on your best behavior."

"Maw, I'm a grown-ass man. I think I can handle taking Ms. Dani here to dinner without getting into any trouble."

"Uh huh. Heard that before." She gives him a look, but quickly changes her gaze to me. "I'm going to apologize in advance for anything he says or does tonight that is out of line." She blows kisses our direction.

We all laugh as we make our way out of the house, saying our goodbyes.

Deacon stops in the large attached garage, pointing to a jeep. "You wanna leave your car and ride with me, or follow? We're gonna go to Pockets. It's a few miles up the road."

"Uh, I guess I'll just follow you since it's getting late. I probably won't work anymore today."

"Okay, sounds good."

I continue to walk around to the front where I parked my car and get in. A minute or so later, Deacon pulls around in a Jeep that has tires bigger than me. It fits him. He revs the engine and rolls his window down to talk to me, so I do the same.

"You wanna race?"

"Drive it like you stole it," I tell him.

He throws his head back laughing and peels out in front of me.

Following him back to the main road, Deacon takes a right—the opposite direction of the motel—and drives about half a mile before pulling into a roadside restaurant. From the looks of the cars in the gravel parking lot, the place seems to be hopping. As the music playing inside filters into the night air, I glance up to see a flickering marquee sign that says "Pockets".

"So, what is this place?" I ask as Deacon steps out of his Jeep.

"You like things that come in pockets?" he asks.

"Um, I guess?"

Deacon must sense my confusion because he continues. "You know, pieces of bread folded together to make a 'pocket'?" He does little air quotes.

"Oh, you mean like pita bread?"

"What the hell's a pita bread?"

Using his line from three seconds ago, I say, "Little pieces of bread folded together to make a 'pocket'," mimicking his air quotes.

Deacon lets out a frustrated breath. "Yeah, but these pockets are *deep fried* . . . and you can have anything you want in 'em. Gumbo, red beans and rice, ham and cheese, barbeque, shrimp étouffée, boudin—you name it! There's even a make your own." He waggles his eyebrows and laughs. "I think you're really gonna like 'em," he says, opening the door for me.

When we walk inside, a girl with curly brown hair bounces in front of us. "Hey, Deke." She smiles, trying to gain his attention, but he quickly dismisses her. "Hey."

"Welcome to Pockets," she says, smiling at me, but it doesn't reach her eyes. She pauses for a minute, looking me up and down. She's probably wondering who I am, if I'm with him, and most importantly, where I'm from. It's what I would be wondering if I were in her shoes. "Who's she?" she asks, pointing at me, but looking at Deacon.

Well, isn't she the bold one.

"*She* is Dani, and we're going to sit in that booth over there. Can you send someone over to take our order?" He speaks to her slowly, as if she's a three-year-old, forcing me to cough into my elbow to hide my laugh. Politely, I smile and offer a small wave as we make our way to the booth. I don't want her spitting in my drink.

When we pass a couple servers, I notice the back of their shirts: *Is that a gator in your pocket, or are you just happy to see me?* I smile to myself, shaking my head. I've always been a sucker for a clever shirt.

I love this place already.

Deacon grabs the menus on the table and hands me one. "Order anything you want. It's on the house."

"Are you showing off, trying to impress me, Deacon Landry?" I playfully accuse him.

"Nope, that just happens naturally. If you must know, Dani Reed, I own this fine establishment."

"You own this place?"

"Well, *we* own this place," he says, smiling. "Me and my brother. You'll meet him later. He's working tonight."

I smile and nod as I take in the place, my wheels turning. I definitely need to find the time to come and take pictures of Pockets. Since it's owned by the family, it should be in the article.

The dark wood covering the floors and the booths immediately draws my attention. There's a wide-open space up by a stage that appears to be set up for live music, but for now, the music is coming from an old jukebox next to the stage. Between the low lights and eclectic decor, this place is a diamond in the rough. It's kind of a shame that it's stuck way out here in French Settlement. A place like this would thrive in a bigger city like Baton Rouge or New Orleans.

"You know what you want to eat?" Deacon asks, interrupting my thoughts.

"Oh, sorry. I kinda got lost checking the place out."

"You like it?"

"I do," I reply, nodding my head. "It's very . . . unique."

"That's a good word for it." He laughs, throwing his arm over the back of the bench. "Can I make some suggestions?" he asks, pointing to the menu.

"Sure."

Deacon begins to excitedly tell me about the menu. His eyes light up as he goes over all of the interesting combinations in the pockets, anything from your average pepperoni pizza, to barbeque, and even gator. Like, they really have a pocket with alligator in it. I'm intrigued, but I end up going with a pulled pork pocket with fresh slaw and order one of their dessert pockets with blueberries and whipped cream.

His pale bluish-green eyes that seem so familiar and friendly, scan the room, but it's the proud smile he wears when he sees me watching I find the most endearing. Well, that, and his over-sized dimples. He definitely gets those from his dad, and the chestnut-colored hair from his mom. It's an identical match to Annie's, even the natural wave is the same.

"I'm going to go to the ladies' room and check my voicemail before our order gets here," I tell him, looking around for a sign.

"Yeah, the bathroom is just down the hall by the bar. You can't miss it," he says, pointing over my shoulder.

I walk down the hall and head straight for the bathroom. When I'm finished washing my hands and patting my face with a damp paper towel, I take a look at myself in the mirror and wish I would've gone back to the motel to freshen up before coming out with Deacon. I run a hand through my hair, trying to tame the fly-aways. I guess it doesn't really matter. It's not like I'm trying to impress anyone.

Once I'm finished in the bathroom, I step out into the hall and turn the opposite way of the dining room to check my messages. I hope Graham has called to check in, but deep down, I know he hasn't. When I see the one missed call is from an unknown number, I go to my voicemail, but there's nothing there. Piper left a text message a couple of hours ago, but I hadn't received it due to lack of service out at the plantation. I shoot her a quick one back, letting her know everything is going well and she should expect some shots in her inbox later tonight.

As I'm pushing send, I turn to walk back to the table and collide with a person and a large tray of food and drinks. Things splatter and spill all over the floor and I find myself lying flat on my back with something warm and gooey stuck to my forehead. When I try to sit up and assess the damage, the slight spin in my head and feeling of unsteadiness forces me back down. *Only me.* I groan, not wanting to face the mess I just made.

"I'm so sorry," I finally tell the person I ran into from my horizontal position, peeking up to see the girl with curly brown hair staring down at me with a scowl on her face. Of course, it would be her. "Are you okay?" I ask, trying to smooth things over.

"I'm fine," she huffs. "Don't worry about it."

She's definitely going to spit in my food.

I attempt to sit up again, feeling the need to help clean the mess, when a pair of strong hands come from behind and gently grip my arms, helping me stand. For a second, I think it might be Deacon coming to my rescue, but when I turn around, dark, messy hair and bright blue eyes greet me.

Micah.

"The better question is, are *you* all right?" The sexy as silk voice from yesterday pours over me like warm honey.

CHAPTER *Four*

MICAH

"LET'S GET THIS MESS CLEANED up."

"Sure thang, Boss," Jamie says, shaking her ass a little extra as she walks off. For my benefit, I'm sure. She'd be happier than a tick on a fat dog if I'd just fuck her already, but she ain't my type. Besides, she's an employee, and I don't mix business with pleasure . . . or, at least, not *that* kind of pleasure.

"Sorry for your little run in with the food," I tell the beautiful woman standing in front of me. I recognize her from the parking lot last night, and my smile turns into more of a smirk. "It looks like you're wearin' a bit of it. Can I get you a clean shirt?"

"Oh, I'm fine. I'll just, um, go back in the bathroom and, uh . . ." She looks down at the gumbo splattered across her chest and midsection . . . and maybe a little étouffée right by the collar. "Uh, on second thought, I'll take that shirt," she says.

There's a smear of barbeque sauce on her forehead, and I have to admit, it's pretty damn cute.

"Micah Landry," I say, offering her my hand.

She blushes and cocks her head, giving me a funny look. "I know. I'm Dani Reed," she replies. "I saw you last night."

"I remember, but we didn't exchange names."

"No, we didn't, but I'm in town doing an article on the Landry Plantation for *Southern Style Magazine*." She gives me a quirk of an eyebrow, like I should know who she is. I do vaguely remember Mama saying something about a magazine article.

"So, *you're* the city-slicker New Yorker who came all the way down here to snap some pictures of our house?"

"Yep, city-slicker New Yorker, that's me." She huffs out a laugh.

"You always so clumsy, Ms. Reed?"

"I have tendencies," she says, looking away and giggling, like she has an inside joke with the wall.

"Lemme get ya a clean shirt."

After finding one that looks to be her size, I walk back into the hallway and hand it over to her. She thanks me and goes into the bathroom to change.

Walking back out into the main part of the restaurant, I see my brother sitting in the corner booth talking to a few of the regulars. While I slide into the booth across from him, I ask, "So, did you bring the city-slicker?"

"Who, Dani?"

"No, that other city-slicker who walked in earlier, 'cause we have so many of 'em 'round here," I deadpan. "Yes, Dani."

"So, you two met?" he asks with a wide grin, and I ignore his waggling eyebrows. My brother loves to stir shit.

"Yeah, she had a little run-in with a food tray. She's in the bathroom cleaning up." I laugh a little under my breath, thinking about her clumsy ass and the barbeque sauce on her forehead.

I look up just in time to see Dani walking past the bar toward the booth where Deacon and I are sitting. She's not just cute. She's beautiful. Her dark red hair falls past her shoulders and kinda bounces. Her head is down and she's walking like she's on a mission—which is probably how she ended up with pockets all over her. If she'd pick her damn head up and look at the world around her, she might not—shit, she almost fell again. Maybe it's a condition.

She's a little on the shorter side, but she definitely has curves in all the right places. There's nothing showy about her, but she's wearing the shit out of the new t-shirt I just gave her.

When she gets closer to the table, I clear my throat and she finally glances up,

"I see you almost bit it again back there," I say, pointing from where she came from. "You should really watch where you're goin'." I smile up at her, waiting to see how she takes the jab.

Her eyes light up a little and she quirks an eyebrow. "Well, maybe you should smooth out these hardwood floors. I swear, it jumped up and tried to trip me. It could be a lawsuit waiting to happen." She laughs, sliding back into the booth. "Honestly, there are days I'm a hazard to myself." She pauses, rolling her eyes. "The crazy thing is I can walk perfectly in heels. Maybe it's because I practiced so hard when I was in college." Her shoulders shrug and she goes for a drink of her beer before continuing. "When I'm not wearing them, it's like a switch is flipped and I'm back to my normal, clumsy self," she says as she laughs and kicks up a leg to show us her Chucks.

I laugh. She's probably the only person in the world who has trouble walking in them. "Has she already been introduced to the bar?" I ask Deacon.

"No, just ordered us some food and a couple of beers. Unless she was drinkin' on the job. I did catch her asleep out by the big oak tree at the back of the property this afternoon."

I whistle through my teeth. "Sleepin' on the job, Ms. Reed?"

"Hey, for your information, I was finished for the day." She holds her own with Deacon and me as we continue to give her a hard time, but she's able to roll with the punches, which says a lot about her. Sometimes we Landrys are hard to handle.

"Whatever you say, Chuck," I tease.

"Excuse me?"

"Nothing. Here's your food," I say, standing up and helping Jamie with their plates before sliding back into the seat across from Dani.

"Mmmm. Unnhhh. Oh, God. This is amazing," Dani moans, tilting her head back and closing her eyes in satisfaction. If I didn't know any better, I'd think she was getting ready to have a Meg Ryan moment in the middle of my restaurant.

"I'll take that as a compliment," I say slowly, unable to take my eyes off her.

She opens her eyes and looks at me. "What?"

"I said, I'll take all the moaning and 'oh, Gods' as a compliment," I reply, giving her a smirk. There's nothing wrong with a little bit of innocent flirting, right? I mean, a girl like Dani isn't usually my type, but I can't deny the attraction I feel toward her. Valerie and I are technically on at the moment, but that never lasts long anyway. And Lord knows she's done her own fair share of flirting while we're together. Just last week, she was hanging all over Jack Wilson at the Owen's barbeque. Even when she saw me, she still kept her hand on his bicep while she winked at me. She wants me to be jealous or some shit . . . go all caveman on her ass, but that ain't me.

"Well, if you made this fuck awesome pocket, then yes, it's a compliment. If not, please pass my compliments on to the chef."

"I told ya you'd have to try them for yourself," Deacon says, his mouth half full. "No one ever believes how amazing they are until they finally have one."

Dani picks up her beer and finishes it off. For a girl from New York City, she's not too bad.

"Test. Test . . . one, two . . . test . . . one, two, three," a familiar voice speaks, emanating over the entire restaurant.

"This thing on?" he asks. "Y'all seen French Settlement's most eligible bachelor? Where's Micah Landry?" Dani looks over at me with a wicked grin, eyeing me expectantly. When he continues with, "he and his glory cock must be 'round here somewhere, charmin' the panties off some unsuspectin' young lady, I'm guessin'," she begins laughing hysterically with her head tossed back.

"For the love of all things good and holy, Tucker," I mutter under my breath. "Wait right here. I gotta kill me a coonass."

I make my way up to the stage where Tucker and his band are tuning up.

"There he is," he shouts into the microphone, earning me a few cheers from the women who have gathered at the tables by the stage. Tucker gives me his gleaming smile—the one that gets him outta more shit than it should.

"For the record, I plan on taking you out back and kickin' your ass later."

"Empty promises, brah. Who's that lovely little lady sittin' with you and Deacon?"

"Oh, Chuck?"

"Dude, her name is Chuck? What the hell kinda name is that? Her parents had to been smokin' some wacky weed."

"Nah," I say, laughing to myself as I glance back over at her. "It's actually Dani. She's just in town for a week or so to take pictures of the plantation. She works for *Southern Style Magazine*."

"Where's she from?"

"New York."

Tucker whistles through his teeth. "Son, she's finer than a frog hair split four ways. You ever been with a Yankee?"

"Nope. Planted my flag in all the states south of the Mason-Dixon Line . . . and a few north of it . . . and Mexico. Oh, and there was that foreign exchange student from France who stayed with the Barrows."

"So, never New York?"

"Never."

"Well, Micah," he says decidedly, slapping me on my shoulder as we both look over to where Dani and Deacon are sitting, "I think you have yourself a mission. You need to go forth and plant your flag in New York. Do it for the greater good. Do it for the south! We shall rise again!" He turns to me and salutes.

"All right, General Fuckin' Lee. Save it for battle." I laugh, rolling my eyes at his dramatics. "She's here on business, and I have a feelin' she's not the type to just hook up with the locals. She may have a city-slicker boyfriend back home waitin' on her."

"Denial ain't just a river in Egypt, y'know," Tucker says, barely loud enough for me to hear him.

"Want me to introduce you to her?"

"Abso-fuckin-lutely."

We start to walk back over to the booth when Jamie steps right in front of us.

"Shouldn't you be takin' some orders?" I ask sternly.

"All caught up, Boss!"

"Well, go find somethin' in the back to clean. Make yourself useful."

"You know, I was thinkin' . . ." she says with mock shyness as she tilts her head to look at me.

"That's scary as hell."

She continues, ignoring my insult. "Valerie's outta town tonight, and I wouldn't want you to be lonely."

Tucker snorts at my side and I jab him with my elbow. Lord knows, she doesn't need any encouragement.

"So," she continues, "I thought maybe I could come over and we could watch a movie or just talk. Maybe you could show me exactly how you stuff your pockets . . . or maybe you'd like to stuff *my* pocket?" She eyeballs my crotch and licks her lips.

"Jamie," I say a little more forcefully than I normally would when speaking to my employees, but I need to get her attention. "Get back to work. I wouldn't wanna have to fire your ass on a busy night like tonight."

Her ponytail almost slaps me in the face as she turns around and stomps off. I swear, she's like a petulant child. If her daddy weren't the mayor, I'd have given her the boot a long time ago. She's one of those girls who was born here and will die here. All she's waiting for is a sugar daddy or somebody stupid enough to knock her up . . . and that somebody sure as hell won't be me.

Tucker and I finally make our way back across to the booth where Dani and Deacon are laughing hysterically.

Dani looks up and wipes tears from her eyes. When she notices Tucker standing next to me, she smiles brightly, and I'll admit, I don't like it. I'm hoping that's not an I'd-like-to-show-you-my-panties smile. If I can't have her, Tucker sure as hell can't have her. If I *can* have her, or want her . . . or whatever, then he *really* sure as hell can't have her. Bottom line: Tucker can't have her.

Fuck, what's wrong with me?

It's like we're seven years old again and I'm trying to prove I'm King of the Mountain.

I run my hands through my hair a few times, willing myself to get a grip before I introduce my best friend to our guest.

"Tucker, this is—"

"Chuck! Nice to meet you. I've heard a lot about you," Tucker says, interrupting me.

Dani looks at me with narrowed eyes. "Chuck, huh?" she asks, a hint of annoyance in her voice. "I *knew* that was what you said earlier." She moves her gaze from me back to Tucker and her lips morph from a hardline to a smile. "Well, it's Sheridan, actually, but you can call me Dani." She accepts his hand and he gently raises hers to his mouth, placing a suave-ass kiss on the top.

Who the hell does he think he is? The Cajun Casanova?

"Nice to meet you, darlin'."

I feel my face heat up. *Damn him.*

"Well," I draw, trying to take her attention from Tucker. "It's because you said you can walk just fine in those fancy shoes you were talkin' about, but when you put on your Chucks, you're trippin' all over yourself. I thought it was cute, so—"

"So, you thought you'd give me a nickname?" she asks, looking back at me. "And Chuck, of all things?" She laughs lightly, rolling her eyes, the annoyance slipping.

"I could've called you Tripsy . . . or Miss Trips-A-Lot."

Deacon laughs while Dani tries to hold her composure, but I see the crack in her façade. "I hate you, Micah Landry. I just met you, and I already hate you." I don't miss the twitch of her lips as she tries to force a scowl on her beautiful face, so I give her another smirk, letting her know I'm on to her.

"I see my work here is done," Tucker says, slapping me once again on the shoulder. "I'm gonna head back to the stage and get this party started!" We all watch as he turns around and does some crazy jump-and-roll bit to get onto the stage. If I hadn't known him my whole life, I'd swear the boy had been dropped on his head or teethed on paint chips as a baby, but the truth is, he just loves life and has a no-holds-barred approach to everything he does. It's one of the things I love most about him. He completely encompasses the *joie de vivre* way of life.

The band starts playing *What's Your Name*, my favorite Lynyrd Skynyrd song, and I'm more than certain the song choice is for my benefit. I make a mental note to thank Tucker for that later . . . while I'm kicking his ass.

For the next two hours, we listen to Hard Limits, drink lots of beer, and exchange smart-ass conversation. The evening feels easy, light . . . effortless. I don't know a lot about Sheridan Reed, but she seems different from girls around here. It could be that new-girl appeal, like a shiny new toy, but something deep inside tells me it's more than that.

Deacon gets up from the table, stretching and yawning. "Well, kiddos, I think it's our curfew."

Dani looks at him like he's lost his mind. "Really? You guys have a curfew?"

"Not technically, but it *is* Saturday night, which means we have mass in the morning. No matter how late you stay out or how drunk your ass gets, you can*not* be late for mass."

"Well, sounds like you boys better get home." She's enjoying this little tidbit of information a little too much, I think.

I catch D's eye, and he gives me a wink. Seems as though Dani thinks she's excluded from Sunday obligations.

Rookie.

I place my hands on the table and lean over closer to her. "That means you too, sweetheart."

"Well, I, uh . . . I don't go to church," she stutters, stumbling over her words. "I mean, I've been to church, but it was a long, long time ago. I wouldn't know the first thing about going . . . I'd probably endanger the whole congregation."

"Just be sure to wear your fancy shoes, Chuck. You'll be fine."

"I'm not talking about tripping, jackass. I mean, God might strike me down with lightning or something of equal biblical proportions."

"We'll say ten Hail Marys just for you," Deacon says as we walk out the door.

"You okay to drive home, Dani?" I ask as I notice her walking toward a black sedan.

"Oh, yeah. I'm good. Besides, it's just a little ways that way, right?" she asks, pointing down the road.

"Yeah, just keep it between the lines." I chuckle, watching her lean a little as she walks. It could be her lack of balance I witnessed earlier, but by the way she's fumbling around in her purse, I'm guessing it's the beer. There's not much that could happen between here and the motel, but I'm not willing to take the risk. "On second thought, why don't I drive you and one of us will swing by and pick you up in the morning on the way to church? You can get your car after."

She looks up at me with one eye open, the other squinted, and her keys dangling from her finger.

"I'm just driving you to the motel, Chuck. No funny business."

"Okay." She huffs and turns to her car. "Lemme grab my camera bag." She fumbles with key and I struggle with wanting to help her and wanting to watch her. Eventually, she gets the door open and leans into the car. I can't help but notice her stellar ass on display—one I haven't witnessed until now. I clear my throat as she stands back up and closes the door with her hip, knocking herself off balance.

"Since you know exactly where it is, I guess I don't need to give you directions to the motel," she says sarcastically. I was kinda hoping she wouldn't bring that up.

I shake my head and let out a hard laugh. "Yeah, I'll get you where you're goin'."

"This is a nice truck." She pats the leather on the dash as I help her in and close the door behind her.

I hop in the driver's side and glance over to see her leaning her cheek against the glass. She's so damned cute, even tipsy.

"Thanks. Try not to throw up in it." We both laugh, but I roll the window down just a little, allowing fresh air to cool her flushed cheeks. Thankfully, she makes it the mile down to the motel, and I try not to laugh as she digs around in her bag again. "Looking for something?"

"Yeah, my big ass room key. Who the fuck has keys? I mean, I didn't even know they made motels like this anymore."

"They don't. This one was made a long time ago." I laugh, using her lingo and fighting the urge to tuck her loose hair behind her ear. "Need me to help?"

"Found it!" she practically screams in triumph, coming up with the gold key, a proud smile on her face.

"That's good. I'd hate to have to wake old man Boudreaux up to let you in."

"Boudreaux," she repeats, like she's mulling the name over. "Valerie Boudreaux. That's the girl you were making bowlegged yesterday."

I can't control the laugh that erupts from inside me. I should probably be embarrassed, but I'm not. "You heard that, huh?" I scratch my head, not sure how I feel about that. Usually, I couldn't care less who knows what about me, but this weird part deep down inside wishes I could rewind to yesterday and not take Val up on her offer.

"I bet someone in Baton Rouge heard that."

We sit there for an awkward second while she fiddles with the key in her hand. "So, are you two a thing?"

"Oh, uh . . ." I toy with how to answer her question. Honestly, Val and I are exactly what she heard. We fuck sometimes. We've known each other forever, and she'd probably like it to be more, but that's not me. "We're good friends."

"Right." Her tone is clipped, final. "Okay . . . well, I better get to bed."

"Hey, Dani, I had fun tonight."

"Me, too. Thanks for the pockets and beers." She smiles and waves. I cringe when I see her almost bite it on the curb, but she saves herself and makes it to her door, turning around and waving one more time before she closes it behind her. When the light in her room comes on, I turn around in the gravel drive, thinking of Dani and her Chucks the whole way home.

CHAPTER *Five*

Sheridan

CHURCH WITH THE LANDRYS IS not nearly as painful as I thought it would be. In fact, it's quite nice, considering I'm fighting a bit of a hangover, but I don't have any regrets. It's been too long since I've had that much fun.

There's a great quality, I've noticed, not only in the Landrys, but in Tucker and other people I've observed so far here in French Settlement. They don't let things bother them for very long. They simply enjoy life—laugh things off, let it roll off their backs. What do they say here? *Joie de vivre.* I think that's what Micah called it last night when I mentioned life seems like one big party down here.

Micah . . .

I'm not sure what it is, but something about him draws me in. It's not that damn nickname he has for me, that's for sure, but there's something.

I quietly laugh at myself for thinking there's only *one* thing I'm drawn to. Okay, so there are at least three things: that messy head of dark hair, those bright blue eyes, and that jaw that's begging to be licked. And those are just the things found above the neck. Once I let my mind wander to what's below . . . well, it's hard to think straight.

In the few hours I spent with him last night, it became obvious that he's smart and has great business sense. It's also obvious other women find him attractive; they'd be idiots not to. The other thing I couldn't miss was the fact that he seems to *like* the attention.

I shouldn't waste my time thinking about Micah Landry. I'm sure he's the playboy of all playboys—out for a good time and not making any commitments along the way. Of course, I could think about Graham, but who the hell knows what he's doing . . . or *whom* he's doing. I mentally scold myself and try to clear my mind. I shouldn't be sitting here thinking about any of this. I'm on a job, and I need to remain professional. To do that, I have to keep a clear mind, which means no Graham . . . and definitely no Micah.

I glance down the church pew at all of the Landrys and my eyes land on the one in question. He's sitting with his arm around his mom, paying close attention to the message being spoken. The definition of his perfect jaw is on display as the fantastic lighting from the large windows pours in over him. I wonder if he's ever considered modeling.

Focus, Dani.

Definitely no Micah.

He's just a man, Sheridan. Get over it.

I feel like I'm channeling my granny with those words. It sounds like a piece of advice she would've given me, and I silently thank her and ask her to help me through this, because I have to focus on this job and doing my very best. Then, I need to focus on getting back to New York and figuring my life out. She'd probably have some wise words about that as well. These are times I miss her the most.

"You gonna go to confession after mass?" Deacon whispers in my ear, effectively breaking me from my thoughts. "You look like you've been countin' up all your sins while we've been sittin' here."

"What? Oh, um, no . . . no confessions for me today, thanks. You go ahead, though, if you need to," I whisper back.

Deacon chuckles, and asks, "Are you even Catholic?"

"Yes, I am. Well, I used to be . . . was. I don't know. It's been years since I've been in a church," I confess. *There, that's my confession. I mean, everyone's gotta start somewhere, right?*

"Now, that's just a cryin' shame. Don't y'all have family time on Sundays up in the big city?"

I look around the church to make sure our conversation isn't bothering anyone before answering. "No, I don't really do family time on Sundays . . . or any other day, for that matter," I whisper, leaving it at that. If I say too much, it'll sound like a sob story, and I hate when people feel sorry for me.

Deacon pulls back from me a bit and his face falls. "Well, Ms. Dani, I'm real sorry to hear that, but don't you worry. The Landrys will make sure you get plenty of family time while you're here with us." He squeezes my shoulder and faces the front of the sanctuary where the priest seems to be finishing up. I glance up and see Micah smiling at me, as if he heard my conversation with Deacon. His blue eyes show kindness and concern. I quickly return his smile and look away, feeling a bit uncomfortable and exposed.

When the main part of the service is over, Deacon excuses himself. "I got some confessin' to do. It's good for the soul, ya know." He slides past me and heads toward the back of the church while everyone else files out of the pews.

Not only is Sunday Mass a requirement when you're with the Landry family, apparently so is Sunday lunch. Annie mentioned either she or Micah usually cook a big family-style spread on Sundays, but since I'm here, they'd like to take me out and show me a little more of the area, which I appreciate. With each glimpse of this place, I grow increasingly excited to share what I find with the readers of *Southern Style*. I don't want to ruin this quiet, quaint town, but people should know how beautiful it is down here.

As I step out of the car at the restaurant, I notice we're at another locally owned establishment. There are two things French Settlement doesn't have: stop lights and restaurant chains. I had forgotten what that was like. After living in New York City for as long as I have, where there's a deli on every corner and a new place to eat for every meal, it seems strange to be so limited, but in the same breath, it's relaxing. Everything about this place makes me feel calm.

When we walk in, we're greeted by not only the owner and the wait staff, but the other patrons as well. The patrons say hello as we pass the tables; a couple people stop Sam or Annie, asking about this or that. Of course, in a town this size, everyone is going to know you. But what I also notice are the glances in my direction. I'm sure they're trying to figure out who I am and where I belong within the family. It's a funny feeling, but I like it. I don't mind being associated with the Landrys. They're good people.

After we're seated at a long table, everyone quickly looks over their menus. I order seafood gumbo and iced tea, making it my own personal mission to eat as much authentic Cajun food as I can possibly stand while I'm here.

Once our meals are served and the casual chatter dies down, Annie asks, "So, what's your work schedule gonna be like this week, Dani?"

"Well, since I knocked out a lot of the exterior shots yesterday, I'd like to start on the interior tomorrow. But I'd also like to come back at different intervals throughout the day to capture the variances in the natural lighting, if that's okay?" I ask, hoping I'm not being too much of an inconvenience.

"Oh, honey, of course that's okay. Whatever you need, Dani, just ask. It'll be our pleasure, and don't feel like you're intruding. Consider yourself one of the family." She smiles, and it's so sincere. "Oh, and these boys will be at your beck and call. If you need an escort to go further out on the property, you just snag one of them. It's not safe to be out too far by yourself, especially since you're not familiar with the land." She smiles down the table at Micah and Deacon, giving them an altogether different smile. One that says, *you'll do as I say or else*. It makes me laugh, but they both smile back and say, "Yes, ma'am," like the good boys they are.

Yeah, right.

Once again, I'm reminded of what Travis told me the first day. *If Mama ain't happy, ain't nobody happy!*

As we're all walking out of the restaurant, deciding who's riding with whom, Deacon groans. "Ugh, my body is exhausted from all this digestin'. It's workin' overtime. I've gotta go take a nap." He rubs his stomach and yawns. "Dani, will I see you again?"

"Yeah, sure. I'll be here a few more days."

"Okay, cool. Maybe you could stick around for Micah's big birthday shindig. Now that'd be somethin' to put in your article." He winks at me as he gets into his Jeep.

That's actually not a bad idea. "I might take you up on that," I tell him, waving as I follow Micah to his truck.

"A big birthday shindig, huh?" I ask Micah.

"Yeah, my mama is always makin' a big deal outta birthdays. You can't tame her. She's a beast when it comes to throwin' parties." He laughs, shaking his head. "But it *would* be pretty cool if you could stick around for the party." His eyes meet mine.

I nod and smile, trying to tamp down my excitement. "We'll see."

Micah and I climb into his truck and he starts it up, but we just sit in the parking lot for a few moments in comfortable silence.

"You're not what I was expecting, Chuck."

I narrow my eyes at him. "Oh yeah? What were you expecting?"

He shrugs before giving me a shy smile. "I don't know . . . someone snooty and prissy, I guess. But that's not you. At least, not that I can see."

"You think you've got me all figured out?"

Barking out a laugh, he replies, "No, not at all. Just makin' an observation."

His eyes are a little too focused on me and the air inside his truck is a little too thin. I clear my throat and face forward, causing Micah to take the hint to put the truck in drive.

Once my heart has slowed to a normal rate, I decide to try to have a normal conversation while learning more about Micah at the same time.

"So, what was it like growing up on a plantation?"

"It's just a house, Dani."

"A very large house," I counter.

"True, and it's special to me because it's been in my family for so long, but I wasn't raised with a silver spoon in my mouth, if that's what you're wonderin'. The Landrys are no better than anyone else. Believe me, my mama would've tanned our hides if we ever tried to act like we were—"

"Snooty or prissy?"

Micah throws his head back and laughs, and I'm mesmerized by the way his Adam's apple bobs up and down.

"Touché, Ms. Reed."

The truck comes to a stop at Pockets, and before I realize what's happening, Micah is outside, opening my door for me. I murmur an awkward, "Thank you," as he helps me out. He just shakes his head at me.

"No matter what you think of me, Dani, I *do* know how to treat a lady."

I want to say something snarky, but I choose to be honest instead. "I didn't mean to offend you, Micah. I guess I'm not used to chivalry."

"Well, that's a damn shame."

I don't disagree, but I also don't respond as I unlock my rental car.

"Hey, Chuck, want me to show you around the grounds tomorrow?"

I look up at Micah as I contemplate his question, his eyes full of mischief and excitement. I should say no, but, "Sure," slips out before I can catch it.

"Well, all right then. I'll see you for breakfast at the house."

I watch as he pulls himself up into his monster truck and motions for me to drive off first. I want to analyze every word we said to each other, but I have to concentrate on driving to the motel first. Rolling down my window, I let the afternoon breeze calm and distract me from the man behind me.

A minute passes before I hear my cell phone beep, alerting me to a missed email. Every time my phone makes a sound, I'm reminded that Graham still hasn't called.

Wherever he is and whatever he's doing, I hope he's having fun. As pissed as I am that he left in the first place, I hope it's worth it to him. If anything, I guess I'm hopeful he comes back feeling rejuvenated and more *human* than he was when he left.

As I pull into my parking spot at the motel, my phone rings. Accepting the call, I nestle it between my ear and my shoulder so I'm able to grab my things and lock up while answering.

"Hey, Piper!"

"Dani! How's Louisiana treating you? Is the assignment going well?"

Piper Grey isn't one to beat around the bush.

"Well, that depends. Are you asking as my friend or my boss?"

"What the hell is that supposed to mean? Spill it, Sheridan."

I get inside my room, place my things down on the small table, and plop myself on the bed, trying to decide which way to answer. Ultimately, I can't lie to Piper, so I tell her everything.

"Answering as an employee, things are wonderful. The plantation is gorgeous, the town is quaint and adorable, and the Landrys are the epitome of southern hospitality."

"That's great. Now, tell me the rest."

I let out a deep, exhausted breath. "I don't know. I guess I feel like I'm struggling to stay professional," I hedge, letting the last part linger like a question.

Piper laughs lightly into the phone. "What's that supposed to mean?"

I growl, feeling frustrated with myself and for Micah for being so damn attractive, but I don't want to say any of what I'm feeling out loud. I shouldn't have even brought it up.

"Sheridan Reed, are you fooling around with one or more of the Landrys?" I can't tell whether Piper is excited or just shocked at the idea of me being so promiscuous.

"Of course not! It's just that the entire family is so nice and welcoming . . . showing me around, feeding me, taking me to church—I'm having a hard time saying no to them. They hardly know me, yet they treat me like . . . like I'm family or something."

"Do you think they might be trying to bribe you so you'll write a flattering article?" It's a legitimate question, but it still makes me bristle.

"No. Definitely not. I'm pretty sure they're like this with everyone."

"So, what's the problem?"

"The problem is I find myself forgetting I'm supposed to be working instead of filling up on delicious food and belly-busting laughter," I pause, thinking I sound ridiculous, but needing to get this off my chest. She sent me here for a job, not a vacation. "I think I'm having too much fun."

I fully expect Piper to make fun of me with that last statement, so I'm surprised when her tone turns more sympathetic than anything.

"Dani, there's nothing wrong with having fun on an assignment, as long as you can remain impartial with your work. It's no wonder you're so drawn to them. It sounds like they're a wonderful family . . . something you've been missing out on for a long time." Although her tone is gentle, Piper's words feel like a punch in the gut. I know she doesn't mean to hurt me, but the truth in her words causes my eyes to fill with tears.

"Yeah, that makes perfect sense, Pipe. Thanks."

"Are you okay?"

"Yeah, I'm fine." I wipe away the few tears trickling down my cheeks and swallow the lump in my throat. "I think I'm just tired. Thanks for the chat, Piper. I'll email you what I have after I go through the pictures I've taken so far."

"Okay, but you'd better call or text me if it gets too overwhelming for you. And I'm speaking as your best friend who just happens to be your boss right now, got it?"

"Yeah, I've got it."

AFTER BREAKFAST, I MEET MICAH in the garage where he's waiting for me, just like he said he would be. He's in a golf cart wearing baggy jeans, an LSU t-shirt, and a pair of Ray Bans.

Holy shit, he looks amazing.

Stay focused, Sheridan . . . task at hand. You've got this. You're a professional.

I get in the golf cart and Micah starts it up, pulling out of the garage and heading straight onto the lush green grass surrounding the property. While he's giving me a brief history of the plantation, I start taking pictures and making notes in my journal. I have him stop when an old, rundown barn catches my eye and spend extra time playing around with the lighting and angles.

We briefly stop at Annie's garden, but I don't spend a lot of time there. It's truly amazing and deserves a whole day dedicated to capturing its beauty.

"The plantation sits on fifty-five acres and there are also two cottages on the land," Micah tells me.

"Who lives in the cottages?" I ask.

"Deacon's in the one over there by the pond. Mine is this one right up here." He points toward the house closer to us. It's white with green shutters and surrounded by trees. I try not to love it instantly, but fail.

"Is this what you want? To stay on the property?"

"Yeah, I do," he answers. "I love it here. It's my home, and I want to share it with my own family, if I ever have one," he answers with confidence. "What about you? Do you plan on living in the big city forever?" he asks, turning the tables.

"Forever? I don't know about forever. That's an awfully long time," I say with a smile, trying to dodge the question.

He lets his sunglasses slide down to the end of his nose and raises his eyebrows over the top of them. "You know what I mean."

"Well," I start, feeling the storm that's been brewing inside kick up a notch, "I've been there for so long, it's hard to imagine living anywhere else. Up until my best friend, Piper, left, I really had it in my head that if I wanted to move up the ladder in my profession, New York was the place to be. But now, I've seen my best friend spread her wings and try something different. I was so caught up in my little corner of the world, I hadn't even considered a different way of life . . . a life outside of the city. Being here, though, I can see why someone would want to spend their life here." I look over at him, but his eyes are straight ahead, like he's deep in thought. "That's what I want to do with my article," I continue. "I want to show others what a wonderful life there is to be had down here and make them fall in love, too."

I'm a bit embarrassed to be opening up to Micah like this, but I feel so comfortable, I can't seem to help it. Shrugging, I add, "That's my job. That's what sells magazines."

"I'm all for people falling in love, but I'm not sure I want a bunch of damn Yankees movin' to the Settlement," he says, grinning.

Micah stops and parks the cart. "Ah, there he is! There's my boy!" He jumps out and jogs toward the cottage, whistling and yelling for someone named Johnny. I assume he's talking about a person, but when I round the corner, I realize the *people* have four legs.

"Dani! Come meet the boys!" I catch up to where Micah is kneeling on the ground, being pawed and licked by not one, but two dogs. His smile is wide and playful, showing off his white teeth.

"All right, all right! Settle down." The dogs begin to calm and Micah wipes his face with the bottom of his shirt, briefly showing me his toned abs and a light smattering of hair traveling down past the waist of his jeans.

Happy trail, indeed.

"Dani, I'd like for you to meet Johnnie Walker and Jose Cuervo," he says, smiling up at me. "Say hello, boys! The brown one is Deke's and the black one is mine," he says, still smiling like a little boy at the rambunctious dogs. They definitely take after their owners.

I can't help but giggle as I start petting both dogs. "You and Deacon named your dogs after liquor? Are you serious?"

"That's nothin'. Tucker has a basset hound named Hiram Walker. And we used to have a fish named Patron."

I let out a snort.

"What's so funny?" he asks, watching me with an amused expression.

"I'm just picturing a little Mexican fish with a poncho and a sombrero," I tell him, and then we're both laughing. After a minute or two, I finally stop and wipe the tears from my eyes. When I look up, Micah has stopped laughing, but a slight, crooked smile is still there. His eyes squint at me, and the twinkle I saw that first day in the parking lot is back.

I feel my knees grow weaker the longer he looks at me. I think we're having a moment, but I'm not sure. I clear my throat, regaining my composure. If I stand here any longer, I'll be in a puddle at his feet and that would be very counter-productive.

"Well," I start, looking into the big black eyes of my new four-legged friends, "it's been lovely meeting you boys, but I must get back to work," I say in my most serious voice, patting them on their heads and giving their ears a good rubbing.

Micah and I exchange another brief look. There's something unsaid hanging in the air, but we both awkwardly look away, and Micah encourages the dogs to move closer to the house. Filling a large bowl with fresh water, he leaves me to my work.

I retrieve my camera from the golf cart and begin walking around the property, taking pictures as I go, gaining a whole new perspective of the main house from this distance. I even manage to sneak in a few pictures of Micah when he isn't looking. I love capturing people in their element. It's so raw and natural. I walk a little farther down a paved-stone path toward the back of the house. There, tied between two big oak trees, is a large white hammock. I let out a little squeal as visions of my childhood come rushing back to me. Brushing my hand along the woven fabric, I close my eyes, and for a moment, I'm in knee-high green grass in the backwoods of Mississippi. Stepping back for a moment, I snap a picture as the sun hits the hammock just right between the thick leaves of the overhanging trees. This one isn't for the article—it's for me.

Micah jogs up to me and gives me a peculiar look.

"Are you okay?" I ask, noticing he's a little out of breath.

"I was just getting ready to ask you the same thing."

"Oh," I say, a slow blush creeping up on my cheeks. "I'm sorry. I haven't seen one of these since I was kid," I explain. "My grandma had one in her yard. I used to love spending summer afternoons swinging and sleeping on it. I guess I got a little too excited."

He laughs and runs a hand through his hair before slapping his baseball cap back on. "Well, by all means." He gestures toward the hammock, encouraging me to hop on.

I gingerly sit on the edge, taking extra care not to fall on my ass in front of Micah for a second time. After successfully climbing in, I kick my legs out and make the hammock rock to life.

"Do you use this thing much?" I ask, glancing up to see Micah leaning against the closest tree.

"Not nearly as much as I should," he replies.

I allow my head to sink into the hammock, my eyes finding a clear patch between the leaves. Once again, I'm mesmerized by how clear and blue the sky is above me. As two white puffy clouds drift by the treetops, I lift my camera and take a few shots from this perspective.

The shade from the large oak trees makes the summer heat more bearable, and as I let my mind drift off for a moment, I forget about boy-friends and jobs. I watch the clouds pass and just let myself *be* until the brilliant blue eyes staring down at me replace the pale blue of the sky.

"We best be making our way back to the house, Chuck."

"Oh, right. Sure." I try to get out of the hammock as gracefully as possible, but I don't succeed. Micah's strong hands keep my camera and me from hitting the ground below. We both laugh, and my head falls to his shoulder as I grasp his thick biceps for support.

"You gonna be all right?"

"Yeah, we've really got to stop ending up like this." I lift my head and swallow hard when his crystal blue eyes are all I see. Those babies should really come with a warning label. I quickly pull back and right myself, smoothing my hand through my hair.

"Like what?" he asks, the smirk on his lips telling me he knows ex-actly what I'm talking about.

"You picking me up, keeping me from falling."

"I don't mind." His smile is wide, genuine, and his eyes shine brightly.

I hate to admit I don't mind it either. For once in my life, I'm kinda glad I have an affinity for falling on my face. With someone like Micah Landry around to pick me up, who can blame me?

CHAPTER Six

MICAH

*L*YING IN BED, TRYING TO motivate myself into getting up and taking a shower, my thoughts drift to Dani . . . which is becoming more common than not. Watching the way she worked her camera, her enthusiasm shining bright in her eyes when she took a shot she loved . . . it felt like I was getting a glimpse at the real Dani . . . her passionate side. The angles, precision, movements . . . the way her mouth worked into different expressions without her realizing it was happening. Without a doubt, I knew I was attracted to her. But up until that point, I didn't realize how attracted I was. Her personality, looks, and even her clumsy nature drew me in, but there was something about seeing her in her artistic element that really drove it forward. And the way her face lit up when she saw the hammock . . . it was so child-like and radiant, pure beauty. I couldn't take my eyes off her.

Her long hair was beautiful in the sun, showing each shade of red, and her skin glowed. She looked angelic lying there, but I have a feeling she's not as angelic as she looks. Every once in a while, I catch glimpses of fire and mischief in her eyes. She's something else—independent, driven, ambitious—definitely a woman who knows what she wants.

And while I really saw her, I couldn't help but *see* her. I know I shouldn't have been looking, but with the way the mounds of her breasts peaked out over the top of her shirt . . . it was hard to look away. I can't help but wonder how they feel . . . how her nipples would react to my touch. And at that thought, I'm hard.

Just the motivation I needed to get in the shower.

I hurry into the bathroom and turn the water on, testing the temperature before hopping in. With thoughts of Dani's tits still in my mind, I quickly step into the spray and lather up my soap. Closing my eyes, I allow myself to imagine what it would feel like to touch her—my hands running over her curvy hips, down her thighs, grabbing her ass, and making my way back up to pay special attention to her tempting breasts.

I firmly wrap my hand around my cock and work it up and down, lathering the soap. The more I think of her soft, round tits, the faster my hand pumps. I picture her long red hair splayed out under me and my hands on her creamy skin. When I think of how my name would sound falling from her lips as she unravels, my balls tighten. One last thought of her naked, writhing beneath me, and I'm done for. My release comes in a few short bursts, hitting the back of the shower wall.

One thing's for sure, if I ever get the chance to fuck Sheridan Reed, I will definitely need to pre-game, or risk the chance of looking like an under-experienced teenager.

After showering and getting dressed, I head out to my parents' house to see if my mama left any breakfast out for me. As I walk inside through the back door, Dani's voice is coming from the formal dining room. I peek around the corner and see her sitting at the table with her phone to her ear.

"Graham," she sighs heavily, "hey, it's Dani. I, uh . . . I thought maybe I'd hear from you by now. I mean, if it were me off on a vacation *all by myself*, you'd be pissed I hadn't checked in by now. For fuck's sake, you'd probably have the FBI hot on my trail." The more she talks, the angrier her voice sounds. "Listen, just call or text me and let me know you're all right. I hope you're having fun . . . or whatever it is you went there for." She pauses, and for a second, I think she's hung up her phone, but then she starts talking again, her voice quieter and sadder. "If you're there with someone else . . . if you're *with* someone else, I wish you'd just tell me. I think I deserve that." Her sigh is loud, and I look around the corner to see her staring out the window. "We really need to talk when you get back. Call me . . . bye."

I hear the phone hit the table, so I peek back into the dining room. With her head resting on her arms, her shoulders move up and down. I refrain myself from bolting out of the house. The tears of a woman will always be my undoing, but no tears have ever made my heart squeeze like the tiny sobs coming from Dani. Without much thought, I'm moving toward her, needing to comfort her in some small way. My hand itches to soothe her with its touch, but I stop myself, afraid I'll startle her.

"Dani . . ."

She turns her head to look at me and quickly begins wiping the tears off her face.

"I'm sorry," she says, trying to cover up the emotions.

"What are you apologizing for?"

"I don't know. For crying, I guess?" she says, laughing through the few tears still running down her cheeks.

She takes a deep, cleansing breath, collects herself, and continues on her exhale. "I'm apologizing for allowing personal matters to interrupt my work. This is very unprofessional of me," she says, standing up from her chair.

"Well, first of all, you wouldn't need to apologize to me anyway. I'm not your boss," I reply, giving her a half smile. "Second, I think it's quite all right for you to have a personal moment, if you need one."

We stand there for a moment, me looking at her, her looking out the big picture window, avoiding my gaze.

"Want to talk about it?"

"I wouldn't know where to start," she replies, letting out a deep breath and rolling her eyes.

"Maybe the beginning?"

"Everything's so fucked up. Honestly, we could be here all day, and it's really *not* the way I planned on spending the day," she says, her demeanor starting to shift back to the Dani I've come to know. "How about you show me some of the house I haven't seen yet? Help me get my mind back on my work?" She puts her cell phone in her back pocket.

"I can do that," I tell her, smiling. The idea of spending the day showing her around again is music to my ears.

I point to a picture of my grandparents on the wall, but before I can speak, the doorbell rings.

"Lemme go get that. I'll be right back. Did you eat breakfast yet?"

"A little, but I could use some more coffee."

"All right. Well, go help yourself, and I'll see who's at the door."

It's Tuesday, and my mama has been in party planning mode, so I assume it's another delivery of some sort. Opening the door, I see it's not a delivery or the taxman—either of those would've been better than the person standing in front of me.

"Hey, Val."

"Hey, Micah," she purrs as she closes the space between us and launches herself at me. I have no choice but to catch her or the sheer force of impact will knock me over.

"What the hell?"

"I missed you! Didn't you miss me?" she asks, giving me a pathetic pouty lip. I hate that.

I turn around and try to shake her off. "*Sure*, I missed your clingy ass," I say, hoping she picks up on my sarcasm and takes a hint. She's so damn manipulative sometimes, always thinking a turn of her lips or a bat of her eye will get her what she wants. Normally, I'd let her have her way and give in, which is how I end up in her bed occasionally, but the fact that Dani is in the next room has me on edge. I don't know why, but I really don't want her and Valerie in the same room.

"Well, I was hoping I could catch you before you left the cottage. I was kinda hoping we could maybe have some breakfast . . . *in bed*." She winks, and I smile at her, shaking my head. "When you weren't home, I decided to come track your ass down."

"Sorry, Val. I've got plans for the day." I look up and my gaze meets a set of emerald green eyes staring at me from the doorway. Her eyes leave mine and zero in on Valerie. The look she gives her is interesting, to say the least.

Her eyebrow quirks and her lips draw together, like she's trying to keep from saying something.

"Dani! I was wonderin' if you'd be out here," Valerie says. Her fake-ass niceness doesn't slip by me.

Dani's eyes narrow and pink tinges her cheeks. "Valerie, it's good to see you." Her words and tone don't quite measure up.

She's not jealous, is she?

The possibility that Valerie pissing on my leg evokes that kind of emotion from Dani excites me. I *want* her to want me, because I sure as hell want her.

Wait. What?

"I take it you two have met," I say, already knowing the answer but hoping to get rid of her before things get too awkward.

"Of course. She's staying at the motel," Valerie chirps, throwing her arms around my mid-section. She's clingier than an octopus. "Dani, did you know Micah is my boyfriend?" Valerie asks in her syrupy-sweet voice, cutting her eyes up at me. She knows she's treading on thin ice. We've had this discussion a million times.

She ain't *my damn girlfriend.*

I give her *the look*, which she knows well because she gets it often.

"Valerie, we're not—"

"Semantics, Micah!"

How she manages to pull a word like "semantics" out of her ass, I'll never know. I'm sure it's something she's picked up off one of those reality TV shows she's always watching.

She brushes past Dani without another look and heads straight for the kitchen. Dani is just standing there, looking puzzled as she glances up at me.

I run my hand through my hair and motion toward the kitchen. I don't trust Valerie to be left alone in the house.

I swear she's going to be the death of me . . . *both* of them . . . for entirely different reasons.

We walk into the kitchen, and Valerie is helping herself to stuff in the fridge as if she owns the damn place.

"Val, we've really got to get busy. I'm supposed to be showing Dani around the house today." I wink at Dani, who's watching the two of us from the doorway.

"Fine." Valerie huffs, not liking the dismissal. She hates when she doesn't get what she wants. "Call me later! I imagine you're just dyin' to have your *itch* scratched," she says, pulling at the front of my shirt as she walks by. "I know you don't like takin' matters into your own hands, so I'm sure you're just about ready to explode."

She begins to walk out of the kitchen but stops and turns on a dime. Touching her finger to her own lips, she presses it to mine, then gives Dani a wave before leaving the room.

What she doesn't know is I took care of that shit in the shower this morning . . . all thanks to Dani and her luscious tits. I keep my focus on the floor so Dani can't see the smug grin on my face or the blush on my cheeks.

"You know the way out, Valerie," I call out after her. "Don't let the door hit ya where the good Lord split ya!"

"Hey, uh, I'm going to get to work," Dani says from where she's been watching the one-sided pissing contest.

"Did you still want me to show you around?"

"No." She shakes her head and fiddles with her camera bag. "I know you have more important things you could be doing around here." She huffs as she finishes collecting her things, and I can't help but sense some hidden innuendo. "Besides, I made some notes from our walk yesterday and I have a few places I want to revisit. That should keep me busy for a while." She smiles, but it doesn't reach her eyes.

"Okay, well, have a good day," I concede, noting the difference in her mood. I'm not sure whether it's the message she was leaving earlier or the surprise visit bothering her, but whatever it is, I don't like it.

"You too. Maybe I'll see you around."

"Yeah, I hope so."

She smiles again, nodding her head as she gathers her things and heads out the door. I watch as she leaves, stopping briefly to speak to my mama, who's working in her garden. The way Dani walks slowly, her head up, swiveling from side to side as she looks for the perfect object to zoom in on with her camera, is mesmerizing. When she disappears around the corner of the house, I slip out the French doors off the kitchen and walk quietly to the garden.

"I was wondering if you were gonna watch from the window for the rest of the day."

"I didn't want to disturb you."

"Since when has that ever stopped you?" Mama asks as she looks up and cocks her eyebrow at me.

"Never," I admit. When Deacon and I were younger, we'd often get right in the middle of her alone time. She was always getting on to us for not being able to be quiet . . ."for even a split second!"

"You looked deep in thought."

"Oh, nothin' that would keep me from wantin' your company," she says as she presses down on the soil around a newly potted plant. Looking up, she gives me that magical smile of hers—one I can't help but return.

"Somethin' on your mind?" she asks, knowing me too well.

I exhale deeply. There's no hiding stuff from her. "I was just thinkin' about a phone call I overheard this mornin', but it's none of my business, really."

"Uh huh. So you were eavesdroppin'?" she asks, giving me a pointed look. "Tell me more."

"Well, it wasn't actually a phone call, more like a message Dani was leaving for someone this morning. I tried not to listen, but she sounded so upset, almost mad . . . and then she got so sad. She was cryin', and you know how I have a weakness for girls cryin'."

My mama's eyebrows furrow as she draws her lips together in a concerned expression.

"What was the message about exactly?" she asks, taking off her gloves.

"Well, I think she was talkin' to her boyfriend, maybe?" I say, shrugging my shoulders. "She sounded upset that he hadn't called her or told her where he was going. Sounds like he's not much of a boyfriend to me."

"Hmm. Well, Dani seems like such a sweet girl. I really hope whatever is going on is resolved quickly. She definitely doesn't deserve that kind of heartache."

"Yeah." Scratching the back of my head, I look around to see if Dani is anywhere near, but I see no hide nor hair of her. "She's too good of a person for someone to treat her like that. I mean, if he's cheatin' or whatever."

"Well, it's not really our business, Micah. I suggest you keep your nose out of things."

"Of course," I tell her, but I can't help the weird feeling in the pit of my stomach. I *know* it's none of my business. And I know my mama's right—she's always right—but I still feel the need to make things better for her.

"Maybe I can talk to her," she says, looking up at me with a knowing smile. "She may just need someone to hear her out or possibly give her a little advice."

"You're good at that."

"Damn right. I've had years of practice," she says, laughing.

I breathe a sigh of relief, knowing Dani is in good hands with my mama.

She stands up, wraps me into a hug, and pats me on the back. "Micah Paul Landry," she whispers, "you wouldn't happen to have feelings for Ms. Sheridan Reed now, would you?"

"What? No!" I exclaim, trying to deny what I'm feeling. "I mean . . . maybe." I sigh, stepping back to look at her. She twists her lips into a knowing smile as I rake my hands through my hair. "I don't really know," I admit, because whatever I'm feeling is new and different, and I haven't really had time to work out the details. "All I know is I like it when she's smilin', and I hate it when she's cryin'."

She pats me on the back and laughs as she walks away, leaving me standing in the garden. "You'll figure it out," she says, turning back around to look at me before heading into the house.

I think about going to find Dani, but I don't want to bother her. Instead, I walk around to the front, hop in my truck, and take off for Pockets. I have some paperwork that's been put on the back burner for a while, and I could really use a quiet morning in the office.

When I pull into the parking lot, I see Deacon's jeep and Joe's truck already parked in the back. Joe is our cook, and he's more dedicated to Pockets than anyone I know. Shit, some days, he's more dedicated than Deacon and me. He's an older guy who's worked in restaurants all his life and probably never been further from home than Baton Rouge. He's a little rough around the edges, but on the inside, he's soft. Seriously, one of the nicest guys you'll ever meet.

I use my key on the back door and let myself in. Deacon and Joe are in the kitchen, so I pop my head in to say hello.

"Shit, dude. I thought you'd be attached at the hip to Ms. Reed." Deacon winks back over his shoulder. His sleeves are rolled up to his elbows as he preps ingredients. "I figured we wouldn't see you until she's gone back to New York."

"No, man." I shake my head, fighting a smile. "Besides, it's not like that. I really did just show her around the property yesterday."

"Uh huh. Whatever you say."

"So, will I get to meet this Ms. Reed I've heard so much about?" Joe asks.

"Yeah, I'm sure she'll be by here again before she leaves." I hope she will, anyway. If Valerie didn't scare her off. "Actually, she mentioned doing a side piece on the restaurant. She wants to do an entire article dedicated to roadside places like Pockets." I nod, thinking how cool it would be to have Pockets mentioned in a big magazine. Then, I start thinking about Dani.

"Dude!" Deacon practically yells.

"What?"

"I asked if you'd hand me that bowl beside you."

"Oh, sorry." I reach for the bowl and hand it over, my mind still on Dani.

"Man, maybe you should go find something to do in the office. You stick around here and you'll be missin' a finger or somethin'."

I chuckle, knowing he's probably right. "Yeah, I've got some paperwork to catch up on anyway."

When I get to the office, I try to put thoughts of the beautiful redhead out of my mind and focus on the numbers in front of me.

I can't say I fully succeed, but I manage to get some work done.

The soreness in my neck tells me I've been sitting with my head down in these books for a while now, and the sounds filtering in from the front of the restaurant tell me business is starting to pick up for the day. I decide to close the books and go make myself useful. Besides, kitchen work is my favorite part of the business. I love cooking up some good food. I guess I'm a lot like my mama in that way. I enjoy feeding people and watching them leave full as a tick and happy as a lark.

As I'm plating up an order, my phone buzzes in my pocket. "Hello." I squeeze the phone between my ear and shoulder so I can continue working.

"Hey, baby, I need you and Deacon out here by six for dinner."

"Mama, we're workin'."

"Yeah, well, you've been at that place all day. I think you can appease your mama and let me feed you."

"Can you do dinner tonight at the house?" I ask, looking up at Deacon.

"I was planning to have dinner with Camille. I haven't seen her since Friday."

"Maw, Deke's going to have dinner with Camille."

"Well, of course she's invited, too. I want everyone together. We haven't had a meal out here since early last week. It's been too long. Don't be late." And with that, she hangs up, leaving no room for debate. We *will* be there.

When I walk into the house from the back door, there is laughter coming from the kitchen, and I notice there are a lot of female voices chiming in. With one look around the corner, I see exactly why my mama insisted on us being here for dinner. Camille is sitting at the bar, but right beside her is the long, dark red hair I've been thinking about all damn day.

"Hey, Micah," Camille says, turning around to give me a nod.

"Hey, Cam. Where's Carter?" I ask, missing the little dude.

"He's with Deke in the living room. They're watching some baseball game."

"Cool." I nod, walking over to kiss my mama's cheek. "You're evil," I whisper against her skin, and I'm rewarded with the most mischievous laugh.

"What?" she asks, looking like the cat that ate the fucking canary. "I just wanted all my kids here for dinner. Can you blame me?" She smirks, raising an eyebrow. I have to laugh and kiss her cheek again. Damn it if she isn't sly when she needs and wants to be. And she can say whatever she wants about me and Deacon getting our orneriness from my dad, but we all know it's her. "Besides, Dani is only going to be here for a few more days, and I really think she should see what a good southern family dinner looks like here at the plantation. Don't you?"

I nod again, giving her a knowing smile.

CHAPTER *Seven*

Sheridan

LIKE EVERYTHING ELSE WITH THE Landrys, dinner is fun, easy, and very entertaining. In fact, I'm having so much fun, I'm able to briefly put aside my irritation with Micah and his *friend*, Valerie.

Whenever I speak with Val at the motel, she's always polite with a splash of skanky thrown in, but this morning, she was trying to mark her territory with Micah, and it made me see red. I'm not ready to acknowledge why her behavior bothered me so much or why Micah only seeming marginally embarrassed by her made me want to vomit.

"I never thought we'd have a damn Yankee sittin' at our dinner table," Deacon says, earning himself some slaps on the back of his head from his mom and Camille. He also gets a glare from Micah, I might add, as well as a nice, hearty laugh from me. I love Deacon. I love how he just says everything he's thinking and never offers any apologies for it.

"Well, Deacon, I haven't always been a *damn Yankee*," I tell him, still laughing.

"Where are you originally from, Dani?" Annie asks.

"Well, uh, I'm from Mississippi, actually." I hesitate for a moment. Any time I start talking about where I'm from, I'm forced to face what I no longer have. It's depressing and usually earns me pity and sympathy from those asking. I hate all of it.

"And your parents?" she asks. "They still live there?"

"Uh, no. My mom died in a car accident when I was younger. I never had any contact with my dad, but he also died. Cancer. It was a few years ago."

There it is. That look. The one people give me when they realize I'm basically an orphan. When I meet Annie's eyes across the table, there's something else there. I can't describe exactly what it is, but mixed with the sadness and sympathy is something resembling resolve.

"So, who did you live with growing up after your mother passed away?" Sam asks, briefly exchanging glances with his wife.

"My granny. She was wonderful." I wipe my mouth on my napkin and lean back in my chair, wishing I had some sort of teleportation device to zap myself from the table. I hate awkward situations. Not only that, I'm so full, I feel like I could slip into a food coma at any moment. The fried shrimp and grits Annie prepared was delicious, and it made me reminiscent of something my granny would've made.

"Was?"

I look up to see Micah staring at me, his blue eyes darker than usual, his brows drawn together.

"Yeah, she died the summer before I graduated college."

The entire table grows quiet, and I feel everyone staring at me—exactly what I didn't want to happen.

"Uh, thank you for inviting me to dinner tonight. And for allowing me to take pictures before everyone dug in." I laugh, trying to break the heaviness in the room.

"Of course," Annie says, reaching across to take my hand. "You're welcome out here any time, Dani. And that goes for after the article is finished, too. If you ever find yourself in our neck of the woods, our door is always open."

"Thank you. I need a few nighttime shots of the exterior. Would you mind . . ."

"I-I could go with you . . . if you want," Micah offers.

"Sure. Yeah. Just let me grab my camera."

"I think Carter and I are going to take off. It's getting close to his bedtime." Camille ruffles his adorable blond curly hair. I love kids, but haven't had much of a chance to be around them. I enjoyed listening to his and Deacon's banter. If I didn't know better, I would think he was Deacon's.

"It was really nice meeting you, Camille," I tell her.

"You, too, Dani. Don't be a stranger." She stands up and pulls me into a hug. "Maybe I'll see you around before you leave."

"Yeah, that'd be great." I squeeze her back and turn to Carter. "Hey, buddy. You take care of your mom, okay? And try to keep this big guy in line," I tell him, pointing to Deacon.

"Okay, Ms. Dani."

Man, he's a cute kid.

"You ready?" Micah asks, standing at the back door with my camera in his hand.

"Uh, you break that, you buy it." I smile at him to let him know I'm just joking.

"Oh, really?" He raises an eyebrow and holds the camera out from his body, acting like he's going to drop it. "Like this?" The camera slips, but he immediately catches it.

"Hey." I reach out and take it from him. "Don't make me hurt you."

"You know, Micah," Deacon says from where he's standing by Camille as she gets Carter's stuff together, "I wouldn't mess with her if I were you. I think she can take you."

Micah laughs and opens the back door for me. "I think you're probably right. She's probably got mad street skills from livin' in the big city." His blue eyes sparkle when he looks down at me, causing me to forget what I was doing or saying.

Focus, Dani.

"After you." Micah stands to the side and sweeps his hand out, signaling for me to lead the way.

"Thanks."

We walk for a few minutes in comfortable silence. Occasionally, I glance back at the house, looking for the perfect perspective for the photo I have in mind.

"I like watching you work. It's very methodical."

Micah's confession makes me blush, and I'm thankful for the darkness.

"So, do you think you'll be able to stick around for my birthday party?"

"I'd like to. My flight back to New York is booked for Saturday afternoon."

"Well, as long as you don't get too wasted, you should be fine."

"Hey, I can't help being a lightweight."

Micah laughs. "I kinda like that you're a lightweight. Drunk Dani is pretty fun." He stays quiet while I take a few shots of the house, working to get the right setting on my camera so the warm glow from the windows comes out the way I want it to. "Sober Dani is fun, too."

"Are you trying to butter me up?"

"What?" he asks incredulously.

"Well, first you tell me how you like watching me work, and then you tell me I'm fun. I mean, a girl can only take so many compliments."

He shakes his head, laughing lightly. "It's all true."

"Well, I think you're pretty fun, too, Micah Landry."

We walk a little farther away from the house when an idea comes to mind. "Hey, do you mind if we walk over by the pond? I bet it's beautiful at night."

"Sure. And you're right. It's beautiful. Especially on a night like tonight."

As we approach the little pond, my heart practically leaps out of my chest. "Beautiful," I whisper, mostly to myself, bringing my camera up to my eye. The full moon overhead dances on the water. I take a moment to get the few shots I want and then sit down on the small dock jutting out over the water.

Micah sits next me, our feet dangling off the side, nearly grazing the surface of the pond.

"Wow," I whisper, afraid to disrupt the stillness of the night.

"Yeah, this is by far one of my favorite places on the property." His voice is low and even . . . soothing, just like the peaceful water.

"I bet you've romanced plenty of girls right out of their morals on this dock," I tease, nudging him with my shoulder.

"Nah, I don't think I've ever brought anyone down here, actually."

I find that hard to believe, but I don't say anything.

"Now, Deacon on the other hand." He laughs lightly. "He's always been the romantic one."

I laugh. "I can see that. He seems like quite the charmer."

"To say the least."

"So, what's the story with him and Camille?"

"Oh, man." Micah pauses for a second, running his hands through his hair. "We were all really tight through school. There's only a few years difference between all of us—Tucker, Camille, Deacon, and myself. We all hung out, and there was always an unspoken *thing* between Deacon and Camille. But neither of them would take the leap and really say how they felt," he says, muttering, "Pussies," under his breath. "So, Cami went off to college in New Orleans, and Deacon went to college in Baton Rouge. They'd see each other when they were home during the holidays, and it'd be like no time had ever passed, but they were both still so damn stubborn. Camille started dating some guy her senior year. I guess they were pretty serious, but when she found out she was pregnant with Carter, he bounced. Eventually, she moved back home to be closer to her family, and Deacon moved back home after he graduated. They've been inseparable ever since."

"He seems like he's really good with Carter."

"Yeah, he's all Carter has ever known. He doesn't call him dad or anything, but he's the closest thing the kid has, and the rest of us are crazy about him."

"I can tell. He has your mom and dad wrapped around his finger."

"You're tellin' me. I've always heard people were different with their grandkids, but I never fully understood it until Carter was born. He gets away with everything." Micah chuckles, looking out over the water.

"Do you want kids?"

"Yeah." It's so easy for him to answer that question. He didn't even hesitate. "How 'bout you?"

"I do." My mind immediately goes to Graham and the nearly identical conversation we had a couple years ago. He admitted he couldn't see himself with kids. I just thought it was because he had never been around them and once we got to that point, he'd change his mind. But a year ago, we had a scare . . . well, a scare for him, not so much for me. I was a few days late and had been on antibiotics that month, which, as it turns out, can affect your birth control. It hadn't even dawned on me until I didn't start my period. Then, I started doing the math and overthinking everything. Graham completely freaked out. He blamed me, saying I did it on purpose. Much to his relief, I started a few days later. We haven't talked about it since.

"Earth to Dani . . ." Micah says, nudging me.

"Sorry. Did you say something?"

"Where'd you go?"

"Nowhere . . . what were you saying?"

"I was just asking, not that it's any of my business, but what was that phone call earlier about?"

"Oh, that." I pause, not really wanting to discuss it, but the peaceful water and Micah's company lulls me into a sense of comfort, so I decide to elaborate. "Uh, it was a message I was leaving for Graham."

"Is that your boyfriend?"

"Yeah."

"Are you guys serious?" Micah shakes his head. "I'm sorry. It's none of my business." He looks back out across the water. "It's just that . . ." he begins again, struggling with what to say. "I overheard you sayin' something about him being with someone else. I know I shouldn't have been eavesdroppin', but . . ."

"It's okay. It's kinda complicated. Graham and I go way back. We've been together forever. Seriously, like since before my granny passed away. We met in college, and since we were taking similar classes, we became fast friends. Lately, things have been a little . . . tense, I guess, with me losing my job and everything."

"You lost your job?"

"Yeah, probably not the thing you tell your current clients." I shrug, feeling comfortable talking to him.

"So, you haven't always worked for *Southern Style*?"

"No, this is my first assignment. It's really my first time ever to take an assignment like this. I've been working for a New York publication since I graduated college. Graham's dad is a big editor in New York, so he got Graham and me internships at *New York Metro*. We were both hired once we completed our internships. Graham worked his way into an editor position right away, probably because of his last name. I, on the other hand, worked my way up from the bottom. I started out as a photography assistant, which means I got coffee for people and held some lights." I laugh because it's true. I started thinking I'd never get to hold a camera again.

"A few years ago, I finally got to start taking my own assignments. It felt good to create something and do what I was meant to do. But after a while, it became stagnant. I actually hated it. It was the same people, same faces, and same places. It was boring."

"Yeah, you seem like someone who needs a challenge."

"I do. It keeps me on my toes."

"I can see that about you." He nods his head, now looking at me instead of the water. "So, what happened?"

"They fired me."

"Just like that?"

"Yeah."

"What about Graham?"

"Oh, he still works there. He claims I made him look bad."

Micah scoffs at that. "That's bullshit."

"I think so, too."

"I *know* so. He should've stuck up for you. If I . . . I mean, if it were . . . well, I would've, if I were in his position."

"Thanks."

"So, what about what you said about him being with someone else?"

I cringe. I should've waited until we were face to face again to bring that up. That's just not something you talk about over the phone, but I was frustrated and annoyed he hadn't even called—*still* hasn't called.

"Well, I don't really know. It's just this gut feeling I have. He went on a vacation without me . . . from me—hell, I don't know."

"Wait a minute. He went on a vacation without you?"

"Yeah, he said he needed to get away."

"Bullshit," Micah mutters under his breath. I'm not sure which affects me more: his sweetness or the way he's defending me against Graham.

"Would you go on a vacation without your girlfriend?"

"Fuck no. I mean, not unless it was a dudes trip or something."

"Definitely not a dudes trip."

"Well, then, that's fucked up."

Hearing Micah's point of view makes me feel better and worse. "I better go," I tell him, gradually standing back up. "It's getting late and I'm planning on getting in some shots of your mom's garden tomorrow morning."

"Okay."

"Hey, uh, thanks for walking out here with me and for listening to all of my drama. I know it might be unprofessional of me, but . . ."

"Don't worry about it. I asked."

We walk slowly back up to the house, enjoying the coolness of the evening. I pop back into the house and say goodnight to Annie and Sam before Micah walks me to the front door and watches me drive off. My mind is still on our conversation when my phone lights up the dark car. I half expect it to be Piper, or perhaps Annie telling me I forgot something, so when Graham's dad's voice comes through the phone, I have to pull it back and do a double take, vaguely recognizing the New York number.

"Mr. Harrison?"

"Sheridan, I'm glad I finally got in touch with you."

"What's wrong? Is something wrong with Graham?" I can't think of any other reason he would be calling me. We're not on friendly phone call terms.

"Yes. He's been in an accident. I should've called you yesterday, but I was waiting to see what the plan of action would be."

My heart sinks into my stomach and twists into a knot. "What happened?"

"It's a long story, and I don't have time to go into details. Graham will have to tell you. But I need you to be at your house in the morning when his plane lands. He's going to be incapacitated for a while, and since his apartment is on the twentieth floor, I figured your apartment would be more feasible for him—"

"Mr. Harrison," I say, cutting him off, "I'm not in New York. I . . . I won't be home tomorrow. You'll have to make other arrangements for him until I can get back."

"That's not acceptable. I have meetings all week." His voice rises, sounding exactly like his son when he doesn't get his way, or perhaps it's the other way around. "You must . . . I *need* you to be here. There isn't anyone else who can assist him. I don't have time to put everything on hold to cater to him."

Fury rises within me. Why does he think *I* have time to put everything on hold? I don't even like Graham right now. Taking care of his every need is not something I *feel* like doing.

"You owe this to him, Sheridan. He's always been there for you when you needed him."

Guilt. That's what I'm suddenly feeling, because he's right. Graham dropped everything the day my granny died. He went with me to Mississippi and held my hand through the preparations and funeral. He forced me to go to class when I wanted to crawl into bed and shut the world out. He brought me pizza and ice cream. He has always been there for me up until recently, and I'm not sure when he stopped.

"Okay," I reply quietly, feeling reprimanded and ashamed of myself. "I'll be there. I mean, I can't be there tomorrow, but I will make arrangements to get back as soon as I can."

His loud sigh over the phone tells me he's displeased with that answer, but he finally accepts it. "Fine. I'll work something out."

"Mr. Harrison, is Graham going to be okay?" I realize I still don't know what happened to him or the extent of his injuries.

"Yes. He has several broken bones, one being his femur. He had surgery yesterday morning, and they placed a rod in his leg with screws at the hip and knee. The recovery time will be extensive. He's still in a significant amount of pain, but he wants to come home, so I've arranged for a private flight. He'll be back in New York tomorrow afternoon." He sighs again, but this time, there's concern laced in there. Somewhere, deep down, he really does care. "I'll take care of him until you make it back. Does he have a key to your apartment?"

"Yes," I reply, a sick feeling bubbling in my stomach. The thought of his leg being broken and him going through surgery makes me feel that much more guilty for the thoughts I've had lately. I can only imagine how much pain he must be in. I feel nauseous just thinking about it. "You said several broken bones, what else?"

"A fracture in his opposite foot and a break in his arm. He also has a few bruised ribs."

It all sounds horrible, and I want to know the details, but before I can ask another question, Mr. Harrison cuts me off.

"Sheridan, I have to go. I'll be in touch."

Looking down at my phone, I realize he already hung up.

I can't even begin to understand what's happening with my life right now, but I know I have to be there for him. He would be there for me . . . I think.

I swipe my thumb across the screen of my phone, bringing it back to life, and make the first of several calls.

"Piper Grey."

"Hey, Pipe. It's me."

"Well, that tone doesn't sound good. What's going on?"

"I just got a call from Graham's dad. Apparently, Graham had an accident while on vacation and has some broken bones. He's flying home tomorrow, which means I have to go home and take care of him." I don't tamper my annoyance. Piper loves me unconditionally, even when I'm being a selfish bitch.

"Wait. Explain to me why you have to go back to New York?"

"I just did, Piper. Graham's badly hurt and he needs me."

"No. He needs a *nurse*. You're doing a job, remember? *He's* the one who went on vacation by himself. Why do *you* have to be the one to sacrifice and take care of his ass?"

My annoyance turns to my best friend. She's pushing my buttons, and she knows it.

"Don't make me feel worse than I already do. I have enough pictures and information to finish my article, and I don't appreciate you questioning my professionalism. As for why I'm the one to sacrifice and take care of him, it's because I'm his fucking girlfriend. That's what girlfriends do."

"Whoa. Defensive much, Dani?" I imagine her holding her hand up, like she's motioning for me to stop. "I don't doubt your professionalism, but as the person who helped you get hired, I have to ask. Also, as your best friend, I want to make sure you're not being taken advantage of."

I know this. I *know* Piper is only looking out for me, but I'm feeling so torn right now—torn between what I *should* do and what I *want* to do.

If I'm being completely honest, I don't want to leave. I'm really enjoying being here alone, working hard, and making my own schedule. Of course, I'm not really alone. The people I've met in French Settlement make me feel more at home than I have in a long time.

My mind flashes to Micah, but I can't allow myself to dwell on him. He seems just fine with his girl-of-the-moment club and I have Graham.

Maybe this will be the kick in the pants our relationship needs. Maybe this will be what breaks us for good. I owe it to him to find out either way, which means I should start packing my bags.

CHAPTER *Eight*

MICAH

*P*ULLING INTO THE GRAVEL DRIVE of the motel feels kinda weird. The only times I ever come here are to see Val, so being here to see Dani definitely makes me think about my life choices. I'm not particularly proud of my track record, but I can't be ashamed of it either. It is what it is. I've just never felt the need to be tied to one girl, and while Val is the girl I've been with the most, I wouldn't be able to stand her on a regular basis. Come to think of it, there haven't been any women I've felt the need to see more than a few times. I've just never clicked with anyone on more than a superficial level and I never really thought about it until now.

Dani, on the other hand, I feel like I could be around her every day and never get tired of her. She's fun to talk to, and I love the way she laughs. I haven't found one thing about her that annoys me. I guess that's why I'm sitting in this parking lot barely after sunrise.

I woke up early this morning with Dani on my mind, and I figured if I could catch her before she started her day, I might be able to steal her away for a few hours to show her something. Really, I just want to see her—hang out with her. We could go walk around the Piggly Wiggly for all I care. After our talk last night, I feel like she could use a friend, and after seeing her reaction to the pond, I know she'll love where I want to take her today.

Jumping out of the truck, I grab the to-go cups of coffee I made before I left the house and shut the door behind me. Since my hands are full, I tap Dani's motel room door with the tip of my boot, trying to be quiet. The last thing I need is for Val to hear me. I don't need to deal with her crazy ass today.

After a few seconds go by and she hasn't opened the door, I kick the door again, with a little more force. A muffled, "Just a minute," comes from inside, so I take a step back, waiting.

When the door opens, I almost drop the cups of coffee in my hands. With the morning sun hitting her red hair, making it shine, she looks absolutely stunning. I wish I could steal that fancy camera of hers and turn it around on her. My eyes move over her, taking in every detail, and my throat drops to my stomach. Dani is completely ready for the day—sunglasses perched on her head and her suitcase right behind her.

"Micah," she says breathlessly. The sound of her voice accompanied with my name goes straight to my dick. *Down boy*. I smirk, because yeah, she definitely affects me like that. It's been a struggle to think of anything else for the past couple days, and I'll be damned if I don't want to reach out and touch her, or at least the strand of hair that's fallen over her shoulder.

"Mornin', Chuck."

"What are you doing here?"

I hold up the two cups of coffee. "I remember you saying how bad the coffee is here, so I brought you some."

The smile that breaks across her face is worth a million cups of coffee. At the very least, one a day for the rest of her life.

"Thank you." She looks down at the coffee and cocks an eyebrow, silently questioning which cup is hers. I offer her one of the cups and her smile grows wider before she carefully brings it to her mouth and takes a cautious sip. Her eyes close and she inhales deeply.

"Thank you."

No, Dani. Thank you. Seriously.

"You're welcome." I can't fight the stupid smile on my face. "So, what's with the suitcase? You finally get tired of this place and come to your senses?"

"Oh," she says, like she forgot where she is or what she's doing. "Yeah. No." She shakes her head and her smile fades away. "I have to go back to New York. This is my last day," she continues, disappointment in her voice. "I called your mom this morning to see if I can squeeze in the last of the shots I need for the article. I'm checking out of here this morning so I can leave for the airport straight from the plantation." She eyes me warily. "I'm guessing you haven't talked to your mom yet?"

"No." She's normally the first person I talk to in the morning, but today, I bypassed the big house and came straight here.

"So, you don't know you have a photo shoot today at five o'clock?" She winces, scrunching her nose. It's the cutest damn thing I've seen in a long time.

"Nope." I shake my head slowly and soften my features into a blank expression. "Afraid that's just not gonna work for me. I already have a photo shoot scheduled for today, so you're gonna have to get with my people and . . ."

Her expression morphs from worried to amused. "Well, maybe I'll see if your *people* mind rescheduling. Do you have an agent?"

We both laugh, each of us eyeing the other as if we have something more we'd like to say.

Please don't go.

Stay.

I wish there was some way I could know what she's thinking.

"Well, this sucks," I tell her, feeling really bummed I'm not going to be able to take her to the river today. She'd love it there. I'm sure of it.

"Yeah," she says, biting down on her bottom lip like people do when they're trying not to cry. She looks just as bummed as I feel.

"Why do you have to leave early?" My question comes out soft and low, almost a whisper. I'm trying not to let her see how much her having to leave is bothering me.

"I got a call last night. Graham's been in a bad accident. His dad needs me to come home and take care of him."

"Oh, damn. I'm . . . sorry?" I say, though sorry comes out more like a question. I don't know this Graham dude, but I don't like him, and it's not because he has something I might want. It's more than that. I don't like how he treats Dani. She's good people, and she doesn't deserve to be treated like she doesn't matter. I'm not even sure she sees it, but from the few things she's told me, I do.

"Yeah, I feel horrible. I'm . . . I'm going to fly back tonight. I guess he'll be staying at my place for a while."

"Well, that's really nice of you."

"He'd do the same for me," she says, but I'm not sure I believe that. I'm not sure *she* believes that.

"Did he call you?" I ask, already knowing the answer but wanting her to really think about what she's going home to.

"No." She looks down at her coffee cup and slowly raises it to her lips, but she doesn't drink. She just inhales. "His dad."

"So you haven't talked to him?"

"No."

"Does he even know you're here?"

"No."

I nod, but I don't say anything else. If I did, it'd be out of line.

We stand there for a few seconds before I take a deep breath and try to accept the fact that she's leaving.

"Let me help you with your bags."

"Thank you." She steps aside and I take the handle of her suitcase while she grabs the bag on the bed that looks like it has her camera equipment in it.

"Got everything?"

She takes one last look over her shoulder and nods.

I put her bags in the trunk of her car and walk backwards toward my truck.

"So, I guess I'll see you out at the house?"

"Yeah, I've gotta turn this key in and pay my bill before I head out there."

I run my hand through my hair before I climb into my truck, feeling frustration and disappointment settle around me. I'm not ready for her to leave. A nervous knot sets up residence in the pit of my stomach when I think of never seeing Dani again. I know I've only known her for a few days, but I want to know her more and I'm not sure how I can do that with her all the way up in New York. There's something special about her, and I can't let her slip through my fingers. I know she has a boy-friend and all, but I'm willing to be whatever she needs me to be.

When my phone rings, I reach over for it and answer. "Hey, Mama."

"Hey, baby. Where'd you take off to so early this mornin'?"

"Town. I needed to, uh . . ." Dani walks out of the motel office, dis-tracting me for a moment. I watch as her forehead wrinkles and her nose scrunches. She's probably wondering why I'm still sitting in the parking lot. When I shrug, she gets in her car and I motion for her to go ahead of me.

"Micah," my mom says into the phone.

"Oh, sorry."

"Did you hear what I was tellin' you?"

"No, ma'am. Sorry."

She lets out a frustrated breath but chuckles to herself, muttering something about nobody ever listening to her. "Be at the house at five. Dani needs some pictures of the family to finish up her article. She has to go back to New York this evening. Something came up."

Now, I'm the one muttering under my breath, but it's more color-ful. "Yes, ma'am. I'll be there. Actually, I . . . uh, don't have much to do today, so I'll probably be around most of the day."

"Uh huh. This wouldn't have anything to do with a certain someone leaving early for New York, would it?"

"No, I finished up the paperwork I needed to yesterday, and we don't have any deliveries coming in today. Joe can handle the prep work." I try to sound indifferent, like I already planned to take the day off, but I know she can see right through my bullshit.

"Whatever makes you sleep better at night."

"Hush."

"See ya in a few," she says, laughing as she hangs up the phone.

I roll my eyes, but I know she's right. I have plenty I could be doing today, but none of it feels as important as spending time with Dani before she leaves.

Dani's rental car pulls up in front of the house, but I continue driving down the gravel road to my house, deciding to give her some space to work.

I walk around to the back of the house, spotting the dogs lazing under the big shade tree where one end of the hammock is attached. They barely open their eyes when they see me coming. Jose rolls over onto his back, offering up his stomach for a rub down. I oblige and then climb into the hammock. Johnny tries to climb up with me, but I stop him before he knocks me out on my ass. When they settle down on either side of me, the three of us sit in silence while I listen to the breeze rustling the leaves overhead and let my mind wander to the redhead whose face has taken up permanent residence.

I spend the better part of the morning piddling around the house: fixing a loose hinge on the screen door, pruning a few branches off the bushes around front, giving the windows a wash down with the water hose. Shit, I even go over to Deacon's and put up the new mailbox he bought over a month ago. Dumbass ran it over with the golf cart after he'd been over here drinking beer one night.

When the afternoon rolls around, I decide I've given Dani enough time to work and head up to the big house. Besides, after all my manual labor, I'm starving.

As I walk in the back door, laughter comes from the kitchen. I pause for a minute in the hallway and listen to my mama and Dani.

"Those dimples," Dani says with a giggle, "I guess he's been using those as weapons since he came out of the womb."

"Oh, sugar. You have no idea," my mom says. "That boy could get away with murder. Hell, he might have for all we know."

They both laugh again. I peek around the corner and see Dani's head thrown back, her slender neck exposed. I know exactly what they're looking at. Normally, I'd hate my mom showing off baby pictures, but something about it being Dani makes it okay.

"Did you really have to pull those out?" I ask.

My mom and Dani both whip their heads around when they hear

me, looking like the cats that ate the fucking canaries. I see that look from my mom quite often, and seeing the exact same look on Dani's face makes me laugh. Two peas in a pod. I shake my head, not sure the world can handle two of them. Seems like a weapon of mass destruction. It's probably good Dani's going back to New York. My insides twist at the sobering thought.

"It's for, uh, research purposes," my mom says, turning back to the book. "Dani needed to see some old family photos." The two of them look at each other and my mom nudges Dani with her shoulder. Both of them giggle again as they turn the page.

"You were so cute in these corduroy pants. Burgundy is definitely your color." The way she looks over her shoulder and winks at me makes me want to do unspeakable things to her. Well, if my mom wasn't sitting right beside her. And if she didn't have a boyfriend.

"Oh, I'm sure you have your own embarrassing baby pictures," I counter.

Dani sighs, shaking her head as she looks back down at the pictures. "Nope."

"Are you tryin' to tell me you were never forced into a pair of burgundy corduroy pants?" I ask, raising an eyebrow. "Or never cut your own hair?" I pause for another second. "Oh, I know. Snaggletooth. We all have one of those pictures where all we wanted for Christmas was our two front teeth."

She laughs but shakes her head. "There are pictures like that, but I don't have them. They're in storage. I haven't been back there since the funeral."

"Where did you say she lived?" my mom asks, turning in her chair to face Dani.

"Laurel, Mississippi. It's just outside Hattiesburg." She nods and presses her lips together, making it obvious there are strong emotions behind the memories.

"You must miss her." My mom reaches over and takes Dani's hand.

"Every day."

"Well, I know she's real proud of you." My mom pats Dani's leg, trying to lighten the mood. "How about we get some lunch?" she asks.

"Micah, you look like you could eat. Wanna join us for some lunch?"

"That's why I came all the way up here." I wink at her.

"I'm tellin' you, Dani, if it weren't for food, I might never see my boys." My mom shakes her head, but we all know that's a lie. Besides, I'm pretty sure she knows the real reason I'm here.

We all get to work on making lunch. The three of us are quite the trio in the kitchen. Soon, our conversation turns to cooking and recipes. Dani is shocked to know I'm the one who comes up with all of the recipes we use at Pockets. I tell her I get it from my mama, but Mom blushes and says it's all me.

"When I was younger, I'd sneak into the kitchen any chance I got. My dad always teased it was because I wanted to be the taste tester and get the first bite, but really, it was because I loved watching my mama and my grandma cook," I admit. "And . . . I liked being the taste tester." I laugh, and so does my mom, pinching me in the side as she walks behind me.

"Your mom or Sam's?" Dani asks my mom.

"Mine. She was a brilliant cook. People would come from miles around to eat her cookin'. That's how Sunday dinners got to be such a big thing, but as the years went on, everyone started goin' their separate ways. She passed away a few years before Deacon graduated high school. Micah was in junior high." She sighs, and I know she still misses her. We all do. Time may heal wounds, but it doesn't make you forget.

"She sounds wonderful," Dani says as she puts plates out on the table.

When our food is ready, we all sit down and dig in, but the conversation continues.

"How about your granny?" I ask. "Did she love to cook?"

"God, yes. Everything I know I learned from her. I swear, I gained five pounds every time I was home for a visit. She'd take one look at me, and say, 'Baby girl, you're too skinny. Sit down and lemme make you somethin'.'" Dani laughs as she mimics her grandmother. "Food was how she took care of people. She hated that I was all the way up in New York, but she sent me a care package once a week." She looks down at her plate and slides the food around with her fork. "I miss those."

"Did she leave you any good recipes?" my mom asks.

Dani smiles around her bite, nodding her head. She takes a moment to chew and wipes her mouth with her napkin. "I think her recipes are my most treasured possessions. When I read over them and see her handwriting, I feel like she's right there with me. Sometimes, when I'm missing her the most, I'll pull one out and just cook. I can hear her voice, feel her presence, and the smells take me back to her kitchen. Those are my happiest memories," she says, a slight mist in her eyes. She smiles, leaning back in her chair with the most content expression on her face. "I know this sounds crazy, but I actually want to publish a cookbook with them. It's my secret project, I guess you could say. Not sure if anything will ever come of it, but I like to dream about it."

"I think that's an awesome idea," I tell her, amazed that she would say that. My mama and I have often talked about taking our recipes from the restaurant and creating a cookbook. It feels strange listening to her verbalize something I've also dreamed about and the connection I've felt with her from the beginning deepens.

She smiles over at me. "You think so?"

"I know so."

"I've only ever mentioned it to Graham, but he seemed to think it would be a waste of my time."

Which is why he's an asshole.

"Well, I think *he's* a waste of time," I say, barely above a whisper.

My mom hears me and gives me *the look* before turning back to Dani. "Your journalism abilities, accompanied with your amazing talent for taking pictures . . . well, and the sheer love you have for these recipes . . . sounds like a recipe for success," my mom tells her. "Excuse the bad pun, but I really think you're on to something, Dani."

"Thank you. Both of you," she says with a smile on her face and hope blooming in her eyes. "I'll be sure to let you know if I ever decide to take that leap."

"I'll be the first to buy one," my mom says, smiling proudly at her.

After we clear lunch away, Dani sets her laptop up on the dining room table and opens up the program she uses to edit her pictures. I watch her as she checks her list in her notebook against what she has on the computer. I try to act preoccupied with the newspaper my dad left on the table this morning, but I know I'm not fooling my mother. She hip checks me when she walks by and I look up to see her smirking at me, shaking her head.

Dani takes several more shots outside and I have to force myself to stay out of her way. I want to soak her up. Knowing she's leaving has me on edge. I feel like there's a huge cliff out in front of me and part of me wants to jump while the other part is playing it safe.

When she's outside, I walk to the window and watch her, stopping at her computer and sneaking a peek at what she's doing, and it's so cool. There's a layout that looks like a magazine spread and she's moving pictures and text around the page. Most of the things on her list have been marked through, which means she's running out of things keeping her here. I wish I could add to the list, but I know she'd have to leave eventually anyway, I'm just wanting to prolong the inevitable.

She walks back in and sits down, popping a card out of her camera and into her computer. "Looks like you're gettin' everything marked off," I say, looking over her shoulder as she downloads the newest batch of pictures.

"Yep. I wish I had at least another day, but I think I'm getting there."

"That's beautiful," I say, looking at a picture taken from my mother's garden with the house in the background.

"Thank you."

"You're really talented."

"Stop it," she says, and I can almost hear the blush in her voice.

"I'm serious! I'd pay big bucks for any of these."

She looks up at me and rolls her eyes.

When a picture of the pond pops up on the screen, my breath hitches in my chest. With the moon beaming down and reflecting off the glass-like water, it's more than beautiful. It's tranquil, peaceful, but most of all, it reminds me of her. I can almost see us there, our feet hanging off the side, our shoulders grazing every once in a while. She looked so gorgeous in the moonlight. I wish I had a picture of that, but this is a close second.

"That looks like something straight out of a magazine," I whisper before I realize what I'm saying.

"Hopefully, it will be." She laughs.

"How much for a print of that?" I ask.

"Really? You'd want—"

"Yes," I cut her off, "I'd love to have one of your pictures."

"Well, it's yours. I'll order the prints once I'm back in New York and have them sent directly to you."

"Let me pay."

"No, it's my pleasure. Really."

"Give me your phone," I instruct, and she willingly hands it over. I put my phone number in as a new contact and shoot myself a text before handing it back. "I have your number now, so I'll text you my address."

"Okay," she says, smiling.

"Okay." For the hundredth time today, I find myself staring at her lips for longer than necessary, wanting to bend down and kiss the shit out of her. She swallows hard and I abruptly break my gaze. Turning around, I leave in search of something to do before I get myself in trouble.

CHAPTER *Nine*

Sheridan

*T*HIS CITY NEVER SLEEPS. AND it stinks.

I miss the quiet and the fresh air.

Thoughts of Louisiana and Micah plagued my mind the entire flight back. When I closed my eyes, I'd see him, blue skies, and green fields. When I opened my eyes, I still saw him. He was in every kind smile or wink of an eye. Even now, as I'm sitting in the back of this taxi, crossing the river, I see him in the way the moon dances off the water.

I don't know how I'm going to get him out of my head, but I know I need to. Nothing happened between us, so I don't have anything to feel guilty for, but the way my heart felt when I was around him—how it still feels when I think of him—feels wrong. Like I'm betraying Graham.

Leaning my head against the cool glass of the window, I watch the city come into focus.

The text I received from Mr. Harrison earlier today stated Graham had made it back to New York safely, and he was setting him up at my apartment with a hospital bed and a nurse to check on him once a day.

The realization of what I'm in for hit me while I was on the plane. If Graham can't walk, I'll be responsible for bathing him, helping him to the bathroom, making him meals.

I outwardly groan.

You can do this, Dani.

Normally, it wouldn't be an issue, but I'm still pissed at him. I'm hurt he never called me while he was away. I'm hurt he didn't call me after his accident. I'm hurt he didn't feel the need to check on me. I'm trying to be the bigger person and put my feelings aside, but it's proving to be more difficult than I thought.

He would do this for me, right?

I wish I could say yes to that question, but something tells me I'd be wrong. Over the last year or so, something changed within Graham. He's not the same man I fell in love with during my freshman year of college. He's harder, less compassionate, and more distant. But maybe this will be what brings us back together, what helps us find some common ground . . . what makes us see what's important in life.

I inhale deeply and blow it out, trying to clear my mind and focus on the task at hand. When I look back up, I see we're only a few blocks from my apartment.

"Forty dollars," the taxi driver says, pushing the button to calculate the final fare. I take out a fifty since he was nice enough to help me with my luggage.

"Thanks," I tell him as I give him the money and grab the handle of my suitcase. Turning around, I glance up at the door of my apartment building. It seems like I've been gone longer than four days.

Has it really only been four days?

On the second floor, a dim light shines inside my apartment.

You can't spend the night out on the sidewalk, Sheridan. Get to stepping.

After giving myself a brief pep talk, I punch my code into the keypad and make my way to the elevator.

Quietly, I unlock the door and ease it open, not wanting to wake Graham if he's sleeping. I'm not sure how well I can handle seeing him before I get some rest. I'm just worn out and my patience is frayed. Too much has happened to deal with all of this right now and I'm not sure I've really had enough time to process the overwhelming emotions.

My head snaps up when I hear someone stand up from one of the chairs at my table.

"Mr. Harrison," I whisper, surprised to see him here. I was sure he'd have hired someone to sit with Graham.

"Sheridan," he says with a nod. He places a business card on the table and walks past me toward the door. "You have my numbers. I'll be in touch."

And just like on the phone, he doesn't give me a chance to say good-bye, or kiss my ass . . . he's just gone.

I leave my suitcase and bags by the door and quietly make my way into the living room. Sure enough, there's a small hospital-type bed set up by the window.

I walk over and brush Graham's hair back off his forehead, silently inspecting him without disturbing him. I gently touch the big black brace secured to his leg and then his arm, which is wrapped in a sling and secured to his chest to keep it from moving. He looks worse for wear, but his face . . . his face is serene and sweet. I've watched this face sleep so many nights, I've lost count. He always looks so young. The hardness is gone, his brows aren't pushed together, he's just . . . Graham.

"Oh, Graham," I whisper, "what in the world happened to you?" I sigh, staring out the window at the street below. "What happened to us?"

Sadness for the person I''ve loved for so long sets in. I hate seeing him like this. His presence is normally larger than life and he's always in control. This is so out of character for him, it's unnerving.

A huge yawn forces its way out of my mouth, so I look around and make sure he has what he needs in case he wakes up during the night. I place his cell phone on the small table by the bed and notice a few bottles of pills on the coffee table. Holding them up to the light, I find one for pain and set it by his phone.

I go into the kitchen, fill a glass with water, and set it by the pill bottle. Then I pull the drapes closed on the window, hoping he'll sleep the rest of the night.

Lord knows I need him to.

My body is so tired, I barely make it to my bed before I fall asleep.

"Hello."

Is someone yelling?

"Is anybody here?" The voice is louder.

Maybe someone is at my door?

I almost yell back, telling them to go away, but then reality hits me. "Oh, shit." I roll over and look at the time. It's still dark outside. The clock on my nightstand says it's almost five o'clock. In the fucking morning. My eyeballs hurt when I blink.

"Dad?" the groggy voice asks, a little louder this time.

"Hold on, Graham. I'm coming." I fumble around, looking for some sweats to put on.

"Dani?" he asks, like he's trying to figure out where he is and what's going on. I'm sure the medication he's on is making him a bit loopy.

I walk into the living room and vaguely make out his form on the bed. "Don't try to get up," I tell him. "Do you need something?"

"I-I just woke up, and it was dark. These pills make me have crazy dreams."

I take a few steps closer until I'm at the edge of his bed. My eyes adjust to the darkness of the room, but the faint light from the covered window allows me to see him a little clearer. Having no idea what to say, I remain quiet.

"When did you get home? Where were you?" he asks, his voice harboring some annoyance.

I can't do this right now.

"Can we talk about this after a few more hours of sleep?" I ask. "Did you need something? Like the bathroom or . . . ?"

"Uh, no. I have this fancy bag," he says, holding up something I assume is a catheter bag.

"Good thinking."

"Yeah, the nurse my dad hired said I needed to keep my leg as still as possible until the incision heals."

"So, did you need anything else?"

"No, I just had a weird dream. Couldn't remember where I was for a second."

"Want me to turn a light on? Or the TV?"

"Nah, I'm good." He settles back down into his pillow. "I'm glad you're home, Dani."

"Thanks. I'm, uh, sorry you're hurt."

That's about as nice as I can be right now.

"Yeah, it's not exactly how I'd planned to spend my vacation."

I want to yell at him—ask him where he was, who he was with, why he didn't take me with him. Instead, I say, "Sleep well. Yell if you need anything. Oh, and I set your phone right here, just in case." I hold it up and then set it back down on the table. "And you have some water and your pain pills if you need them."

"Thanks, Dani."

The tone in his voice is soft, genuine, and the way his eyebrows pull together as he looks at me lets me know he means for more than just the water and pills. It's his way of saying thanks for being here—for taking care of him. A glimpse of the old Graham shines through, but as much as I've missed this older version of my boyfriend, I'm not ready to forgive and forget just yet.

When I'm settled back in bed, even though I'm dog-tired, I can't seem to go back to sleep. My mind is swirling with thoughts of what I'm going to actually say to Graham tomorrow, because whether he's injured or not, I can't ignore the elephant in the room. He's going to have to give me something . . . some sort of explanation and reason behind him leaving and not calling. We can't pretend like our relationship is fine and sweep everything under the rug. It's making me feel uncomfortable in my own home.

THE SUN GLARES THROUGH MY curtains, beating against my eyelids. I blink open my eyes and glance at the clock, relieved I was able to sleep in so late. I take my time sitting up, preferring to stretch across my bed and revel in how good it feels to be back in my own space, until a sound from the living room pulls me out of my reverie.

Oh, shit. Graham.

I jump out of bed and throw my door open, stopping when a woman's voice coming from the living room catches me off-guard. "Mr.

Harrison—" she says before Graham interrupts her.

"Call me Graham." I hear the syrupy tone in his voice and it makes me bristle. I've always hated when he pours on the charm like that. Especially, when he does it with other women. She'll be a pile of goo before she leaves.

When she giggles and sighs, my eyes practically roll out of my head.

I walk farther into the living room, making my presence known.

"Good morning," I say, smiling.

"Hello," the lady says, looking a little startled to see me.

"I'm Sharon." She glances back at Graham. "I'm the nurse *Mr. Harrison* hired," she says, distinguishing between Graham and his father. "I'll be here once a day until Graham begins physical therapy."

"She came by yesterday and helped get me set up." Graham smiles up at her like she's Mother Teresa.

"Well, that's great." I try to sound positive, but I know my tone is clipped.

I need some coffee.

She turns back to Graham and continues talking as if I'm not even in the room. "So," she begins, tucking the blanket around his legs gently, "I'll be back tomorrow to clean this wound again. The immobilizer must stay on. You *must* stay off it for the next seven to twelve days, depending on how quickly the wound heals. After that, you'll be able to start some minimal physical therapy. Remember to call if you have any problems with the catheter. Anytime the bag gets to this level," she says, pointing it out on the bag, "it must be emptied." She glances over her shoulder at me. I nod my understanding. "I've left detailed instructions here," she says, patting the folder on the end table. "A nurse is on call twenty-four hours a day . . ." she pauses and reaches into her bag, "but this is my personal number, and I don't live far from here. So if you need *anything*, don't hesitate to call." She doesn't look at me, only at Graham. I don't miss the sparkling smile he gives her in return. He's eating this shit up with a spoon.

You've gotta be fucking kidding me.

"Thank you, Sharon," Graham says, his dimples out in full force.

I huff a deep breath and walk to the kitchen to make coffee, hoping I can find some alcohol to mix with it. I'm going to need something strong to make it through this day.

A few seconds later, the door shuts and I assume Sharon let herself out.

"Can I get you anything?" I call out to Graham, forcing down my irritation. "Are you hungry?"

"No, I'm fine. Sharon brought me a bagel and coffee."

Of course she did.

I finish making a pot of coffee and remember I threw out almost everything in my refrigerator before I went to Louisiana because I didn't want it to go bad. I settle on a granola bar out of the cabinet, but the entire time I'm eating it, I'm wishing I were sitting in Annie's kitchen, eating a big plate of her breakfast.

I definitely need to go grocery shopping.

When the coffee is ready, I pour myself a large cup and walk back into the living room. As much as I loved Louisiana and being there, I really missed my comfy chair and bed. I curl up in my oversized chair and pull the coffee mug to my lips, inhaling the nectar of the gods. The aroma immediately soothes my frayed edges and calms me.

"So, where were you?" Graham asks, accusation in his tone.

I pull the mug back to my lap and wrap my hands around it.

I guess we're doing this now.

"Well?" he asks.

"I can't believe you're asking *me* where *I've* been."

"Well," he says slowly, "you were gone when I got here. I-I thought you'd be at the airport . . . or at least waiting here for me." He has the nerve to look hurt. The fact that he expected me to be home waiting, like the faithful girlfriend I've always been, makes me even more defensive.

"I called you," I say, point blank, staring at him. "I called you every day and you never answered."

"The reception was shit, Dani." He tries to sit up a little straighter in his bed and a look of frustration crosses his face.

"I left messages, as in more than one. You never even called me to tell me you made it safely to wherever the hell you were. You didn't even call me after you got hurt!" Tears sting my eyes and I take deep breaths, trying to keep them at bay. "If nothing had happened to you, who knows when I would've heard from you."

"I was going to call you as soon as I got good reception."

"That sounds good now," I murmur, picking at the imaginary lint on my pajama pants, unable to look at him.

"It's the truth."

I laugh, but there's no humor in it.

"What the hell is this all about? You act like I did this on purpose!" he yells, pointing to his leg. "Where were you that was so important you couldn't be here for me when I got home?"

I shake my head, trying to keep my temper in check. I want to beat some sense into him and make him hurt like he's made me hurt.

Well, I guess karma kind of did that for me.

"I'm still pissed you went somewhere without me," I tell him truthfully. I'm tired of him thinking my feelings don't matter. They fucking matter.

"I told you. I just needed some guy time . . . a breather." He huffs, running a hand down his face, his annoyance obvious. "Everything is stressful around here. I just needed away from it all for a while."

His choice of words makes me pause. "Guy time?" I ask. "But you were *alone*, right? Or at least that's what you said."

"No—I mean, yeah. I was alone, yeah . . . but it was just *me* . . . doing *guy* stuff. You wouldn't have liked it anyway."

"Yeah, Graham. I would've hated it!" I yell, throwing my hands in the air. "Getting away from all the stress and the city. That sounds horrible!" Like my life hasn't been stressful. I now know a few days away from this place gave me a completely new perspective.

"I just figured you'd want to stay and look for work. You can't stay unemployed forever, you know. That savings account of yours will run dry one of these days."

Thank you, Captain Obvious.

"Did you even call the list of magazines and newspapers I left for you . . . or my dad?" With that question comes the condescending tone he loves to use when we talk about work. "I know you didn't call him to ask for any leads."

I bark out a harsh laugh, shaking my head. "For your information, I *was* working when I got the call from your dad." I carefully place my mug on the side table and brace myself for where the conversation is headed.

He frowns and gives me a disbelieving look. "Then why weren't you home?" he asks, and it's more of a challenge than a question.

"Because I took a freelance job in Louisiana. For Piper. She called the day you left and asked me to do an article on a plantation down there."

"A *freelance* job?" he asks, rolling his eyes. "Dani, you know those don't lead to anything permanent." The way he shakes his head at me makes me feel about two inches tall. I want to scream or hit him—or both.

"I-I've never felt more creative and free." I stand up and pace the living room. "Since college, it was the first time I actually loved what I was doing." I turn to him, silently pleading for him to get it—to get me. I *need* him to understand. "I'd lost it, Graham. Whatever *it* is—my passion, my mojo, my muse—I didn't feel inspired anymore. Every day was mundane, and I was so bored. I know that's why I was fired. I wasn't bringing anything fresh to the table. But while I was on that plantation, I got *it* back. Taking that job was the best thing I could've ever done."

"Well, it sounds miserable to me." He shifts his shoulders and stares at the ceiling, no longer facing me.

"It wasn't. It was great."

He looks toward the window, his face contorted into a frown. I'm not sure whether he's mad because I didn't tell him about the job or because I took the job in the first place. "Who the hell wants to be in all that heat and humidity every day? I hope they at least paid you well."

His words fall heavy on my heart. I feel the lump in my throat trying to surface, but I tamp it down. "It's not always about the money, Graham," I whisper, shaking my head. Realizing we're not going to see eye to eye on this, I let the subject go. I don't have it in me to argue with him anymore and he probably shouldn't be getting worked up like this in the first place.

I walk back to the kitchen and only once I'm in there do I let my tears fall. The fact that Graham can't be happy for me, that he can't just be happy that I'm happy . . . it hurts. I've always celebrated his accomplishments and supported him in his endeavors. If he'd have told me he wants to quit his job and start peddling papers in Central Park, I would've been on board. I continue to hide out in the kitchen until I feel like I can walk back through the living room without letting him know how much his words affect me.

An hour or so later, I'm showered and dressed, feeling marginally better.

"I'm headed to the market. Do you want anything specific?" I ask Graham, who's propped himself up in bed and is going to town on his phone with his good hand. I'm surprised the pain pills he took earlier haven't knocked his ass out yet.

"I'll take some sparkling water and those little rice crackers if they have them," he says without looking up at me. "Oh, and could you get me some hot and sour soup? I've been craving that."

"Sure," I say, nodding. "You gonna be okay while I'm gone?"

"Yeah, I'll just call Sharon if I need anything."

Of course you will.

When I get out on the sidewalk, I take a deep breath in an effort to clear my mind and regroup. If I don't let this shit with Graham go, we'll be at each other's throats for the next month. I had hoped this would bring us closer, help us remember what's important. Hopefully, now that everything is out in the open, we can begin to work through it.

Hopefully.

I exhale a heavy breath, willing myself to believe it.

Standing at the corner, waiting for the light to change, I feel the vibration from my phone in my pocket and pull it out to check the incoming message.

Micah: In your absence, I've taken over the role of family photographer.

I glance up to see the light has changed and it's now safe to cross. After I'm on the other side, I open up the message and see the picture attached. It's of Deacon and he's sleeping with his mouth open and drool on his chin. I laugh out loud and text back a laughing emoticon with tears coming from its eyes.

A few seconds later, my phone buzzes again.

Micah: Hope NYC is treating you well. If not, La will gladly take you back. ;)

CHAPTER *Ten*

Sheridan

THINGS BETWEEN GRAHAM AND ME have calmed down. We haven't argued anymore, but we also haven't talked much, either. I get him what he needs and help him when he needs me, but other than that, we're just sharing space. Instead of this bringing us closer, I feel like we're drifting further apart.

Other than a few phone calls from Piper, my texts with Micah are the highlights of my days.

> *Me: How's the party?*

> *Micah: Deke and Tucker are doing drunk karaoke, and the dogs just swiped a plate of pork off the table. Mama has declared the party "utter chaos" and is searching for more wine.*

> *Me: Sounds like fun to me.*

> *Micah: Yep, just a typical Friday at the Landry Plantation. Too bad you can't put that in your article.*

Me: I could make a last minute change.

Micah: I'd hate for you to compromise your integrity. It's really something you should experience firsthand.

Me: Wow, you sound . . . sober.

Micah: Autocorrect is a great thing, Dani.

Me: LOL. Happy birthday, Micah.

Micah: Night, Chuck.

CHAPTER
Eleven

Sheridan

G RAHAM'S PHYSICAL THERAPIST STOPPED BY yesterday and introduced herself as Kaitlyn Thomas. She was a younger woman, pretty, with long dark hair, almond-shaped dark brown eyes. I groan, knowing the flirting won't stop when Nurse Sharon is out of the picture.

Couldn't they have sent some big, burly dude to be his physical therapist?

Kaitlyn is supposed to start with some simple exercises at the beginning of next week. If everything goes according to plan, he'll have his cast off in four more weeks, and that should be the same time he'll start the more intense physical therapy.

We've only been at this for two weeks, but I'm already counting down the days. I'm not cut out for the nursing field. Luckily, Micah is never too far from his phone. I tap out a text, realizing just how much I count on him to keep me sane.

Me: So glad I didn't go into the medical field.

Micah: Being a nurse ain't your thing, I take it?

Me: Definitely not. I'm not sure whether it's me or the patient, though.

Micah: How's what's-his-face doing?

Me: Graham is as grumpy as ever.

Micah: You know I'll gladly kick his ass for you, right?

Me: It's not quite that bad. I won't deny dreaming about hiding his wire hanger so he can't scratch his leg, though.

Micah: Damn, you're meaner than I realized. I like it.

CHAPTER *Twelve*

Sheridan

AUSAGE.
Oil.
Flour.
Milk.

I check to make sure I have all the ingredients to make my granny's recipe for sausage gravy. This morning, I woke up craving it. Maybe I really need her, or the memory of her—regardless, some serious breakfast cooking is about to go down in my kitchen.

I take out my granny's old cast iron skillet and pile the ingredients on the counter beside the stove. Graham is preoccupied with Nurse Sharon, who brought him a chocolate croissant and an Americano for breakfast. She didn't ask me if I wanted anything. Come to think of it, she pretty much acts like I'm not even here. But that's okay. Croissants are great, but nothing beats my granny's gravy.

I overhear Sharon telling Graham he no longer needs to use the sling for his arm, which makes him happy and more mobile. He's starting to go stir crazy, but I can't blame him. I mean, at least I get to go out and run errands. He's stuck in that bed. I help him change positions as frequently as possible, but there's only so much you can do when your leg must remain completely immobile.

To save time, I pop open a can of biscuits and place them on a baking sheet.

"Hush, Granny." I smile to myself, knowing she probably wants to march down here, scold me for using biscuits out of a can, and make her famous cathead biscuits, which gained their name from literally being the size of a cat's head. "I don't have time, nor enough flour," I mutter, bending down to make sure I have the flame just right before pouring a little cooking oil into my skillet.

As I slice off half the roll of sausage and get ready to put it into the hot skillet, I hear her voice in my ear.

"Now, sister, what have I told you about the sausage?"

"The more sausage, the more flour I'll have to use. And the more flour I use, the more milk."

"With that much sausage, you'll have enough gravy to feed an army."

I smirk, knowing she's right. I pinch off half of what I was originally going to use and put it in the skillet. When the sausage is nice and browned, I begin spooning in a little flour, eyeballing it just like she would. The smell filling my kitchen is also filling my heart. I can feel her here with me, and it's just what I need after the week I've had.

Soon, the flour and sausage are a perfect shade of brown, so I begin to stir in the milk. I watch as the few simple ingredients meld together to make something so delicious. The timer on the oven and the correct thickness of the gravy coincide with Sharon's departure. I pop my head into the living room and ask Graham if he's still hungry.

"What are you cooking?"

"Gravy and biscuits," I tell him, raising my eyebrows with excitement.

"Ew. No thanks. I've never liked that stuff."

"Are you kidding me?" I ask, laughing. "What's not to like about biscuits and gravy?"

"I guess it's a texture thing."

I shake my head at him. "Have you tried it in the last ten years? Your taste buds change, you know."

He smirks up at me and shakes his head. "No, but I'm full from the breakfast Sharon brought."

I turn around and huff out my frustration, walking back to the kitchen to make myself a bowl of delicious breakfast goodness.

As I take a second to enjoy the masterpiece, I'm suddenly very aware of how Graham never seems to appreciate anything I do these days.

Before I take a bite, I snap a quick picture and text it to someone who I know will appreciate this moment with me.

Before I can bring my fork to my mouth for another bite, my phone dings with an incoming text.

Micah: Are you sexting me now?

Me: What?

I laugh.

Me: No. I'm not sexting you.

Micah: Yeah, you are. That's food porn. It's considered sexting. Stop it.

Me: Well, congratulations. You're my first.

Micah: Good to know. ;) Looks delicious! I'll be over in ten minutes.

Me: There's plenty!

Micah: Don't tease me like that, woman. You better hope my mama made breakfast.

Me: Channeling my inner granny.

Micah: She'd be proud. :) Cooking for the boyfriend, I assume?

Me: Nope, just me. The boyfriend doesn't like biscuits and gravy. "It's a texture thing."

Micah: *rolls eyes* Who doesn't like biscuits and gravy? Are you sure he's not a Communist?

I laugh and begin to cough, choking on a mouthful of my breakfast.

"What's so funny?" Graham asks when I walk back into the living room and curl up in the chair with my bowl.

"Oh, um, Piper just sent me a funny picture."

He grunts and rolls his eyes. He and Piper have never really seen eye to eye. According to her, he's too serious. According to him, she's too *flighty*.

After breakfast, I clean up the kitchen and put on some soup I know Graham likes. More than anything, cooking keeps me from going stir crazy. Sitting around this apartment makes me miss Louisiana. At least I still have a few photos to edit from the plantation shoot. I've spent quite a bit of time looking through them and getting lost in the images. Yesterday, I picked out a few of the ones Micah had said were his favorites and sent off an order to be printed. I also added in a couple I know Annie will enjoy. I thought about mentioning the pictures in one of our text messages, but decided I'd rather it be a surprise.

"I'm going to call a few of the magazines and newspapers you gave me numbers for," I tell Graham, knowing it will make him happy. "I figure if I put my name and application out there now, I should have a new job by the time you're back on your feet." It's not what I want to do, but it's something, and who knows? Maybe I'll find something that inspires me like the plantation did.

"That's really great, Dani," he says, sounding enthusiastic about something I've said for the first time since I've been back home.

I sigh, my mind immediately drifting to lush green grass, trees, blue skies . . . blue eyes. I shake my head to redirect my thoughts.

"Hey, we should watch a movie or something," Graham suggests. I look up to see him propped up on his good elbow, smiling over at me. "I wish I could take you on a date to thank you for all you're doing for me right now, but . . ." he hesitates, pointing down to his leg, "unless you've got a wheelchair and you want to wheel me down the sidewalk . . ."

"Uh, no. Your ass is staying in that bed until Nurse Sharon says otherwise." I smile back at him, enjoying the easiness. "We could have a date here. I'll even change out of these sweats." I pull at the baggy sweatpants I've been wearing since yesterday.

"Oooh, really? Are you going to put on a pair of those yoga pants?"

"Maybe. If you're lucky."

"I'm feelin' lucky." He winks.

"You weren't feelin' so lucky a couple weeks ago, were you, buddy?" I tease, walking over to check his bandages and make sure his bag doesn't need to be emptied.

So romantic.

After I've made sure everything is good, I give him the bowl of soup and set him up with a tray before going to take a shower.

"I'll be right out," I tell him, glancing back over my shoulder.

The way he smiles back at me reminds me of better times, better days. Maybe everything isn't lost. Maybe this last ditch effort will work after all.

After a shower and a change of clothes, I feel like a new person. Sometimes it's the little things.

I pop a bowl of popcorn and move the big chair closer to his hospital bed. Holding up a couple DVDs, I ask, *"Tommy Boy* or *Black Sheep?"* Both are two of our favorites from our college days. We've watched them a hundred times and still laugh every single time.

"Black Sheep," he says.

Falling comfortably into the world of Chris Farley and David Spade is easy and familiar, like an old pair of worn jeans. I lean my head back on the chair, getting comfortable. Graham reaches over with his good arm and runs his fingers through my still damp hair. Normally, it would put me right to sleep, but I can't keep from laughing at the idiots on the television. Hearing Graham's snort behind me makes me laugh even harder.

My side aches, my cheeks hurt, and it just feels good.

When the movie is over, we put *Tommy Boy* in, deciding to make it a marathon. The more we laugh, the more the funk we've been in seems to dissipate. Graham continues to stroke my hair and rub my shoulder. I intertwine my fingers with his and give them a light squeeze. For the first time in a long time, it feels good to be with him.

"I missed you, D."

"I missed you, too, Graham." It's the truth. Despite the hurt and disappointment, I missed him—I missed this.

CHAPTER
Thirteen

Sheridan

AFTER MAKING SOME CALLS AND emailing my résumé to a few newspapers and magazines, I was relieved to get some call-backs. While the nurse and physical therapist are here today, I'm going to a couple of interviews and will hopefully land a job, which will get Graham off my back and get me out of this apartment for more than a grocery shopping trip or food run. I'm thankful that Graham is improving and needing me less and less, because I don't know how much more of this I can take.

As I'm dressing for my interview and trying to figure out which skirt to wear, my phone buzzes from the dresser. I'm guessing it's another text from Piper. I put her down as a reference and she's been texting or calling every time a newspaper contacts her, letting me know how it went and what she thinks about them.

Southern Style was so pleased with my work on the Landry Plantation article, they're considering the idea I pitched to Piper a week or so ago about roadside diners. Piper thought it would make a fantastic spread for the first fall issue in September, but if that's going to happen, I'd have to start working on it within the next month or so, since it's already June.

Though, until I know for sure, I have to keep looking for something else.

Just thinking about the article hitting the shelves next month makes my stomach feel like birds are taking flight. I'm equally scared to death that it won't be as good as it needs to be and over-the-top excited that something I created is going to be in a publication like *Southern Style*. It's a dream come true. The fact that the success of that article will determine whether or not I get more opportunities like that makes me nervous. I want that. I want to feel inspired and do what I love. I want it so bad.

Grabbing my phone and bag off the bed, I try not to think about the what-ifs and focus on what I have to do today. That's pretty much been my motto these last three weeks: one day at a time.

When I walk into the living room, Nurse Sharon is already fussing over Graham, so I say my goodbyes and head out to the elevator. I push the button for the first floor and look down at my phone to shoot Piper a quick text back, but it wasn't her after all.

Micah: I'm bored. Let's play a game.

Me: I'm headed out to an interview. Can I have a rain check?

Micah: An interview, huh? Does this mean you're out of the freelance game?

Me: No, but I have to keep looking. I'll be living off Top Ramen if I don't get a job soon. LOL

Micah: I'm sure you could come up with lots of good ways to make noodles.

Me: Subject for another cookbook.

Micah: Now, that's what I'm talking about! How's that going, by the way?

Me: Still on the back burner.

Micah: I think you need to bring it to the front, let it come to a boil. ;)

Me: Maybe someday. Right now, I'm about to get my ass run over by a taxi. Gotta go!

Micah: Be careful! Good luck on the interview!

Me: How about that game?

Micah: How'd the interview go?

Me: Okay, I guess. Not really what I want to do, but it'll pay the bills. IF I get it.

Micah: Well, I hope you find something perfect for you. Nothing but the best for Sheridan Reed!

Me: The game?

Micah: Oh, right. The game. You ready?

Me: Yes, but I have to tell you, I could go pro with my pinochle skills.

Micah: Duly noted. How about 20 Questions?

Me: Sure. Are you a person, place, or thing?

Micah: What? No, not that 20 Questions.

Me: There's more than one version of 20 Questions?

Micah: Holy hell, woman. I just meant we should ask each other questions to learn more about each other.

Me: Oh, well, that's not really a game. That's called getting to know each other.

Micah: Are you always a pain in the ass?

Me: Is that your first question?

Micah: You're lucky you're hot.

Me: You think I'm hot?

Micah: Is that your first question for me?

Me: Maybe.

Micah: Then my answer is yes.

CHAPTER
Fourteen

Sheridan

GRAHAM'S LIGHT SNORES FROM HIS bed make me look up from the television show I've been zoning out on for the past hour. I don't even know what I'm watching, some survivor show on Discovery. I yawn and consider closing my eyes. Watching Graham sleep makes me tired, even though I shouldn't be. I haven't done shit today.

The nurse came earlier this morning and helped Graham shower . . . well, I guess she just supported his leg while he showered himself. Then Kaitlyn came by for his physical therapy session. So, I guess technically, Graham has been the more productive one today. Although, while he was doing his PT, I did run down to the store to grab a few things for nachos later, so I wasn't a total bum.

When another loud snore erupts from Graham's sleeping form, I glare at him, willing him to stop breathing.

Everything he does lately annoys the shit out of me. He smacks when he eats. He breathes heavily. He snores. He also does this weird hacking thing all the time. And hearing him whine about not being able to work or go do his guy things makes me want to stab my eardrums. He should've kept his ass at home and we wouldn't be in this predicament.

Maybe it's me?

Maybe I need out of this apartment.

Maybe it's time for Aunt Flo to visit. I think, counting back days since my last period. I don't really keep track of it since my sex life has been non-existent.

I miss sex.

I could definitely stand to get laid. It's been . . . shit. It's been a long damn time.

Since that's out of the question, I do the next best thing and shoot Micah a text.

> *Me: Is it possible to go crazy just by listening to someone breathe? And how am I just now learning he's an occasional smacker?*

> *Micah: Your man's a mouth-breather and a smacker? That's gross. I have to admit, I'm disappointed in your choice of boyfriends.*

> *Me: Well, they can't all be southern playboys, you know?*

> *Micah: That's a damn shame.*

As I'm getting ready to send back a response, a loud knock from the front door echoes through the apartment, I consider turning the television down and pretending I'm not at home. I'm not expecting anyone and Graham has had all of his scheduled appointments for the day, so I can't imagine who it would be. I'm definitely not in the mood for solicitors or anyone else who might be out there, but after another loud knock, I pull myself off the couch and shuffle to the door.

"Who is it?" I ask, through the door, while simultaneously unlatching the lock. I don't know why I do that. I'm pretty sure you're supposed to ask and then open. Peeking through the crack, I see a man in a brown uniform.

"Ms. Reed?" he asks.

"Yep, that's me," I answer, opening the door wider.

"I have a package for you. Please sign here." He hands his clipboard over to me and a smile breaks across my face. *Piper Grey.* Piper sending me a package must mean . . .

I squeal, quickly sign on the dotted line, practically throw the clipboard back to him, and grab my package in return.

"Uh, have a nice day," the delivery man says, a bit taken aback by my sudden outburst.

"Thank you!" I yell through the now closed door.

"What's all the screaming about?" Graham asks, still half asleep.

"I got a package from Piper!"

"Well, yippee," he says, his voice laced with annoyance and sarcasm.

Ignoring Graham, I plop back down on the couch and rip the seal on the package, taking care not to bend or damage anything inside in my haste. When I get my hands on what's inside, my heart beats faster and my mouth falls open.

When my phone starts singing about huge asses, I jump.

"Hello?" I say, putting it up to my ear without even seeing who's calling.

"Do you love it?" Piper asks.

"I do. How'd you—why didn't you tell me?" My voice is barely above a whisper, unable to take my eyes off of the magazine in my hand. My photo—my creation—is on the front cover of *Southern Style Magazine*.

This can't be real life.

Piper's giggle from the other end lets me know I probably said that out loud. "It's real life, and it's gorgeous, Dani! I wanted to tell you a couple of weeks ago when they decided to use it, but I figured the surprise would be worth keeping it a secret."

"You have no idea . . ." My voice trails as it begins to crack. "You just don't know what this means to me." A small sob breaks free, but it's okay, because this is Piper, and she knows me. She's been there through all sorts of tears, but these are good ones, and she made them happen. "Thank you."

"Hey, I just opened the door. The kickass job was all on you. They absolutely loved you, by the way. My senior editor said they want to use you for the roadside diner article."

"Shut up!"

"Yep! I don't have a start date yet, but don't get too comfy in New

York, Sheridan Reed. Your ass is gonna be back in God's country in no time."

"I don't know what to say."

"Say yes! And, 'thank you, Piper. You're the best friend a girl could ask for.' Also, say I'll get to see you on this trip. I don't think I can go another six months."

"Yes. To all of that."

"Good."

She sighs contentedly into the phone. She's happy. She's happy that I'm happy. And I am *so* happy.

"You just turned a shitty day into the best day ever."

"That's what friends are for."

The call waiting beeps in my ear and I feel Graham shift beside me.

"Hey, Pipe. I'm getting another call. Lemme take this. I'll call you back later."

"Okay! We'll celebrate over Skype. Grab a bottle of wine before you call me back."

"It's a plan!" I switch the call, effectively hanging up on Piper.

"Hello?" I say, not recognizing the other caller's number.

"Sheridan Reed!" I'd know this voice anywhere.

"Annie!"

"Sweetheart, I just got a package from *Southern Style*, and I'm speechless! I can't tell you how much this means to me. And your picture of the house on the front cover . . ." She lets out a deep breath, "honey, it's the most beautiful thing ever. I'm so proud of you."

"Thank you."

"No, sweet girl, thank you! This is just . . . well, I can't wait to kiss you when I see you next."

I laugh into the phone, basking in her warmth and goodness. "I can't wait for that."

"I'm cooking for you, too. Anything you want."

"That sounds amazing."

The phone grows quiet for a moment before Annie starts again. "We miss you down here, you know."

"I miss down there."

"What's keepin' you?"

"Oh, you know, life . . ."

"Well, don't forget to take care of yourself. What Dani wants is important, too."

"Thank you. And I won't. Oh, and I just spoke to my best friend who works for *Southern Style*, and she told me she got the green light on the roadside diner article I want to write."

"Oh, that's great news! So, we will see you, right?"

"Of course! I can't come down there without visiting my favorite family." Graham clears his throat, reminding me I'm not alone. I'm guessing he doesn't like me making plans without him. *Interesting*.

"Well, you let me know the details and I'll set up a room for you. You're not staying at that dump of a motel."

I laugh. "I'll take you up on that! Not sure when or how long I'll be in your area, but I'll let you know."

"Sounds great. Take care, Dani."

"You too, Annie."

When I hang up, I stare at the magazine in my lap, feeling my excitement bubble up all over again.

"Well, let me see it," Graham says, holding out his hand.

I hand it over to him and watch as his eyes take in the cover.

"That's mine," I tell him, pointing to the cover. "I did that."

"That's great, Dani," he says, smiling. "Congratulations."

"Read the article," I tell him, shifting in my spot to face him. I can't keep the excitement out of my voice.

"Okay." He laughs and then begins to flip through the pages while I hover over his shoulder. When he finally lands on my article, I draw in a sharp breath. It's exactly what I had hoped it would be. The photos tell it all. There's no need to read the words on the page, although I hope people do. I want them to see how wonderful it is there. I hope they feel the sense of home and comfort I felt.

Graham sits in silence for a few minutes while he reads through the article. "It's really good," he finally says, looking up at me.

"Thank you," I tell him, leaning a little closer to get a better look at the far page.

He turns his body until we're eye to eye. I don't move as his hand reaches up and brushes my hair from my face, pushing it over my shoulder. Then, his lips brush my cheek . . . and then my mouth. It's soft and gentle, barely more than a kiss you'd give a friend, but it takes me by surprise.

My eyes grow wide and I pull back from the unexpectedness.

"What?" he asks, laughing nervously while his hand still touches my cheek.

"What was that for?" I ask.

"Congratulations . . . a job well done . . ." He pauses and his eyes search my face. "Can I not kiss my girlfriend?" he asks, rubbing his thumb against my skin.

"Yeah," I say, a bit taken aback by his actions and words. "Of course you can."

When I settle back onto my side of the couch, my fingers touch my lips, trying to process how I'm feeling. This shouldn't be weird. I've been kissing Graham for years. He's the only person I've kissed. So, why does it feel weird?

"I really am proud of you, Dani."

Turning to look at him, I see a touch of sincerity in his eyes and something else I can't quite put my finger on. Jealousy, maybe?

"Thanks, Graham."

I watch him as he continues looking through the magazine. His eyebrows furrow and his mouth twists. "Is this the family who owns the plantation?" he asks, pointing to the family picture.

"Yeah, that's the Landrys."

"You really like them, huh?"

"Yeah, they're *such* good people."

"Who's this?" he asks, pointing to the biggest guy in the family, with the biggest dimples.

"That's Deacon."

"And this?"

"Micah." Just saying his name makes my stomach flip flop and my pulse quicken.

Graham snorts. "Spoiled rich brats," he says, turning the page.

Um, hello. Pot, meet kettle.

"They're nothing like that."

"Right."

"They're not!" I semi-playfully swat his good arm and bite my tongue before I start a full-blown argument.

"Well, the house is really pretty," he says, closing the magazine and tossing it onto the table. "And you did a good job on the pictures."

"Thanks."

I grab my phone, anything to distract me from telling Graham he's one to talk about rich, spoiled brats. His dad may be an asshole, but he's always given Graham everything he's ever wanted. The Landry boys might be spoiled, but it's with love. I've seen the way they help and care about others. You can be spoiled without being rotten . . . well, Micah and Deacon definitely have their rotten moments. I smile and shake my head.

I miss them.

Me: Did you see the article?

Micah: Looking at it right now. You're amazing!

Me: Thank you.

Micah: I'm serious, Dani. I can't even tell you how proud I am of you. Everything from the pictures to the words on the page . . . it's so fucking good.

I beam at his words. They make me feel good—better than when I opened the package and saw *my* photograph on the front cover.

CHAPTER
Fifteen

Sheridan

Micah: When you fart in public, do you fess up?

Me: It's one-thirty in the morning.

Micah: Did I wake you?

Me: No.

Micah: Then answer my question. I feel it shows a person's true character.

Me: No.

Micah: No? Do you pin it on someone else?

Me: OMG, Micah. I can't believe we're having this conversation. I don't confess or blame anyone else because I try very hard not to do THAT in public!

Micah: But what happens when one slips out?

Me: That's never happened before.

Micah: Bullshit.

Me: What do you do when one slips out?

Micah: I claim it if I need to. That shows I'm honest and responsible, don't you think?

Me: No, it shows that you're gross.

Me: Happy 4th of July! Don't do anything I wouldn't do. ;) Actually, please live it up and allow me to live vicariously through you, because I have no life.

Piper: I'm drinking in your honor tonight, Sheridan Reed! I hope you get vicariously drunk. I might need you to vicariously hold my hair in the morning. ;) Love you, D! Happy 4th! Wish you were here!

Two different texts come through simultaneously.

Piper: P.S. Who's 225–555–7319?

Micah: Who the hell is 205–739–0005?

I roll my eyes, knowing I just opened a can of worms. I guess I wasn't really thinking clearly when I sent the group text.

Me: Piper, meet Micah Landry. Micah Landry, Piper Grey, the best friend.

Micah: Hello, Piper.

Piper: Ah ha, Micah Landry. Well, isn't this fun. ;)

Micah: Not to be one-upped by the best friend, I'll be drinking in your honor as well, Ms. Reed.

Piper: Well, isn't that chivalrous.

Me: You've gotta watch him, Pipe. He has some southern playboy voodoo charm.

Piper: I'll remember that.

Piper: Micah Landry. Spill.

Me: It's 8:05AM. Why are you awake? Did you never go to bed?

Piper: I'm not quite the party animal I once was. *sigh*

I laugh, missing my best friend so damn much.

Me: Aww! Does that mean you didn't get vicariously drunk for me last night and sleep with some random guy? Because I desperately needed to get laid. I forgot to tell you that part.

Piper: I'm sorry I failed us. I'll do better next time.

Me: I'm gonna hold you to it. Did we at least get tipsy?

Piper: My lips were numb for a couple hours.

Me: Nice.

Piper: So, Micah Landry?

Me: He's a friend?

Piper: Why was that a question?

Me: I'm not sure. He's a friend. We have a lot in common. He's fun to talk to. That's it, really.

Piper: Uh huh. Ok.

Me: Have I ever lied to you?

Piper: No, but you did let me dance on top of the bar at Fat Woody's with toilet paper stuck to my shoe!

Me: Ah, good times.

Me: Tell me something no one knows.

Micah: That's pretty deep for this early in the morning. Are you okay?

Me: Yeah, it's been a long week, just feeling overwhelmed and confused. I could really use a distraction, I guess.

Micah: I never actually passed my driving test.

Me: So, you've been driving without a license for over ten years?

Micah: No. I got my license. I just never took the driving test.

Me: Explain, please.

Micah: Instead of driving, I fingered the instructor while we were still in the parking lot. She liked it so much, she gave me an A. And a blowjob.

Me: *I don't even know what to say to that.*

Micah: *Not one of my best moments, I agree, but what 16yo boy would turn that down?*

Me: *Good point.*

Micah: *I also wanted to be a dancer on Broadway when I was a kid.*

Me: *WHAT?!*

Micah: *I remember saving my allowance so I could order this spandex bodysuit covered in sparkles. I hid it under my bed and would stare at it every night before I went to sleep.*

Me: *You're not serious.*

Micah: *Nope, but you're distracted now, right?*

Me: *LOL. Yes, thank you.*

Micah: *Anytime.*

CHAPTER *Sixteen*

MICAH

"ORDER UP!" I YELL THROUGH the small window, sliding a couple of plates onto the counter. Joe has the weekend off because his daughter is getting married and it's taking both me and Deacon to fill his spot. We've spent the day prepping food and gaining a whole new appreciation for what he does, that's for sure. Not that we didn't already appreciate him, but we pretty much have him at worship status right now. I'm dog tired, and from the looks of Deacon across the kitchen, he's feeling it too.

We recently had to fire our manager at Grinders, our restaurant in Baton Rouge, so it's been taking up more of our time as well. Between there and Pockets, we're being stretched thin these days.

"I've never been so excited to see Sunday roll around as I am this week," Deacon says as he stands beside me, assembling a few plates.

"No shit, dude. I feel like I'm dead on my feet."

"Hey, boss," Jamie says, waltzing into the kitchen. I groan and roll my eyes before turning around. She's been relentless in her advances lately, and it's getting on my last nerve.

"What?" I ask, shooting her a glare. She should be working.

"Don't shoot the messenger," she says, holding her hands up in surrender. "I'm just back here to tell you a long-legged blonde is out front lookin' for ya," she says with a sneer.

I cock an eyebrow at her, wondering why she even bothered coming back here to tell me.

She quickly flashes a ten between her fingers. "A girl's gotta pay the bills."

"Tell her I'll be out in a minute."

Jamie nods and turns for the door, taking a tray of food and her pissy attitude with her.

"Do you know who it is?" Deacon asks.

"No."

"Well, don't ya wanna find out?"

"In a minute."

"You need to get laid, bro. You've been a moody bastard the past few weeks."

I *have* been moody. But nothing seems to make it better. I tried hooking up with Valerie, but couldn't even make it to the motel room. Everything about her grated my nerves—her voice, her perfume, even her sticky lipstick—so I dropped her off and made up something about feeling sick.

It probably doesn't help that Dani infiltrates every facet of my being these days. I hear her voice in the silence. See her when I close my eyes. Sometimes, when I'm trying to go to sleep at night, it's like I can feel her there with me. I'm glad I didn't kiss her when she was here because that would've made things even worse.

At least I have her text messages. If I'm missing her too bad, I'll shoot her some crazy text and wait for her response. Sometimes, she'll text me first. I don't like when the messages sound sad, though. One night last week, she texted saying she was confused, and I could tell there was more going on than she was admitting. Nights like that, it's all I can do to keep my ass off a plane headed for New York.

I've never been like this—some guy who sits around pining for a girl. I've been a fuck-'em-and-leave-'em kind of guy. I've been upfront about it and completely unapologetic. Having a good time has always been my main objective. Sure, there've been a few girls who have been around for more than a one-night stand, like Valerie, but even they know there are no strings attached.

All of them have been replaceable.

All of them, except the one I haven't even been with. I just can't seem to get her out of my mind. But I don't want to. I don't even try.

"I guess I'll deliver these next two orders and see who's callin'."

"Go get 'em, Tiger," Deacon jokes without looking up from the pocket he's assembling.

Walking out into the main part of the restaurant, I instantly see who Jamie was talking about. It's been a long time, but I'd know those legs anywhere—the screamer.

"Hey, Alex," I say smoothly as I walk past her.

I set the two plates down in front of the customers sitting closest to the stage and ask, "Is there anything else I can get for ya?"

When they tell me everything looks good, I turn my attention back to the table behind them.

"What brings you around?" I ask. I haven't seen her legs in a very long time. Or her face, for that matter.

"Oh, you know, I was in the area and couldn't pass up a visit to my favorite restaurant." She bats her eyes, tossing her bleached-blonde hair over her shoulder. "The place seems to be doing well, Micah. You must be proud."

"Yeah, we're not doin' too shabby."

"How's everything else?" she asks, but what she really wants to know is whether I'm still available—still up for a good time.

I think the universe knew just what I needed to get out of my funk. A quick fuck with an old friend, for old time's sake. No strings attached. No guilt. No "call me later". I know exactly what to expect with Alex, and that's comforting in a weird way.

"Good."

She looks at me for longer than necessary, letting her eyes take in everything from my scuffed up boots to my messy hair. "So, you feel like gettin' together later?"

"Sure."

As soon as the word is out of my mouth, I want to take it back.

When she runs a finger down my arm and then casually over to the waist of my jeans, my dick stirs, reminding me of why I'm agreeing to this. I swallow thickly, trying to get my head in check.

She stands from the booth and leans in until her lips are practically touching my ear. "I was hopin' you'd say that."

Images of red hair and green eyes flood my mind.

What would Dani think about this?

Would she care?

No. No, of course not.

That's stupid. She has Graham. We're just friends.

I grimace, feeling guilty, but not knowing why.

"You know where to find me," I tell her, forcing a smile onto my face.

"I'll be back around closin' time."

I nod and smirk before turning around and practically running back to the kitchen.

I do *not* know what's come over me. It's like there's a war going on inside me. My heart and my head are ganging up against my dick, but I have no idea who's going to win.

The feeling in my gut kinda resembles having bad tacos or driving past a bad wreck, but since I haven't done either of those, I'm having a hard time understanding it all.

For the next two hours, I keep myself busy in the kitchen and force my head and heart to give my dick a break. He's lonely, for fuck's sake. Surely they can understand that.

Later that night, after everyone has left, even Deacon, I'm sweeping under the tables near the bar when someone taps lightly on the front door. I don't even have to look up to know who it is. Stepping up to the door to unlock it, I open it so she can walk inside. Her perfume is assaulting, and I find myself holding my breath when she gets too close.

"Hey," she says, invading my space and pressing her tits against my chest. Her cheeks are rosy and her eyes are glazed over. She's definitely tipsy. I can smell the alcohol on her breath.

Tequila, if I had to guess.

Fuck.

Once again, I'm at war with myself. Standing here, staring at her, knowing she's very capable and willing, I'm having a hard time saying no. But, on the other hand, the sick feeling I had earlier is back in full force.

Alex flattens her hands against my chest. "You've filled out."

"The last time we were together, I was still wet behind the ears." A hint of nostalgia washes over me and I allow myself to really look at her. Her tits are bigger, hips are fuller . . . she's filled out too.

"Oh, but you were so very talented, even then. I'm really looking forward to what else time has improved." She licks her bottom lip and her eyes drop to my dick. "Are we doing this here?" she asks, looking around, confirming exactly why she's here.

She's a sure thing. She always has been.

"How about we go back to my office?"

"Much better."

I let her walk in front of me and I take in her ass as we make our way down the hall and to my office. When we walk in, she turns on me. "Off," she commands, pointing to my jeans. The second my hand goes to the first button on my jeans, the voices in my head get louder. Before I get them completely unbuttoned, there's a full-on war raging between my head and my dick. When she sees me hesitate, she takes over for me, making fast work of the last two buttons. They're half-way down my ass before I realize this isn't what I want.

"I can't do this," I say breathlessly. My heart is beating so fast I feel like I just ran a fucking marathon.

"What?" The look on her face is confusion and disbelief.

"I-I can't do this," I tell her again, a bit more calmly this time, because she's no longer touching me.

"What the *fuck*, Micah?"

"I-I'm seeing someone," I stutter, completely making this shit up as I go. "She doesn't live here, but I'm seeing someone, and I know we've done shit in the past, but I can't anymore. I'm sorry I led you to believe otherwise," I finish, knowing it sounds like a line of bullshit, but it's the only thing I could think of.

"I don't believe you. Micah Landry doesn't do relationships."

"Well, I didn't used to, but I do now."

"So, you're really seeing someone?" she asks, still skeptical.

"We're not *technically* official." *Fuck.* We're not anything. "But I want us to be, and I obviously can't do that if I fuck it up by fucking you."

What the hell am I saying?

She smirks, her surprised expression morphing into something else. "Well, she must be pretty damn special."

"She is."

I want to roll my eyes and call myself out on my own bullshit. Dani isn't mine, and she may never be. But my heart wants to believe what my mouth just said.

Alex fixes her skirt and looks in the mirror on my office wall to check her makeup. "Well, I'm sorry this," she waves a hand toward my dick, "didn't work out, but I'm happy for you."

I walk her to the front door of the restaurant and watch her walk to her car. Turning off the house lights, I quickly make my way out the back door to my truck. The need to take a shower is so overwhelming, I can't get home fast enough.

But what I need even more is a thousand miles away.

I pull out my phone before turning onto the main road.

Me: Hey, Chuck. You awake?

I wait a second, hoping she responds quickly, but she doesn't. Looking at the clock on the dash of my truck, I see it's after midnight, which means it's after one there, so I pull out onto the road and head home.

After I shower and almost scrub my skin raw, I put on a pair of pajama pants and throw myself onto my bed. When my phone rings beside me, I don't even bother looking at the screen.

"Hello?"

"Micah Landry." Val's sugary-sweet voice comes through the speaker.

Fuck! I want to scream. She's the last damn person I want to talk to right now.

"Val."

"Are you busy?"

I know where this is heading. It's always the same questions. *Am I busy? Can I do her a favor?*

"Micah?"

"Yeah?"

"So?"

"I'm not busy, Val, but I just got in from a really long day and I'm exhausted," I tell her, and it's the God's honest truth.

"Well, I know just what would make you feel better." Her voice dips, changes to sultry and seductive. It has worked in the past, but not anymore.

"I can't."

"How about I come out there?"

"No." The word comes out a little too forceful, but I can't help it. I don't want to see Val, and I especially don't want her at my house.

"What's wrong with you, Micah?" she asks, acid lacing her words. She's been changing lately, becoming clingier and clingier. Val and I have always had a firm agreement—no strings attached.

"You've been blowing me off for the last month," she says, followed by a frustrated huff.

It's true. I have.

"I think it's time for us to go our separate ways, Val."

"Why?" she asks with a pout in her voice.

I pull at my hair, frustrated and exhausted. "This is exactly what I wanted to avoid. You've always known what we had was just fun. But lately, you've been taking things more seriously." I pause, trying to find the right words—trying to let her down easy and not break her heart. "I don't want to hurt you, Val."

"I'm not getting attached," she says, indignant.

She sniffles into the phone and I feel like the biggest asshole on the planet. Maybe I'm reading her wrong? But I don't think I am. Besides, I know Val isn't who I want.

"I know you're going to hate hearing this, Val, but I'm going to be truthful with you." I take a deep breath and prepare to bare my soul to her, hoping it doesn't come back to haunt me. "We've been friends a long time, right?"

"Yeah," she says quietly.

"Friends long before we were anything else?"

"Yeah."

"And I've always told you I don't want to be tied down. I'm having a good time and I don't want to be in a committed relationship."

"I know. I don't want that either."

"You say that, Val, but I know you want more. You might be fighting it, just like I am, but it's there. You practically pissed all over my leg when Dani was here. And what about last week when you went off on Jamie for talkin' to me at the restaurant?"

"She's a whore." I snicker into the phone. She's kinda right. Jamie has been around the block a time or two. "She doesn't deserve to touch you."

"See, but that's the thing, you don't have any claim to me."

I can literally hear the breath leaving her, the gasp audible over the phone. "I didn't mean to get attached," she whispers. "I never meant to want more."

"We don't have control over those things. One of these days, you're gonna find someone who loves you more than anyone else on this planet. You deserve that, Val."

She sniffles again and I continue to feel like shit, but I also feel like there's a weight lifting off my chest.

"I always thought that might be you."

Her words cut me to my soul, and I kinda want to cry right now, too. I'm breaking her heart and I never meant to do that.

"I never meant to hurt you."

"I know."

"You gonna be all right?"

"Yeah." She takes a deep breath in and lets it out. "I am." A few seconds of silence go by before she speaks again. "Thanks for being honest with me."

"You're welcome."

"I'll see ya around."

"Yeah, see ya around."

I toss my phone to the nightstand, roll over, and hug my pillow, wishing it had red hair and green eyes. The vibration from my nightstand startles me. I rub sleep from my bleary eyes and look at the alarm clock: 1:37.

Dani: You still up?

Me: I am now.

Dani: Sorry I woke you. Pretend I didn't send this. Go back to sleep.

I laugh. She's so damn cute.

Me: I don't want to. I want to talk to you.

Dani: Good because I can't sleep. What do you want to talk about?

Me: Anything. Everything.

I know that sounds vague, but it's the truth. I want to know everything about Sheridan Reed. Come to think of it . . .

Me: What's your middle name?

Dani: Paige. I was named after my grandmother. It was her maiden name. Lillian Opal Paige.

Me: I like it.

"Sheridan Paige Reed," I whisper, allowing her name to roll effortlessly off my tongue. I *really* like it.

CHAPTER
Seventeen

MICAH

205–739–0005: What are your intentions with my best friend?

I STARE AT MY PHONE, trying to process this early morning text message. Who it's from finally dawns on me and I snicker as I type out my response.

Me: Who are you? And what the hell are you talking about?

Before she has a chance to respond, I swipe my finger across the "add new contact" button on my phone and add her in. *Piper—The Best Friend.*

Piper: Don't mess with me, Micah Landry. I can be your closest ally or your worst enemy.

I scrub my face with my free hand, chuckling to myself.

Me: Are you always this hostile in the morning?

Piper: It's nearly 10:00. That's barely considered morning.

Me: *Not when you don't go to bed until 3:00 AM.*

Piper: *And just what were you doing at 3:00 AM? This is exactly why I need to know your intentions with my best friend. She's been dicked around enough in her life.*

I already love her. She's obviously fiercely protective of a girl I care a lot about and she used "dicked around" in a sentence.

Me: *For your information, I had to close down my restaurant by myself last night, and then I was texting YOUR best friend until she fell asleep on me. And I don't have any "intentions". We're friends. She makes me laugh. We have a lot in common.*

Piper: *Hmmmm. That's bizarrely similar to the answer I got from her when I asked about you. Did you kiss her?*

Me: *First, I don't kiss and tell.*

I pause, not sure what my second is, but I've already sent the text, and you can't have a first without a second.

Me: *Second, I don't kiss and tell.*

Piper: *Do you want to kiss her?*

Me: *She has a boyfriend.*

Piper: *You didn't answer my question.*

Me: *Yes, I did. Sometimes, you have to read between the lines.*

Piper: *Touché. That was kinda deep for just waking up.*

Me: *I'm not just a pretty face.*

Piper: *I'll have to be the judge of that.*

Me: Am I still on trial?

Piper: Yes, until I give further notice. Also, I tried stalking you on Facebook, and the only Micah Landry I could find was bald and gay. I'm assuming that wasn't you?

I laugh out loud. Who admits to stalking people on Facebook?

Me: No, definitely not bald. And definitely not gay.

Piper: Why don't you have a Facebook page? Everyone has a Facebook page.

Me: I don't have time for one, and I don't want people stalking me. ;)

Piper: Well, you know what this means, right?

Me: No. What?

Piper: I'll have to stalk you in person.

Me: Should I go ahead and file the restraining order?

Piper: Won't stop me. Good day, Micah Landry.

Me: Good day.

What the fuck was that?
I have a feeling Piper is a force to be reckoned with. I'm looking forward to meeting her. And maybe a little scared.

Me: Should I be worried about Piper?

Dani: Oh, no. What did she do?

Me: Apparently, since she can't stalk me on Facebook, she's going to stalk me in person. I'm kinda scared.

Dani: God! She's such a nosy bitch. I told her to leave things alone. I'm sorry. And don't worry. She's all bark and no bite. Well, unless you try to come between her and her pizza. You might lose a finger.

Me: Good to know.

Me: 20 questions. Rapid-fire. You start.

Dani: Favorite movie?

Me: Die Hard. Favorite song?

Dani: The Climb by Miley Cyrus. Favorite color?

Me: Red. Favorite holiday?

Dani: Halloween. Favorite Pocket?

Me: Fried oyster. Favorite sport?

Dani: Football, duh. Favorite childhood memory?

Me: The time Deacon shot me in the chest with a BB gun and I pretended I was dying.

Dani: You're an awful person, Micah Landry.

Me: Hey, I didn't comment on your piss-poor taste in music!

Dani: Ignoring that. How old were you when Deacon shot you?

Me: I was eight, and he was ten. Not gonna lie, it stung like a sonofabitch, but it was worth it to see my big brother crying like a baby to our parents.

Dani: Did you ever tell him you were faking?

Me: Oh, yeah. It was pretty obvious when there was nothing but a pink dot on my chest. He was pissed at me for a while, but believe me, he's gotten his revenge since then.

Dani: Do tell.

Me: That's a story for another day.

CHAPTER
Eighteen

Sheridan

Me: I want the other story.

J'M IN A LONG LINE at the pharmacy, waiting on Graham's prescriptions. They told me over the phone they'd be ready, but when I got here, the guy at the window said they were running behind and I'd need to take a number.

Graham is finally out of his immobilization cast and has started more intense physical therapy on his leg, but with that comes added inflammation and pain. The good news is his mobility is coming back and he's improving every day. He no longer has any casts and all of the bruising is gone. At this pace, he'll be back to work and out of my apartment in no time.

A few minutes go by before my phone dings.

Micah: What other story?

Me: Deacon's Revenge.

I smile as I type. It sounds like the title of a very intense, serious novel, and I know Micah's response will be anything but. Anything involving him and Deacon, especially when they were kids, deserves to be in a sitcom.

Me: I'm waiting in a long-ass line. Entertain me.

Micah: As you wish . . .

Another minute goes by . . .

Micah: Last year on Father's Day, I got a card in the mail congratulating me on being a dad, and it was signed by a girl I barely remembered being with. Stupid me opened it in front of my parents too, so to say I was shitting bricks was an understatement. I was freaking the fuck out! Sweating, chills, sick to my stomach . . . all that shit. That is, until I saw my precious brother standing behind my parents, doubled over, laughing his ass off.

Me: Damn! Remind me never to piss Deke off!

Micah: I've always used condoms, but it still scared the shit out of me. Fucking asshole.

Me: I thought you said you wanted a family.

Micah: I do, but not like that. I mean, I'd love my kid no matter the circumstances, but I'd rather wait until I was in a committed relationship, you know?

Me: Absolutely.

Why does the subject of Micah and kids turn my insides into jelly?

Micah: So, where are you waiting in a long-ass line?

Me: Pharmacy. I'm here getting Graham's prescriptions, but I might need to get myself something while I'm here. I'm not feeling so swift.

Micah: Fuck the line and the pharmacy. If you're not feeling well, you should get home. Do you think you have a virus or something?

Me: Simmer down.

I laugh, shaking my head. He's adorable.

Me: I didn't eat breakfast, so my head hurts and I feel kinda sick to my stomach. I'm sure I'll be fine after I take some Tylenol and eat some lunch.

Micah: I'll be texting you later to check on you. If you don't respond within five minutes, I'll call 911 on your behalf, so you better keep your phone close.

He is his mother's child.

Me: Yes, Annie—I mean, Micah.

Micah: If you could see me right now, you'd know I'm giving you "the look".

I laugh and pocket my phone, deciding to take Micah up on his suggestion. I'll come back later when it's not so busy. Excusing myself past the people behind me in line, I make my way out of the pharmacy.

I think about stopping for something to eat on my way back, but I really just want some of the leftover meatloaf I made yesterday. Once again, Graham didn't eat any of it because "it's *gross*". Meatloaf isn't gross. Meatloaf is awesome. And leftover meatloaf sandwiches are fantastic . . . and currently calling my name.

Several people are waiting for the elevator, so I decide to bypass the crowd and take the stairs. When I push open the door of my apartment, I almost make a beeline for the kitchen, but a loud bang back near the bathroom makes me jump.

"Graham!" I call out, moving toward the noise.

Another bang.

"Graham!" I say even louder, my worry building, fearing he may have fallen.

When I walk into my bedroom, my jaw drops to the floor . . . with my stomach . . . and my heart.

"Graham?"

Yeah, he's fallen all right. Right onto his back. In my bed. With Kaitlyn.

My heart pounds faster, my breaths coming quickly, nostrils flaring. I close my eyes, trying to erase what I've just witnessed.

The headboard of my bed hits the wall one more time before Kaitlyn notices me standing in the doorway.

"Oh my God!"

"Yeah, baby. Let me hear you."

"No, Graham!" she screams, slapping his chest as she tries to climb off him and hide herself at the same time.

"What?" he asks, sounding pissed off.

He lets go of Kaitlyn's hips, allowing her to move off him. Then he opens his eyes and looks at her face, but she's looking at me. His gaze follows hers and then our eyes meet. I can't turn away. It's like a car wreck. You know it's bad and you know you don't want to see it, but you look anyway.

"Dani?" he asks in disbelief.

I shake my head, still trying to process what's happening while keeping myself from flipping the fuck out.

I will not cry. I will not cry. I will not cry, I chant over and over in my head while biting the inside of my cheek to keep the tears at bay.

"Dani, this isn't what it looks like." He shakes his head profusely, trying his damnedest to pull his pants up.

I press my lips together, pushing down the emotions threatening to spill over.

"Don't," I say, holding up my hand to silence him as I try to keep my voice even but firm. I don't want to hear his excuses. There aren't any good enough.

"Sheridan. Baby."

"I am *not* . . ." I pause, closing my eyes and willing myself to stay in control. "I'm not your baby. Don't . . . don't say that. I want you to get out." I hear myself talking, but I feel like I'm watching from somewhere high above. "Get your fucking shit, and get out."

"Sheridan!" he yells, sounding desperate, but I don't want to hear it.

I turn around and bolt for the front door, throwing it open. I need out. I need air.

Somebody give me some fucking air!

"Sheridan!" Graham yells in the distance as I quickly make my way down the stairs, not even stopping to shut the door.

My feet take each step so fast, I nearly fall on my face when I get to the bottom. I run out the front door, shoulder checking some guy who won't move out of my way fast enough. I push my way down the street and continue through the next intersection. I keep going until my throat and lungs feel like they're on fire. When I feel like I'm about to pass out, I lean up against the side of a building and I cry.

What the fuck just happened?

I sob.

People stare.

I slide down the concrete wall and sit on the ground.

I cry some more.

People walk by like I'm not even here.

And I feel alone. Really and truly alone.

For the first time in a long time, I feel like I'm walking the planet all by myself, even though I'm surrounded by millions of people.

I read in a book somewhere you don't really know who you can count on until your world is turned upside down . . . until you're at your very lowest point. The people who are there for you at that time are the people who will be around for the long haul. I thought the day my grandmother died was the lowest point in my life. My world literally shifted on its axis.

I remember crying when my mom died. I was five. I remember wearing a pale pink dress that day. I had been with my grandmother, where I was on most days. Now, looking back, I think I cried because my grandmother was crying. I didn't know how final death was. I didn't feel the grief because my grandmother was there to cushion my fall. I always thought if I had her, I could handle anything.

When my grandmother died, I felt like I couldn't breathe. It was a little easier to swallow because I knew she had lived a good, full life, but it didn't make it hurt less. She was all I had ever known. But Piper and Graham were there for me. They picked me up, dusted me off, and helped me keep going when I didn't want to.

Then, my dad died.

But I wasn't a stranger to grief. The day I found out, I remember thinking if I could survive my mother and my granny's deaths, I could survive anything. His death didn't feel personal, because I didn't even know him. The only thing he'd ever done for me in my life was donate some sperm when my mom was eighteen. When I went to his funeral, I felt like I was attending a friend of a friend of a friend's funeral.

A month later, when I was walking to one of my classes on campus, I saw a mother and father with their little girl. It was so simple, so normal, but in those three seconds, as they held her hands and swung her between them, I realized I was alone—an orphan. I had no one. That's when I finally cried over my dad, or maybe just over the idea that there wasn't anybody left on this earth genetically linked to me. Sure, I have some aunts and uncles somewhere, but I'm not close to them. That's what happens when you're the only child of an only child. But Graham was there for me. He came, found me on a bench, and held me, told me he'd always be there for me, that I'd never be alone.

But he lied.

And here I sit on a disgusting sidewalk in New York City with my best friend a thousand miles away and the only other person who's been there for me is seventeen blocks behind me . . . fucking the physical therapist.

A semi-psychotic laugh erupts out of my chest, along with more tears. I want to scream. I want to run back to my apartment and break Graham's other leg. I want to get on a plane and lie in my best friend's bed while she feeds me Ben and Jerry's.

The only other person I want to talk to right now is Micah, but I'm not ready to talk to anyone yet.

I want a drink.

One thing I know for sure is I can*not* go back to that apartment.

Pulling myself up off the sidewalk, I stand in the middle of the street, holding my hand up for a taxi. When one pulls over, I quickly get inside.

"Where to?"

Where to? I hadn't thought that far.

"Uh . . ."

Shit.

"Where to?" he asks again in his thick foreign accent.

Fuck. He's going to kick me out of his taxi if I can't come up with an address.

Looking up, I see the sleek glass building in front of us. "I need to go there," I say, pointing toward the building. "The, uh . . . Trump Hotel, I think."

"Trump?"

"Yeah."

I don't know why I say it. It's way over my budget, but I decide I'll find a way to make Graham foot the bill. I still have access to all of his accounts and credit cards. I even know his passcodes.

Digging in my bag for a tissue and some money to pay the driver, I see Graham's credit card and his driver's license from when I went to pick up his prescriptions earlier.

Yeah, that cheating bastard is totally paying.

As I walk up to the desk, I take in a deep breath. I should be ashamed of what I'm about to do, but I'm not. I'm just nervous because I'm about to lie my ass off.

"Welcome to the Trump," a lady with light blonde hair says, smiling. "Do you have a reservation?"

"Um, no," I say sweetly, tilting my head and scrunching my nose. "My husband is here on business and his meeting is running late, so he sent me to see about getting a room for the night."

"I can help you with that, Mrs . . ."

"Harrison," I say, swallowing down the bile forcing its way up my throat.

A few minutes later, I have two keys to a room on the fourteenth floor. That was way easier than it should've been. I lamented to her how bare my hand felt without my rings and how I couldn't wait to get them back from the jewelers after they were properly soldered together. She even bought my story that we were "kinda on our honeymoon", which was how I explained away the fact that my name and address had yet to be changed. She sympathized with me on having to follow him around while he jetted the country on business, but I told her when you're in love, you'll do whatever it takes, to which she literally sighed . . . out loud.

It was all I could do not to throw up in the plant next to the elevator.

I am such a lying liar who lies.

I'm going to hell.

No, Graham is.

And Kaitlyn.

I should have punched him.

Or her.

Or both of them.

Before I even get my card in the slot, tears are pouring down my face again. I open the door and gently close it behind me, sliding down the back while the betrayal and disappointment set in anew.

I sit there on the floor, leaning against the door, for what could be minutes or hours. The ridiculously loud growl from my stomach is what finally pulls me out of my trance. I think about cleaning my face and walking downstairs to find something to eat or calling room service, but nothing sounds particularly good.

Walking over by the bed, I begin opening cabinets and drawers. A place this nice is bound to have a mini bar, right?

Bingo.

Tiny bottles and packages of snack foods line the shelves. I peruse my options: tequila, vodka, rum, spiced rum, wine . . . yuck . . . beer . . . not my brand.

"Hello, old friend," I say, twisting the cap off the bottle of Jose Cuervo.

The name on the label makes me think of the big black Labrador living on an expanse of land in Louisiana, which makes me think of said black Lab's owner.

I think about texting him, but how would I even start that

conversation? *Remember my boyfriend? Yeah, he fucked the therapist.*

And I am *not* calling Piper. No way. I'm not ready for her "I told you so". Not that she ever told me Graham was going to cheat on me. Actually, she's probably going to be shocked about that. And had she thought he would cheat on me, she'd have cut his balls off before he had the chance. However, she's never been his biggest fan. They got along pretty well during college, but since we've been together, not so much. She saw the changes in him long before I ever did.

"I should've listened," I whisper to the tiny bottle in my hand. "I'm probably going to regret this at some point, but here goes nothing." I empty the bottle into my mouth, wincing at the distinct burn as it coats my throat.

I really should eat something. Gathering the contents of the mini fridge, I carry the items to the bed, dump them in the middle, and settle on a can of Pringles and a package of almonds. It's a unique combination, but it does the trick of shutting up the bear in my stomach.

The chips and almonds make me thirsty, so I reach for something else to drink. "Hey, Jack. Long time, no see," I say as I hold up another bottle. "How about you treat me a little smoother than Jose? Although, I guess neither of you have fucked me over as hard as Graham." I down the second bottle and sigh. My throat doesn't burn nearly as badly as with the first, so I go for a third. I've never taken a shot of rum, but what the heck? There's a first for everything, including your boyfriend fucking his therapist.

After bottle number four, I rummage through my pile, looking for something else to eat. I grab a bag of cheese crisps, which I've never heard of before, but they look tasty.

I could really go for that meatloaf about now.

Fucking Graham. Fucking ruining my chances for a meatloaf sandwich. Fucking ruining my life.

The cheese crisps make me thirsty again, so I down another tiny bottle. Spiced rum. Much tastier than the first bottle of rum. It probably would've tasted even better mixed with the can of Coke lying there, but who has time for that?

My options on tiny bottles are dwindling. I saved the gin for last, because fuck me, I hate gin.

Half an hour later, I'm still sitting in the middle of the gigantic bed with half empty packages of pretzels and nuts, and one, two, three, four, five, six . . . seven tiny empty bottles.

Lying back on the bed, I try to focus on the ceiling, using it as my point of reference, because the room feels a little shifty.

"Oh, Dani, Dani, Dani . . . what have you gotten yourself into?" I ask the empty room.

When I turn my head to look at the clock, I see it's only 6:00 PM. But at least it's past 5:30. Because I'm drunk. And I think there's some unwritten rule that says you're not supposed to be drunk before 5:30. Or was it 5:00?

My phone buzzes on the nightstand and I glare at it, the sound offending. *If it's Graham, I swear I'll throw that fucking phone out this fourteenth floor window.*

Thinking of Graham pisses me off, fueled even more by the liquor coursing through my body. I almost hope it *is* Graham. I have a few things to say to him, and it'd be a lot easier to get them out in my current state of mind.

Pulling my phone to my face—entirely too close to my face—I try to focus on the screen.

Micah.

> *Micah: Sheridan Reed, you have two minutes to tell me you're not passed out in some back alley in New York, or I'm calling the cops.*

"Well, aren't you Bossy McBossypants." I try hard to type that into a message, but after fucking autocorrect is finished with it, it's more like: *"Well sent you nosy mc postpone."*

I hit send anyway. My arms feel like jelly and I don't feel like retyping it.

> *Micah: Are you okay?*

> *Me: drunk*

I go for simple, one-word responses. Those, I seem to be able to do.

Micah: Are you serious? It's 5:00 in the afternoon.

Me: 6

Micah: Okay. 6:00. Why are you drunk?

Me: ducking hrshm

When the phone rings, it scares the shit out of me. Micah's picture shows up on the screen and I stare at it for so long, the call goes to voicemail. Luckily, he calls back.

"Hellooo?"

"Dani?"

I pull the phone to my forehead and press it against it. The coolness feels good; almost as good as his voice feels in my ear. This is the first time I've heard his voice in two months. It makes my heart ache and my throat tighten.

"Dani?" I hear his voice, but it's too far away. *Where did he go?* I pull the phone off my forehead staring at it for a minute before bringing it back to my ear.

"Hello?"

"Are you okay?"

"Um, yes . . . no . . . I don't know," I say, drawing out my words as my voice weakens with each response.

"What's wrong?" There's so much caring and concern in the way he's asking, it makes me feel like crying. I try holding it back, but it makes my throat hurt so I let out a small sob, releasing some of the pressure.

"Dani, you're scaring me. Please, tell me what's wrong. Are you hurt?"

"Graham . . ." I barely get it out past the gasps and tears.

"Did Graham do something?"

I nod my head.

"Dani, did Graham hurt you?"

"Yes," I whisper.

"What did he do?" he bites out, anger replacing the caring and concern. Controlled anger, but anger, nonetheless.

"He fucked the physical therapist."

"Did he tell you that?"

"Nope," I say, the scene playing back in my mind. "I saw them. In my bed. I walked into the apartment, and I heard a loud bang, and . . . and I thought Graham might be hurt," I say, breaking into a loud sob. "S-so, I yelled for him, but didn't get an answer. It sounded like it was coming from the bathroom, so I went back there and . . . they were in my bed."

The tears are gone, replaced with numbness. I lie back on the pillows and lay my head on the phone. My arms are too tired to hold it, but I don't want to hang up.

"Where are you?"

"Hotel."

"Which one?"

"Trump. Soho."

There's a long pause on the phone, neither of us talking.

"I'm so fucking sorry, Dani."

"Don't apologize. You didn't fuck the therapist, did you?"

He laughs, but there's no humor there. "No. But I'm sorry he hurt you." His words sound pained, like he's the one hurting.

"I don't know how to feel. One second, I'm crying. The next second, I want to go back there and beat the shit out of him. And the second after that, I want to use the key I have to his apartment and go burn all of his clothes. And then, sometimes, I laugh at the complete absurdity of it all."

There's another long pause, and I press my ear close to the phone, listening intently to Micah's breaths.

"I felt like I was having an out-of-body experience. When I told him to get the fuck out of my apartment, I felt like I was hovering above myself, watching it all happen."

"What did he say?"

"That it wasn't what it looked like."

Micah laughs humorlessly into the phone and mutters something under his breath.

"If I hadn't felt like crying so bad in that moment, I would've laughed. As he was saying it, his dick was standing at half-mast and hanging out of his pants."

"*Fuck*," Micah groans into the phone.

"Yeah, that's what they were doing."

"I'm so sorry."

"Yeah." So am I. I'm sorry I ever trusted Graham. I'm sorry I wasted so many years loving him. I'm sorry I believed him when he said he would be there for me.

"What are you going to do?"

"I have no fucking clue. This wasn't really in my five-year plan."

I begin to cry again, but we continue to talk, and every once in a while, we just sit in silence. I don't need him to say anything. I just need to know he's there, even if he is a thousand miles away.

"I feel so alone," I whisper into the phone.

"You're not alone, Dani."

"I am. You . . . you have no idea how this feels." My voice cracks and I swallow the cotton ball lodged in my throat. "You have a family, who you see every day, and friends and . . ." He has everything. Everyone. Anyone he wants. I have nobody. Except Piper and . . .

"You have me."

I *wish* I *had* you, Micah Landry. "Thanks for saying that and for being a good friend."

"Is there anybody you could call . . . ?"

"No. I mean, Piper, but . . . oh, God. Please don't tell Piper about this. I mean, don't try to do some good friend thing by hanging up with me and calling her," I ramble frantically. "I'll call her. Just not tonight."

"Do you have any other friends close by?"

"No." Admitting that makes me feel even more pathetic. "But I'm fine. I mean, I *will* be fine. Don't worry about me. It's not like I'm going to jump out of this fourteenth floor window or anything. I'm not a jumper."

"That's good to know." His soft laugh makes me smile, and for a moment, I imagine what he looks like right now. He's obviously not at work, so that means he's probably in a rumpled LSU t-shirt and jeans, like the day he took me on a tour of the property. The warm feeling that idea gives me turns cold when I realize he could also be getting ready to go out on a date. Maybe he's going to drive Val right through that fucking door this time.

"You don't have to keep talking to me, you know."

"I want to."

"I don't want to keep you from any plans you may have. You don't have to babysit me, Micah."

"Babysit? What are you talkin' about? Believe it or not, I *like* talking to you."

"But, if you have a date or something . . ." I can't even finish that sentence. I don't want to hear about his flavor of the month.

"Dani, I haven't been on a date in a long time."

What?

"A long time? What's that, like, a week?"

Why the fuck am I doing this to myself? Oh, yeah . . . booze.

"If you must know, Ms. Reed, it's been two months since I've *been* with a woman."

I feel flushed from my head to my toes, and I'm not entirely sure it's because I'm tipsy. Speaking of alcohol, I need to replenish my buzz while I contemplate what Micah just said. I pop the cork on a bottle of champagne, making a toast to all the physical therapist-fucking bastards of the world.

At some point, after the sun has gone down outside my window, my eyelids feel like they're coated with sand. They're so heavy, I finally give in to sleep with my phone pressed to my ear.

When a loud pounding echoes through the quiet, I press my hand to my exposed ear, willing it to go away. I can't even open my eyes, they hurt so badly. The knocking continues every thirty seconds or so, and I worry it's inside my head. I haven't been drunk in a long time; maybe this is what a real hangover feels like?

"Dani," a muffled voice calls from the other side of the door.

Oh, shit.

CHAPTER
Nineteen

MICAH

I PRESS MY EAR TO the door, trying to hear any sign of life on the other side. I tried calling on the taxi ride here to make sure I remembered the room number and to give her a heads up I'm in New York, but her phone must've died. For all I know, she could've been wrong when she was singing about it, drunkenly, over the phone last night.

"Room 1414 . . . such a lucky room . . . too bad I'm not getting lucky in 1414."

She sang it over and over for a good two minutes. I laughed at her, and she asked if I was laughing because I didn't like her singing. I told her I liked it very much. It was horrible, actually, but adorable at the same time.

I knock a little louder, hating that I'm probably waking her up, but I can't stand outside this hotel room forever. A maid with a cart has already been by once, eyeing me warily as she passed.

What if she was so drunk she didn't really know where she was?

What if she doesn't want to see me?

"Dani," I call through the door, hoping she can hear me.

A loud thud inside the room makes my ears perk.

"Dani? Are you okay?" I ask a little louder. "It's, uh . . . it's Micah."

A few seconds later, the door slowly opens, and behind it is the best thing I've seen in two months. She's a little worse for wear, but she's still beautiful . . . and perfect . . . and holy shit, I've missed her.

"Micah?" she asks, looking at me through squinty eyes. Squinty eyes with black smudges under them. A few of the smudges go all the way down to her chin and there are spots of black on her cream-colored shirt.

And . . . she's not wearing any pants.

I clear my throat, looking down to her bare legs and then back up to her face. *Fuck.*

"Micah?" she asks again, like she doesn't trust herself to believe what her eyes are seeing.

"Yep."

"What the fuck are you doing here?" She turns to look inside the room, back out to me . . . and then sticks her head into the hallway. Realization starts setting in.

"Oh, fuck," she whines, covering her face. "Did I ask you to come here?"

"No."

"I didn't?" She peeks through her fingers. "Then why are you here?"

"I wanted to check on you. Make sure you're all right."

"You could've called me."

"Your phone's deader than a doornail."

"Shit," she hisses. "God, I'm so embarrassed."

"Why?"

"Because . . . well, because you're here and . . ." She bends down and rests her hands on her knees. "Oh, God. I think I'm gonna be sick." She straightens and cups a hand over her mouth, releasing the door in my face as she runs toward the bathroom. Fortunately, I act fast and catch it before it shuts.

"Don't come in here!" she yells after slamming another door in my face.

I chuckle to myself and lean against the wall beside the bathroom.

Well, isn't this a warm welcome.

"I came here to help you, but I can't really do that if I'm standin' out here, now can I?" It's a rhetorical question—one I don't plan on her answering since she's throwing up at the moment. At least she made it to the toilet. Tucker threw up in my bathtub once. And don't even get me started on Deacon's messes I've cleaned up over the years.

But I've never taken care of a sick girl before.

I quietly open the door and my heart clenches. I really hate seeing her like this. She's sitting in front of the toilet with her arms and head resting on the seat. Wetting a washcloth, I wring it out and place it on her neck. I pull her hair out of her face, cringing at the dampness. Taking another washcloth, I wipe through her hair, getting as much of the vomit off of it as I can, then I twist it around and shove it down the back of her shirt to keep it out of her face.

"Want some water?" I ask.

"No," she mumbles, her voice weak and sad. "I'm sorry you have to see me like this."

"I wouldn't be here if I didn't want to be."

She sniffles a little, wiping her nose on her arm. "Yeah, but I can't believe you want to be here." She's crying now, like full on girl-crying, and it breaks my fucking heart. "Yo-you didn't call Piper, did you?"

"No. You asked me not to, so I didn't."

"Thank you," she says, her forehead still pressed into the crook of her arm with her cheek on the toilet seat.

I take the rag, wipe the side of her face, then rub my hand down her back. My mom always used to rub my back when I was sick, and it made me feel better. Hopefully it'll work on Dani, too.

A second later, she throws up again, trying to push me away with her free hand, but I don't budge. She cries some more, her sobs echoing from inside the porcelain bowl.

I'd like to track Graham Harrison down and break both his fucking legs.

When she feels like she's done getting sick, I turn the shower on for her, check the temperature, and help her shed her shirt. She doesn't bother taking off her bra or panties. She just climbs in the shower and lets the water pour over her.

"I'll be right outside the door. Holler if you need me."

I step out into the hotel room, giving her some space. The only evidence that someone has been here is the pile of empty packages and bottles on the bed. There's a small, clear space by the pillows where she must've slept. Her phone is lying on the pillow.

I hate that she was here all alone last night. I stayed on the phone with her for as long as I could, even on the drive to the airport, but I never said anything about coming. I just got online and booked the first flight I could find. The fastest I could get here was by driving to New Orleans early this morning and leaving from there. If I hadn't had a fucking layover in Atlanta, I would've been here earlier.

Flying here was a no-brainer. I would do anything to take her pain away right now.

While Dani is still in the shower, I clean up the bed, tossing the trash and doing a count of all the empty bottles. Seven. Well, eight counting the empty champagne bottle. The shit she didn't eat or drink, I put back in the mini bar, saving a pack of crackers and a can of Sprite, just in case.

I brought her some breakfast pockets I made at home yesterday, but I doubt she'll want to eat those until her stomach feels better.

I laugh a little as I glance over the pricelist for the items in the mini bar. Forty fucking dollars for the small bottle of champagne she drank. Ten bucks a pop for the tiny bottles of liquor. She rang up a nice little tab for Graham.

"Hey," I hear from behind me. I turn around, finding her peeking around the door with a towel wrapped around her. "Um, I have a problem. I kinda don't have any clean clothes to wear."

With a laugh, I look away. Her not having clothes to wear should not be a problem, but it is. She's the most beautiful creature I've ever seen, sick or not, but I didn't fly to New York to fuck Sheridan Reed. I flew to New York to be her friend and help her through a hard time. I grab the backpack I left by the front door and pull out a pair of boxer shorts and a t-shirt. "Here, wear these. We'll send your clothes down to be cleaned."

"Yeah, Graham can pay for that, too." She gives me a half-smile before shutting the door.

That douchebag deserves it. He deserves a whole hell of a lot more than a five-hundred-dollar hotel bill. Dani has been at his beck and call for the last two months, taking care of his every need, and he repays her by sleeping with the fucking physical therapist.

She deserves so much better.

Dani slowly walks back into the room and sits on the bed, looking so exhausted. My arms itch to wrap around her, but the way she's fidgeting with the t-shirt and shorts she's wearing makes me worried she's uncomfortable. As much as I don't want to, I offer to leave.

"But you just got here!" Her outburst surprises both of us. I try to hide my grin as she bites her lip and turns her face toward the window.

"I don't *want* to go, Dani, but if I'm makin' you uncomfortable, I will."

She covers her lap with the blanket and begins picking at a stray thread. "I'm just embarrassed."

"What on earth for?"

It takes every ounce of strength I have to keep from laughing when she rolls her eyes at me and says, "Duh!" She pauses for a moment before looking up at me. "Micah, this is it." Her voice is so matter-of-fact and sad. "This is the lowest of the low. I've officially hit rock bottom, and I hate being so pathetic, especially in front of you."

"Now, you stop right there. You think I've never felt like this before? You think I've never seen other people I care about hurt like you're hurting right now? Well, I have on both accounts, and I know it sucks."

"I still can't believe you flew all the way up here."

Forcing that dreaded F-word out of my mouth, I reply, "It's what friends do." A flash of disappointment crosses Dani's face, but she quickly recovers. I'd love nothing more than to kiss that look away for good, but I remind myself that's not why I'm here.

"Do you want me to brush your hair?" I ask, trying to lighten the mood "I mean, isn't that what girls do with their friends when they're sad?"

She laughs. "Maybe sometimes. I'm more of an eat-and-drink-my-self-stupid kind of girl, obviously. But I'm still pretty tired. Mind if I take a nap?"

"Of course not. You sleep, and I'll see about gettin' your clothes washed, okay?"

Nodding, she scoots completely under the blanket and closes her eyes. Unable to help myself, I bend down and kiss her forehead.

When she's good and asleep and the only thing I can hear is the small snore coming from the little ball under the blankets, I call housekeeping and request them to come clean the bathroom. The lady is fast and quiet and she takes Dani's dirty clothes with her to have them laundered.

After housekeeping leaves, I lie down on top of the blanket next to Dani. No reason to tempt myself any more than I already have. Maintaining a platonic status between us is going to be a lot harder than I thought, or maybe I didn't think. Honestly, my only thought since she called me yesterday was getting to her.

Early this morning, during my layover in Atlanta, I called my mama to let her know I left and I'd be back on Friday. She sounded worried, asking me if something was wrong. I told her a little bit about Dani, just enough for Mama to understand my need to see her for myself without betraying her trust. She told me to promise to give Dani an extra hug for her and, I quote, "take care of our girl". *Our girl.*

I swear, when my mama gets something in her head, there's no gettin' it out. The fact that Dani has, or *had*, a boyfriend seemed inconsequential to her. She said she has a sixth sense about these things.

Rolling over to my back, I laugh softly. She has a sixth sense about a lot of things.

A couple of weeks ago, when I was moping around the house, she told me when you really care about someone, you have to show them, not just tell them. *Show* them. I looked at her like she was crazy. I hadn't even said anything about what or how I was feeling, but somehow, she knew my foul mood had something to do with Dani. When I asked her how I was supposed to do that, she told me I'd know when the time was right. And she followed it up with one of her many philosophical sayings: *Matters of the heart can't be rushed.*

I have no idea where she gets all that shit, but every once in a while, something she's told me over the years comes back to me, and it suddenly makes sense. Like now. I think what she was trying to tell me was if you really care about someone, you have to be patient. If I would've rushed things with Dani, I could've messed everything up. Lying here beside her, I realize I'm okay with just *being* next to her. Of course, I want her, but I'll take *this* over anything that doesn't include her and me in the same room any day.

For a while, I just watch Dani sleep, brushing the hair away from her face and memorizing each freckle on her nose and cheekbones.

Sometime later, a phone ringing wakes me. I'm completely disoriented at first, forgetting where I am, but once I've taken in my surroundings and find Dani's phone where I left it charging, I see it's Piper calling.

"Hey, Piper. This is Micah Landry," I say, trying to clear the sleep from my voice.

"Well, butter my butt and call me a biscuit. That's one sexy southern drawl you have there, Micah. What the hell are you doing answering Dani's phone?"

I manage to hold in the sound, but my laughter still shakes the bed, so I climb off and sit in the chair by the window, not wanting to disturb Dani.

"Spoken like a true southerner. I almost couldn't tell you're a Yankee."

"Ha ha. Answer my question."

Damn, she's bossy.

"Well, she's sleeping right now. I heard her phone ringing, saw it was you, and decided to answer it."

"But *why* are you there . . . or is she in Louisiana?"

"I flew up here to help Dani for a couple days." I choose my words wisely, not wanting to say anything Dani wouldn't want me to.

"Help her do what?" she asks, and I pick up a bit of sadness and maybe some jealousy in her tone.

"She's just going through something right now and I wanted to help her."

"I'm sure you did." Her words are clipped and she huffs into the phone. "Why didn't she call me?" There it is—that girl jealousy thing. Why do they have to be so damn sensitive? Deacon and Tucker would never pull this shit. If things were reversed and Dani was back in Louisiana helping me and they found out, they'd be buying her beers for taking care of shit so they didn't have to.

"Look, Piper, I know Dani's your best friend, but she has her reasons for not calling you first. She asked me not to say anything, so I'm not going to. She'll tell you when she's ready." I try to be as diplomatic as possible and hope like hell I don't piss her off.

She's quiet for a minute, and I brace myself for the ass chewing I assume is coming my way.

"Very good, Micah Landry. You've passed Round Two," she says with satisfaction.

"Round Two?" I ask, confused.

"It is the duty of a girl's best friend to test potential boyfriend material on her behalf."

Oh, shit.

"What was Round One?"

"You're not Graham Harrison."

I laugh into the phone and lean back in the chair.

Have I mentioned I like her?

"Listen, I've gotta go," she says. "Can you have Dani call me when she wakes up? If I don't hear from her, I'll call her back tomorrow."

"Will do."

"Oh, and Micah . . . take care of our girl."

There it is again—*our girl.*

CHAPTER
Twenty

Sheridan

MY BODY IS AWAKE, BUT I'm afraid to move. I want to stay wrapped in this nice, expensive duvet all day, but I know I can't. Last night wasn't really my version of fun. I don't usually drink myself stupid, but it kept me from thinking about Graham, and for that, I'm grateful. Unfortunately, now that I'm sober, I realize I can't avoid him forever, which means I have to start moving.

I squeeze my eyes to keep them shut, trying to will away the killer headache and bring back the dream I was just having about Micah. It felt so real. A manly groan erupts beside me, starling me.

Someone's in my room.

Or am I in someone else's room?

Oh, God, Sheridan. You take the phrase "go big or go home" to a whole new level.

As if getting sloppy drunk wasn't enough . . .

Wait.

The fog slowly begins to dissipate from my brain, my thinking becoming clearer. Reality sets in, and I'm actually more embarrassed about the truth coming into focus—Micah Landry flew all the way to New

York to take care of my drunk, sad ass. I threw up in front of him. I'm currently wearing his t-shirt and boxers because my clothes were covered in vomit. He's sitting next to me in bed, I'm sure I have the worst case of bedhead ever, and don't even get me started on the fur growing on my tongue.

This is worse than a walk of shame.

I don't even have time to try to make myself look presentable.

I decide to pretend like I'm still asleep for a while, prolonging the inevitable, but my body revolts. I hop up and run across the room.

"Dani?" I hear behind me as I jet to the bathroom. Micah's voice sounds concerned, but it's not what he thinks.

"I gotta pee!"

His laugh echoes through the room, and it sounds so good. Even though I'm embarrassed by my actions that brought him here, I'm really happy he's here. As I shut the door behind me, I catch a glimpse of myself in the mirror and the sight makes me cringe. Shit. I look even worse than I feel.

I pee for forever. I don't know how I even have this much pee in me, but just when I think it's over, it starts back up again. When I'm finally pee-free, I wash my hands and splash water on my face, swiping away the last traces of my mascara. My hair looks like a rat is living in it, so I rake my hands through it and use the ponytail holder that's been on my wrist for three days to pull it back off my face. Unfortunately, I don't have a toothbrush. Fortunately, this fancy-schmancy hotel has tiny bottles filled with things other than liquor. I gargle with mouthwash for a long time, and when I spit it out, I drain the bottle and gargle again, even swallowing some of it in hopes my breath won't smell as bad as it tasted a few minutes ago.

Before I open the door, I flip the light off and take a deep breath, leaning my head against the cool metal.

It's not as bad as it feels.

He wouldn't be here if he didn't want to be here.

And then I repeat the one thing I remember him saying to me before I fell asleep: *This is what friends do.*

I just need to think of him like Piper. A really hot, manly Piper.

Yeah, that doesn't help.

I groan in frustration and crack open the door. I hear the moan again and accompanied with it, the smell of something delicious. My stomach still feels a little woozy, but I'm also starving.

Peeking my head around the corner, I see Micah propped up on the bed, making out with some sort of flaky pastry.

Fuck me.

I don't know which one I want more—Micah or the food—so I go with the one I know won't cause me any regrets.

"Is that a pocket?" I ask accusingly. How dare he hold out on me like that? I'm a recovering drunk who needs her grease and protein.

"Don't get testy, Chuck," he says, smirking with crumbs on his scruffy chin. "I brought plenty to share. Actually, they're for you, but you slept so long, I got hungry."

My embarrassment forgotten, I plop down on the bed. "Gimme."

"So demanding. I'm glad to see you're feelin' better."

He pulls out another flaky pocket and wraps a napkin around the bottom. When I reach for it, he pulls it close to his chest, causing me to fall forward. We're so close, our noses are practically touching. I've never been this close to Micah Landry. The proximity makes me swallow hard, trying to focus on the task at hand—pockets. That's what I'm after, right?

"Say please." His voice is low, and he doesn't make an effort to put any space between us.

"Please." The word leaves my mouth, but I've already forgotten what I'm asking permission for. Is it the lips centimeters from mine or the food Micah is holding out of reach? Well, I *could* reach it, but then I'd be on top of him and that isn't very conducive to keeping things platonic.

"Please what?" he asks. The semi-dazed expression on his face matches how I feel inside and I wonder if he feels it too. *It* being this pull between us, like two magnets—my north to his south.

One second, he's staring longingly at my lips, but the next, he's backing away from me and shoving a pocket in my hand, all the rouse of teasing nowhere to be found.

"Eat."

"Now who's being demanding?" I grumble.

He laughs again, shaking his head.

My attention is quickly diverted to the food in my hands. I eyeball it like I'm on death row and it's my last request, or like a girl who hasn't had a real meal in two days. The first bite has me mimicking Micah's moans from a few minutes ago. "So fucking good," I say around a mouthful of food, not caring about manners or impressing anyone. Besides, I'm sure whatever damage can be done is done. He saw me throw up. It doesn't get much worse than that. "Thank you," I tell him when my mouth isn't so full. I make eye contact with him so he knows I mean for more than this amazing pocket. "For everything."

He nods and smiles, looking down at the bag in his lap and pulling out another pocket for himself. If I didn't know any better, I'd think there's a slight blush on his cheeks, but the scruff is camouflaging it. And Micah Landry doesn't blush.

"What's in here?" I ask, practically inhaling the deliciousness in my hand.

"Boudin."

"I think it's my new favorite."

"You'd eat a pig belly pocket right now."

I laugh and chew at the same time. "True."

I lean back against the headboard next to him and we eat in comfortable silence. My mind drifts to Graham, but I don't even feel sad anymore. I'm still pissed, I'd still like to cut his balls off, but I'm not sad.

"I called down to the front desk and told them we'd be staying another night," Micah says between bites.

"Oh, right." I glance over at the clock and see it's after the normal checkout time. "Damn. Sorry I slept most of the day."

"S'okay. I figured you needed it."

"Yeah. I mean, I slept last night, but it wasn't good sleep."

"Feel better now?"

"Yeah, much better, thanks to you."

"I didn't do anything."

"Yes, you did. You're here. That's enough."

He throws his arm around my shoulders and pulls me into his side. It's kind of like a hug, and when he squeezes me to him, I realize I missed this. It's the best hug I've had in a long time.

"Are you crying?"

"I—yeah, sorry." I sniffle and wipe my face on the sleeve of my shirt . . . or Micah's shirt. Whatever.

"I'm sorry, Dani."

"No," I say, waving my hand in the air. "It's not what you think. These tears aren't for Graham."

"What are they for then?"

I sigh, unsure how to answer. "Me, I guess." I shrug my shoulders and lay my head on his chest. He pulls me closer to him, wrapping his arms securely around me.

"Did you love him? Or do you still?"

"Yes and no."

"Well, which is it?"

"Yes, I did love him, but I haven't been *in love* with him for a while. And no, I don't anymore."

He kisses the top of my head, rubbing my arm in a soothing gesture. And it works. He's warmth and comfort; I feel like I could melt into him.

"Well, just because you aren't still in love with him doesn't mean it hurts any less," he says, his lips moving against my hair.

"Yeah. But . . . I think I was almost waiting for something to give me the green light to leave him. Half of my heart was hanging on for old time's sake, but the other half has been gone for a long time. That doesn't mean I didn't feel completely crushed walking in and finding him and Kaitlyn like that." I bite the inside of my cheek to keep from crying again. I'm done crying over Graham. "I might have to burn my bed. And I love that bed."

Micah chuckles and tightens his hold. "We'll get you a new bed."

I like when he says *we*.

A knock at the door makes me stiffen. My mind starts to race with possibilities. Could Graham know where I am? Could Mr. Harrison track me down? Maybe the hotel knows I'm not really Mrs. Harrison?

"Housekeeping."

I sigh a breath of relief and get up. Micah laughs. "Who'd you think it was gonna be?"

"I don't know. I think I'm paranoid from all the lying I did when I checked in."

I swing the door open to a lady holding what looks like my clothes, minus the vomit.

"Here's your clean laundry, Mrs. Harrison."

"Thank you," I say, faking a smile.

"It'll be charged to your room."

I smile again and nod, quickly shutting the door. "God, I would make a horrible criminal," I say, leaning against the closed door.

Micah's laughing even harder now. "You *are* a horrible liar, but it serves the bastard right."

"I think I'm gonna shower again and change, so you can have your clothes back."

"Don't change on my account. I think they look good on you."

His comment surprises me, and I'm sure the expression on my face tells it all. If it doesn't, then the blush creeping up my cheeks will.

"Uh, I'm gonna . . ." I stumble around my words and turn toward the bathroom.

I need a shower. A very cold shower. Because if Micah Landry makes any more comments like that, I will not be held accountable for my actions. And I'm not sure that's such a good idea seeing as I just caught my boyfriend of four years cheating on me less than two days ago. I think there's some unwritten rule about how long you have to wait before jumping into bed with someone else, or maybe it's an unspoken rule that you *do* jump into bed with someone else.

But I know me, and I know Micah Landry. After one night with him, I'm not sure I'd want to give him up—and he's not into long-term relationships. He does casual sex. He fucks girls up against motel walls.

I might want to be . . .

Stop it, Dani!

"SO, WHAT DO YOU WANNA do tonight?" Micah asks, flipping through the magazine he found on the desk.

I groan, covering my face with a pillow. "I'm a horrible host! Is this your first time in New York City?"

"Yep."

"And you're stuck in this hotel room with me?"

"It's kinda why I flew all the way up here."

"I'm the worst friend ever."

He chuckles. "Stop it, Dani. I didn't come to see the sights. I'll save that for another trip." He tosses the magazine onto the ottoman in front of him and uncrosses his long legs, standing up. "Wanna watch a movie or something?"

"Yeah, sounds good. Unless you wanna get out? I'll show you around a little." I sit up, trying to sound less like a Debbie Downer.

"Is that what you wanna do?"

"Sure, if you want to."

"You're *such* a horrible liar."

"I know. I suck."

"So," he says, bouncing as he plops down on the bed beside me. "What movie are we watchin'? We should rent some porn. That shit's always expensive."

"What?" I screech.

"Porn."

"I heard you, but we're *not* renting porn."

Because there is no way in hell I can watch other people having sex and keep my clothes on, and it's already been predetermined that I will be keeping my clothes on.

"Aw, you're no fun. We need to charge as much as we can to this room before we leave."

"Well, we can rent two movies. And order room service. But no wine. I can't even look at alcohol right now."

"Okay, two movies it is. And steak for dinner. And dessert, since we can't have booze."

"Deal."

AFTER OUR MOVIES AND ROOM service, we're full as ticks, as Micah would say, lying on the bed with all the lights out. The curtains of the hotel room are pulled back and the city lights twinkle through the window.

"Man, New York really is a city that never sleeps, huh?"

"Yeah, nothing like French Settlement."

"Definitely not," he says, shaking his head. "I bet you miss it when you're gone. It was probably weird being in such a small town."

"Actually, I didn't. After I got used to it and found out where I could get good coffee, I didn't miss anything about this place. Well, maybe my favorite Chinese restaurant, but that's about it."

"Really?"

"Yeah. I mean, I haven't always lived in New York. There was a time in my life when all I knew was small towns."

"I kinda forgot that."

"Being in French Settlement awakened something inside me. I don't know whether it was the change of pace or being closer to where I grew up, but it made me love my job again, and for the first time in a long time, I felt at peace."

Micah grabs my hand and holds it, not like a boyfriend and girlfriend hold hands, just like someone who's telling someone else everything's going to be okay.

"HEY, MICAH?" I WHISPER INTO the dark room. "Are you asleep?"

"No."

"Will you go with me to my apartment in the morning?"

"It is morning."

"Later, then?"

"Of course I will."

"Thank you."

"You're welcome. Get some sleep."

AN ANNOYING BEEPING WAKES ME from a deep sleep. I swat toward the noise, trying to get it to shut up. When my arm hits something that's not the alarm, I sit up quickly, staring down at the beautiful man in my bed.

Micah.

I almost thought I had dreamed him up, but here he is in all his glory.

He rolls over and hits the alarm clock and then looks back at me with a sleepy, half grin. "Good mornin'."

Those two words make my stomach tighten.

"Good morning," I reply, burying my face in the pillow and hoping like hell I don't have bad breath.

"We should probably get going. Busy day ahead," he says, his voice still gravely.

I can't quit looking at him. I know he's not trying to be sexy, but he is. Maybe the fact that he's not trying makes him even more so.

"I'm going to hit the shower, unless you need in there," he says, walking toward the bathroom, giving me a great view of his ass.

"That's fine," I tell him, needing a few more minutes to wake up and get my head on straight. Besides, I took a shower last night. I just need to wash my face and brush my teeth. While Micah's in the shower, I find my brush in my bag and try to make my hair look halfway decent. Once he's out, I do my business and then we're ready to go, with half an hour to spare.

"Wanna get some coffee on the way?"

"Sure." He holds the door open for me and we make our way to the elevator.

"Excited to see what New York looks like from outside the hotel?" I ask, poking him with my elbow.

"I saw it from the taxi on my way here."

"Oh, well, this will be much more fun. Nothing like the smell of city streets in the morning."

He laughs, shaking his head. "I think I'll take my plantation."

Yeah. Good choice.

We grab a cup of coffee from a café down the street and hail a cab instead of walking to my apartment. When we pull up in front of my building, I take a deep breath before stepping out on the curb.

"You good?" Micah asks, placing his hand at the small of my back. The gesture makes my knees feel weak.

"Yeah," I say, my voice shaking a little, but it's not due to nerves.

There's no one waiting on the elevator, so we hop in, and I press two.

"Think he's still here?" Micah asks.

The elevator door opens and we step out.

"He better not be, but I wouldn't put it past him. Besides, he had a lot of shit to get out. And even though he's walking, he's not fast."

I pull out my key and unlock the door. The second the door is open, I smell coffee, which gives me my answer.

That son of a bitch.

"Graham?"

"Dani?" he asks, his voice coming from the kitchen. "Is that you?"

I walk in and he's balancing on one leg, a set of crutches leaning up against the counter beside him. When he sees me, relief washes over him. He leans forward and holds his hand out, wanting me to take it. "Dani. I'm so sorry. I knew you'd come back."

"Of course I was coming back. This is my fucking apartment!" I try to hold back my anger, but I hate that he's still playing house . . . in *my* house. "What part of 'get the fuck out' did you not understand?"

"You were mad. I didn't think you really meant it." Picking up his crutches, he begins to hobble toward me, but stops as Micah steps around the corner and places his hand at the small of my back again.

Graham's eyes grow wide as recognition sets in. "What the hell is he doing here?" he growls.

"None of your fucking business," Micah replies coolly.

"Dani, we need to talk," Graham pleads.

"There's nothing to talk about. I said everything I had to say two days ago."

"*I* need to talk!" Graham says, raising his voice and taking a couple steps closer.

Micah places his body at an angle in front of me. "She said she's finished talkin'."

"Well, I'm not," Graham says, standing as tall as his injured leg will allow.

"Well, you lost the privilege to call the shots around here when you fucked your therapist," Micah retorts.

"It's not like that!" Graham says, leaning on one of his crutches and pulling at his longer-than-usual hair in frustration. "Which is why I need to talk to *my* girlfriend," he says, reaching around to grab my arm.

"Don't touch me, Graham," I say through gritted teeth. "I want you out. Like, yesterday. Who do I need to call to make that happen?" I reach in my bag for my phone and begin to scroll through it, looking for Mr. Harrison's phone number when it rings. Piper's name pops up on the screen, but I decline the call and look back up at Graham.

"Who are you going to call?" he asks, his tone mocking.

"Your father. The law. I don't really fucking care if they'll get you out of my apartment."

"You need to calm down," he says, reaching a hand out to me. It makes me retreat back, and he sighs in frustration, leaning on the wall for support. "Please give me a chance to explain and tell you how fucking sorry I am."

"Go ahead," I tell him, just wanting him to say what he need to say so I can leave. "What do you want to tell me?"

"Not with him here," he says, pointing to Micah, who is still standing next to me, seething. His jaw is clenched tight and his arms are crossed over his chest like he's holding himself back.

"Anything you have to say, you can say in front of him," I tell him, locking eyes with him and holding his gaze, showing him I'm not backing down.

His face contorts into a sneer. "Are you fucking him?" he asks incredulously. I watch as his shoulders go rigid and he tries to stand to his full height, his eyes shifting from me to Micah.

"Whoa, whoa, whoa!" Micah says in an authoritative voice, taking a step forward and uncrossing his arms. "You need to back the fuck up and don't talk to her like that."

Graham ignores Micah and looks around him at me. "Answer me, Dani," he demands. His face twists with emotions and I know I don't owe him anything, but I don't want him to think that it's like that between me and Micah. I don't want him to think I'd stoop to his level.

"No, Graham," I say firmly. "We're not fucking. Or anything else. We're friends. That's it."

Micah's shoulders tense a little more. For a few awkward seconds, we're all in a stare off, until I finally can't stand it anymore. I just need out of this place and away from him.

"So, back to you getting the hell out of my apartment," I say, grabbing my bag and pulling it up on my shoulder. "Where do we stand on that?"

Graham's face falls and he lets out a deep breath, defeat hanging thick in the air. "Give me a couple hours," he mumbles.

"Good. Micah and I are going to lunch. I expect you to be gone when we get back."

I grab Micah's hand, pulling him toward me and the door. He finally relaxes a little and walks with me, but keeps an eye on Graham. Before we make it out the door, I remember the credit card and driver's license in my bag. Pulling it out, I turn around and slap it down on the table, looking up at Graham with a blank expression. "Thanks for the hotel room."

Once Micah and I are back out onto the sidewalk, he puts his arm around my shoulder and pulls me into him, kissing the top of my head. "Are you okay?"

I let out a deep sigh and melt into him. "I've been better, but I'm glad that's over with."

"What do you want to do?" he asks.

"I want some Mongolian beef."

He chuckles and places his lips to my head again. "Mongolian beef it is. Where can we go to get that?"

I take us to my favorite Chinese restaurant and we walk up to the counter. Before I can open my mouth to order, Micah steps up and tells them we'll have two Mongolian beefs. "Want anything else?" he asks, looking back over his shoulder.

I shake my head and try to not think about how much I love that he just ordered for me. He's here and he's taking care of me. If I think about it too much, I'll start crying and Lord knows I've shed enough tears over the past couple days to last me a lifetime.

We find a table by the window and have a seat. I'm watching Micah while he watches people when my phone rings.

Micah's eyes snap to mine. "Sir Mix-a-Lot? Really?" he asks, quirking an eyebrow and smirking at me.

I manage a laugh and roll my eyes. "Hello, Piper," I say into the phone.

"Sheridan Paige," she says, first and middle naming me like she loves to do.

"I know, I know. Please don't lecture me," I groan, rubbing my temples. "Micah told me you called. I've just been dealing with stuff . . ." I pause, looking out the window.

She sighs sadly into the phone. "What's going on with you, Dani?" Her voice is soft and low. I know she's hurt because I haven't called and confided in her. "And don't tell me nothing."

"Promise you won't say I told you so?" I ask, not wanting a lecture from her today. I've had enough fuckery for one day.

"Promise," she says.

"Graham's an asshole of epic proportions," I start, stating the obvious.

"I told you so."

"You're such a bitch," I tell her, but I can't help the small smile forcing its way onto my lips.

When her laugh flitters through the phone, it makes me laugh too, but then her voice turns solemn. "What am I going to kick his ass for?"

"He cheated on me with the physical therapist." I just spit it out. No sense mincing words.

The line is quiet for a moment and I pull it back to make sure we're still connected.

"What?" she yells, making me pull the phone back again, but this time, to save my hearing. "What the fuck, Dani? Where . . . how?" she asks, drawing out the last question.

"Well, he was putting his d—"

"Stop! Don't make me use my brain bleach. I didn't mean that. You know what I mean. He's staying at your apartment. You're with him every second of the day."

"Well," I sigh, not wanting to rehash the whole sordid story, but I know I'll have to do it sometime. I look across the table to Micah with an apologetic smile. His eyes are watching me intently and his jaw is tight, but he shakes his head and mouths, "It's fine." So, I continue and tell her everything.

Once I'm finished with the recount, there's a long pause on the phone and then a growl coming from Piper's end. "That fucking bastard."

Micah clears his throat as the waitress sets our food down in front of us and I see his nostrils flare.

"Fuck. Dani, I'm so sorry, honey," she says softly. "Even I couldn't have predicted that. I knew Graham was a douchenozzle, but I didn't know he'd stoop that low. Do you know how long it's been going on?"

"I don't know. I don't want to know. I just want him out . . . of my life, of my apartment . . ." I tell her, rubbing my temple with my free hand.

"He's still there?"

"Well, I told him to leave and he said he would."

"Where are you now?"

"Eating lunch with Micah," I tell her, looking up and making eye contact with him again.

"Do you want to talk about it?" she asks.

"No."

"Call me later."

"I will."

"And if that motherfucker isn't out of your apartment when you get back, tell Micah to break his other leg."

I laugh and shake my head. "Hopefully that won't be necessary."

"I've got another call coming in. I've gotta go," she says as her office phone rings in the background.

"Get back to work," I tease.

"Talk to you soon."

I end the call and put my phone in my pocket.

"Piper?" Micah asks.

"The one and only."

"Well, this looks delicious," Micah says, looking down at his steaming bowl of food.

"Seriously, the best Mongolian beef you'll ever put in your mouth."

He quirks an eyebrow. "Well, I'll have to take your word for it, because it'll be the first Mongolian beef I've ever put in my mouth."

"No way!" I look at him like he's crazy.

"Exactly how many Chinese restaurants did you see in French Settlement while you were there?" he asks, leveling me with his gaze, his fork in the air.

"Touché."

He laughs and digs in for his first bite. "There was this great Chinese place in Baton Rouge Deacon and I used to go to when we were in college, but I always ordered this house special they had. I don't even know what the fuck was in it, but it was delicious."

I laugh and watch him as he experiences his first bite of the best Mongolian beef he'll ever eat. And what a lovely sight it is. He chews for a second and then darts his tongue out to lick his lips. His eyes roll and he finally groans out his approval. "So fucking good."

I nod and clear my throat before taking a bite of my own. "I told you," I say after I swallow, unable to take my eyes off his mouth.

Music playing from my pocket causes Micah to smile around his fork and I'm actually appreciative of the distraction.

"Hello," I say a little too eagerly, especially since I just talked to Piper less than ten minutes ago.

"Get your ass on a plane. ASAP," she says in her bossy tone.

"What?" I ask, dropping my fork to my plate.

"I just got off the phone with my boss," she says, and I can hear the smile in her voice. It causes me to smile back. "He wants you to start on the article no later than next week."

"Are you serious?"

"I figured this news couldn't have come at a better time."

"Oh my God, Piper. I could kiss you right now." Those tears I talked about not crying today are trying to break through the dam, but I blink them back.

"You'll get to soon enough. I'm coming to see you when you get back down here. Once you've figured out your game plan, give me a call."

"So, next week?" I ask, my heart practically beating out of my chest at the thought of getting the hell out of this city.

"Yes, so pack your shit and get your ass back down here."

"Thank you," I say, trying to keep it together.

"Don't thank me. It's your awesome idea and amazing talent that sold them on it. You only have yourself to thank."

I end the call and drop the phone onto the table. Looking up at Micah, I meet his pale blue eyes and they look happy, mirroring my own emotions. When I'm mad, he's mad. When I'm sad, he's sad. Right now, I'm happy and he's happy. The thought of being able to go back with him makes the last bit of tension and dread leave my body.

"I got the job. I'm flying home with you."

CHAPTER
Twenty-One

MICAH

*I*F YOU WOULD'VE TOLD ME when I left Louisiana on Wednesday I'd be flying back home with Sheridan Reed two days later, I would've laughed in your face. But that's exactly what's happening.

Once Graham was finally out of Dani's apartment, she started packing while I searched for flights and gave my mama and Deacon a call, letting them know I'm coming home. I was able to change my New Orleans flight to the same one Dani booked to Baton Rouge, and now, here we sit, together, thanks to Mr. Wilson.

Mr. Wilson was originally sitting next to Dani, but after some major groveling on my part and the promise of a couple of cocktails, he eventually switched seats with me, pissing and moaning under his breath the entire time he walked to the back of the plane. I don't care, though. I'd be willing to put up with a lot more than that in order to be this close to Dani.

Last night, she refused to sleep in her bed, but didn't want to bother with another hotel room, so she slept on the couch while I slept in her recliner. It wasn't the best night's rest for either of us, but we've managed to stay somewhat coherent. Until now. Thirty minutes in the air, and she's already sleeping with her head resting against my shoulder.

My eyes start to droop as I look down at her beautiful face. She has no idea how fucking amazing she is. She's the strongest, most talented woman I know, besides my mama, and I'm so proud of how she handled that dipshit Graham.

Hours later, heading toward baggage claim, my hand automatically finds Dani's lower back. I know she isn't looking to start anything serious right now, but I can't help wanting to stake a claim on her in some way. I've never wanted to do that with a woman, and I know I have no right to assume she'd even want to be with me, but I'll be damned if I step aside and let some other asshole get to her.

Just thinking about Dani with someone else makes my pulse race.

"What's wrong?" Dani asks, looking up at me. "You're clenching your jaw pretty tight there. In deep thought or something?"

I look down into her big green eyes and instantly relax. "Oh, um," I stutter, trying to think of something to say, other than *I really hate when other guys touch you.* That sounds creepy. "I just remembered I left my truck at the airport in New Orleans. I guess Deacon'll have to give me a ride over there later this week. And we'll have to rent a car to get home."

"No big deal," she says with a shrug of her shoulders, looking so damn carefree. "I'm going to need a car for my road trip anyway, so I'll rent it. I really should've thought about that sooner, but I feel like I'm in vacation mode."

"Ahh, that's just bein' in the south," I tell her with a wink. "The slower pace and relaxin' attitude settles into your bones, suckin' you right in and makin' sure you never want to leave," I say, pulling her to me for emphasis. She laughs, and it's the most beautiful sound I've heard all day. "The only acceptable reason to rush is when you're goin' to a party or somewhere to eat, but even then, it's more of a quick stroll rather than a sprint."

Dani continues to laugh the more I carry on, and I'm addicted to the sound. "Well, whatever it is, it's working its magic on me."

"Well, now, don't get me started on the Voodoo around these parts,"

I joke.

Dani spots her luggage and I quickly grab it before she can. The sound of my brother's voice booming through the building cuts her protest short.

"Is that Sheridan Reed I see?" Deacon yells, causing everyone around us to stop and watch as he lengthens his stride to reach us. He wraps Dani in his arms and twirls her around in greeting. "Bro, you didn't tell me you were bringin' Dani home. I would've brought the whole family with me!"

"We're goin' straight home so we'll surprise them when we get there. We were just gettin' ready to go over and see about renting a car. I didn't know you were comin'."

"No worries. I'll just follow you home. I spent the night at the apartment last night after a late shift at Grinders, so I thought I'd stop by to see if you needed a lift. But first, let's get down to business. Where's my surprise?"

"What the hell are you talkin' about?" I ask, knowing exactly where this is going.

"My surprise . . . souvenir . . . present . . . whatever you want to call it, I want it. Hand it over." Deacon's face is a wall of stone and he quirks an eyebrow at me. Dani shifts nervously beside me and the look of panic on her face makes me want to laugh, but I don't.

I play dumb for as long as I can before putting Deacon out of his misery and handing him the cheesy, but traditional, "I heart NY" shirt I bought him at the airport. He loves it, of course, and is too busy gushing over it to see me mouth the words "pay up" to Dani.

She rolls her eyes and mumbles, "Fuck," as she reaches into her pocket and pulls out a ten-dollar bill.

I'm happily stuffing the money into my own pocket when Deacon notices and starts wagging his meaty finger at us. "What's this? What's goin' on here?"

"Ms. Reed here didn't believe an almost thirty-year-old would throw a tantrum like a toddler if I didn't bring him back a gift, so we made a little wager."

"Micah, you're supposed to bring back souvenirs whenever you travel. It's common knowledge. I'm just keeping up the tradition," Deacon claims.

"Bullshit. You wouldn't talk to me for a week if I came home empty-handed. Damn, maybe I should've kept the shirt for myself."

"Don't listen to him, Deke. I love giving people gifts, which is why I got you this Statue of Liberty snow globe!" She pulls the globe out from behind her back and holds it up like it's made of gold or something. Deacon's eyes glisten at the sight.

"You're the best, Dani! Thank you."

Watching Dani step on her tiptoes to kiss his cheek makes me jealous in ways I can't even explain, and probably have no business feeling, but I can't help wishing it was my skin her lips were touching.

Deacon waited around while Dani rented a car, just to make sure we didn't have any problems, and is now following behind us as we drive home. I, of course, opted to ride with Dani, as if it were even up for discussion. When the three of us were standing at the counter, waiting for the car rental place to get the keys, Deacon shot me a knowing wink over the top of Dani's head. I tried to hide my smile, but it was futile. Just her being here with me right now, in Louisiana, makes me feel like a kid on Christmas.

When we pull up to the house forty-five minutes later, Dani parks in front and Deacon pulls up right beside her.

"You're gonna be in so much trouble for not telling Mama about this," Deacon says, jumping out of the car.

"Nah, she's gonna love me even more than she already does. This," I say, pointing to Dani, "is my insurance policy for maintainin' my favorite child status."

Dani rolls her eyes and Deacon punches my shoulder.

The front door swings open and my mom walks out with her hands on her hips, staring us down.

"Micah Paul Landry."

"Ha!" Deacon says, running up the steps and picking Mama up to swing her around. "I'm not the one who just got full-named." He grins and places Mama back on her feet.

"Sheridan," my mama gushes, double-timing it down the steps.

"Sweetie, I'm so happy to see you!"

"I'm sorry your son decided to keep me being here a secret," Dani says, falling into my mom's embrace. "I told him he should call and let you know, but he's a stubborn ass."

"Oh, honey. You're preachin' to the choir. No apologies necessary. Besides, you don't even need to call. All you gotta do is show up." The smile my mom gives Dani is pure love. She and I have had several conversations about the beautiful redhead wrapped in her arms, and if Dani was of adoption age, I'm pretty sure my mama would be first in line.

"I THINK WE NEED TO have a cookout today."

After staying up late last night playing cards with my family and Dani, I decided I was too tired to go to my own house, so I slept in a guest room. Truth is, I wasn't ready to leave Dani yet. Even though we were in separate rooms, unlike our two nights in New York, I was at peace just knowing we were under the same roof.

I'm in the kitchen starting a pot of coffee when my mama walks in and declares we need to be social.

"A cookout? Okay. Who are we invitin', and more importantly, what are we cookin'?"

"You and Deacon can decide what to cook and who to invite, for all I care. I just want to show Dani a good time, especially since she's had a rough week. That girl needs a hefty dose of southern hospitality."

I couldn't agree more.

After Dani wakes up and we've all had breakfast, she and I make a trip to the grocery store for cookout supplies. Grocery stores in this part of Louisiana are different than other parts of the country. They have the usual foods found everywhere, but you can also find seafood, hard liquor, and delicacies such as cow tongue, alligator, and pickled pig's feet. I'm having so much fun watching Dani's reactions to all the things she finds, I almost forget what we're supposed to buy for this afternoon.

Deciding to keep the party low key, we only invited a few close friends over for boiled shrimp and crab. I'm excited for Dani to share today with us, just hanging out and having fun, and I know she's looking forward to it too, especially since Piper will be here. They'd already made plans to see each other before Dani's next assignment, so it only made sense for Piper to join us. I'll admit, I'm curious about her. She seems like she'll fit right in, and I can't wait to finally meet her in person.

As we turn down the last aisle to grab a few cases of beer, I stop short before nearly running over a lady picking up a case of wine coolers.

"Oh, hey, Micah! What are you up to today?"

Ah, Trisha Bradley. Sophomore year in college. She liked it when I pulled her hair.

"Hey, Trish. Not much, you?"

"Oh, I'm in town for a girls' weekend and my parents are watching my kids. Wanna meet up later?"

She licks her lips as her eyes travel up and down my body. I don't like it. And I really don't like that Dani is witnessing it. I glance her way and watch as she cocks an eyebrow. Her nose scrunches slightly when Trish touches my arm, and I'm not sure whether she's grossed out by Trisha or me, but I hate seeing that look on her pretty face, especially knowing I may have caused it.

"Yeah, I don't think so, but thanks for asking. Tell Jimmy I said hey."

When we're out of earshot, Dani leans toward me and whispers, "Who's Jimmy?"

"He's her husband. I guess she forgot she was married."

"How convenient. I have a feeling you make a lot of women forget they're married, Micah Landry." She nudges me with her shoulder before leading our buggy into the checkout lane, right up to Becky. The Hummer.

Damn it to hell.

Thankfully, Becky only says "hi" and "have a nice day", but I swear, nothing gets past Dani.

"Is she one of your girls, too?" she asks in the parking lot. Her clipped tone doesn't escape me.

I finish loading the groceries in the back of my mom's SUV before answering.

"You ask that like I have a harem or something."

"Well, if the condom fits . . ." She pauses. "You *do* wear condoms, right?"

Ouch.

I pull my baseball cap off and run my fingers through my hair before putting it back on. We're still standing in the parking lot and the Louisiana sun is heating up the blacktop, causing sweat to run down my back.

My social life is obviously bothering her, and I'm not liking how she's judging me.

"Yes, Dani, I've been with a lot of women, and yes, Becky was one of them, but it's not like I have a group of girls waiting on stand-by for me. I like to have fun. I always have. I'm always honest with the girls I'm with, and for your information, I *always* wear a condom."

She sighs and drops her hands from her hips down to her sides. "I'm sorry. It's none of my business. And I didn't mean to imply you mistreat the women you're with, either."

I open the door for her and make sure she's buckled in before getting behind the steering wheel and turning the air conditioner on full-blast. The cold air cools my skin and nerves. When I turn to face Dani, she looks guilty and a little sad.

"Look, I don't have a sob story . . . no built up walls around my heart or anything like that. I've had a great life and things have always come easily for me. I'm not overcompensating for anything. I just like to have fun. It's never my intention to hurt anyone or lead a girl on, but I know it sometimes happens, and I'm not proud of that. The truth is, I've never been with a girl I've wanted *more* with."

"I get it, Micah. You don't owe me an explanation."

"See, that's where you're wrong, because I do—or, at least, I want to give you one." I take a deep breath and decide now's as good a time as any to lay it all out there for her. Shit or get off the pot, right? "I've wanted more with you from the moment you called me out on my shit on the way back to your motel room," I say, laughing at the memory of a tipsy Dani in my truck. I look over, trying to judge her reaction, but I'm having trouble reading her expression. She looks over her shoulder at me, biting her lip like she does when she's either trying not to cry or thinking about something really hard, so I keep going. "I know I don't deserve you, Dani, but I *want* to. I need you to be patient with me, though. I'm trying to do things right. But this," I say, motioning between us so she knows I mean *us*, "it's all new to me."

"Well, you know my story," she says, turning in her seat to face me. "I've been in a committed relationship for four years." She releases a deep breath, her shoulders sagging as she looks out the windshield. "I'm sure most people would say the last thing I need right now is to jump into a relationship with anyone. Or into bed." She laughs. "Unless you're Piper. She would suggest revenge sex." She rolls her eyes, turning her gaze back to me. "I can't deny the pull I feel toward you, but I don't want you to be a rebound or revenge sex. I really like you, Micah Landry. And I know you have a past. And I'm okay with that . . . in theory." Her smile is contagious, and knowing she *likes* me makes my head spin.

"So, we'll take things slow," I tell her, reaching my hand across the seat, wanting to touch her.

"Yeah. I mean, that's normally how *y'all* do things down here, right?" She winks, and it's adorable. I repeat *slow* over and over in my mind to keep from climbing over the console and kissing her stupid.

I want to taste her lips so bad it hurts, but not here. Not now. *Slow.*

We both sit there for a second, staring at each other before turning to look out the window. I know there's a lot more that needs to be said between us, but that was a start, and I'm hoping we'll have plenty of time to figure this out while taking our time to do it right.

Rolling up to the two-lane highway that leads back home, I see there aren't any cars coming in either direction. When I give the truck a little extra gas, the back tires spin and squeal causing Dani to do the same.

"Stop showing off."

"I'm just naturally this cool."

Her laugh fills the truck and it's a sound I want to hear every day.

JUST A LITTLE BEFORE SIX o'clock, a knock on the front door inter-rupts our loud banter in the kitchen as we prepare the food for the boil.

"I'll get it!" Deacon yells, swatting Cami's ass with a kitchen towel as he walks by. She retaliates by throwing a half ear of corn at his head and the fight is on. He has her up and over his shoulder before she even knows what's coming.

"Deacon Samuel, if you make a mess in my kitchen, I'll beat you into next week!" My mom is shooing them out the back door when the knock at the front door grows louder.

Dani is shucking corn at the table and laughing her head off at the entire display. I shoot her a wink as I walk by, and she smiles even wider, shaking her head. Our normal playful flirting has turned a little more heated since our talk in the grocery store parking lot. I notice her watch-ing me. I see her eyes grow dark, and I know what she's thinking—or, at least, I hope I know what she's thinking. I hope she wants me as much as I want her, or even a fraction of how much I want her. But more than that, I hope she wants to *be* with me, because for the first time in my life, I want someone for more than just a one-night stand or occasional hook-up. I want to *be* with her. I want her here with me on nights like this. I want to go to the grocery store with her. I want to take walks and sit and talk for hours. And all of that scares the shit out of me because it's new and uncharted territory.

"Someone get the damn door!" my dad yells as he walks out of the kitchen carrying bowls full of crab legs and shrimp.

"I'll get it," I say, wiping my hands on the towel over my shoulder.

I run the rest of the way to the door and swing it open.

"Were you going to let me spend the night out here on the front porch?"

"Piper Grey?" I know exactly who she is, but as usual, I decide to give her a hard time.

"Of fucking course, the one and only. You have *got* to be Micah Landry," she says, sticking her hand out for me to shake. Her shoul-der-length brown hair and pale brown eyes are exactly how I pictured her—spunky and cute.

"The one and only," I reply, shaking her hand and appreciating her tenacious grip. No one likes to shake a wet noodle.

"Where's our girl?" she asks, poking her head around my shoulder. "As much as I like standing here talking to you, I miss the shit out of her." She pushes me aside and walks past me like she owns the damn place.

Yep, I like her.

"Sheridan Reed!" she calls as she walks through the foyer.

I chuckle at the display, shut the door, and follow her into the kitchen. When I get there, Dani is out of her seat and wrapped up in Piper. The two of them are talking so fast, I can't make out what they're saying, but it's obvious they're happy to see each other, and seeing Dani so happy makes me happy. This is exactly what she needed.

My mom catches my eye from across the kitchen and smiles.

Yeah, I know, Mama. Mission accomplished.

The night is filled with good food, good friends, family, and lots of laughs. It's a pretty typical Saturday night for all of us, but it's a new experience for Dani and Piper, and they seem to be soaking it up.

Dani looks so content sitting in the chair beside me. The fire in the pit flickers, making her skin glow. Her red hair is piled on top of her head and her cheeks are a little flushed, probably from the heat. Her arm hangs over the side of the chair, stroking Jose's fur. He's just as content as she is, making no plans to leave her side.

And I'm now jealous of a dog.

"Thanks again for the amazing dinner, Mr. and Mrs. Landry," Piper says, kicking back in a lounge chair beside Dani.

"What did we tell you about that Mr. and Mrs. thing?" my dad asks, quirking an eyebrow.

"Sam. Annie. Got it. Sorry." She smiles, and I glance over to see Tucker watching her intently.

"I'm going to get something else to drink," Cami says, standing up. "Anybody else want anything?"

My dad, Deacon, and I all call out for another round of beers. Dani and Piper say they'll go with her to help carry them all. My mom follows behind, saying something about needing to put a few things in the fridge.

"So," my dad says when all of the women are out of earshot.

"Go ahead, Dad. I know you've got somethin' to say."

He laughs, shaking his head. "I was in the kitchen earlier, and I overheard your mom and Dani talking about your trip to the grocery store today."

I groan, afraid of what he might've overheard. "I swear, it's like everywhere I go, there's someone from my past." It's the truth. The Trishas, Beckys, and Valeries are everywhere; I can't seem to escape them. And it scares me. What if my past keeps me from having a future with Dani?

"You can't change your past," my dad says as he leans forward, resting his elbows on his knees.

"That's for damn sure," Tucker chimes in, laughing. "And Micah's got a past." He scratches the back of his head, leaning back in the chair. I'd like to kick his ass.

"Like you don't have a past, Tucker the Fucker."

He picks up a loose piece of gravel and throws it at me, but I dodge it.

"But you want this, don't you? Like *really* want this?" Deacon asks, eyeing me from across the fire. "You're not just stringing Dani along like those girls, right?" He pauses, and my dad chuckles. "Because if you are, I'll have to kick your ass."

"No! Fuck no. I want this." I stand up from my chair and pace in front of the fire. "It's just a lot harder than I thought it would be. And I don't know what the fuck I'm doing."

"Listen, son," my dad says, standing up and placing his hands on my shoulders to force me to look at him. "If it's got tits or tires, it's gonna require some work." He looks me square in the eyes. "And I know you're not afraid of a little hard work. So, if this is what you want, work at it. Show her you're serious."

Laughter coming from the back door causes us to shift gears. I know what my dad is saying is true. In his own way, he said the exact same thing my mom has been saying. She didn't pull out the *tits and tires* line, but she said I'd need to work at it. So I will. I'm going to show Dani how much I want this.

"So, where are you from?" Tucker asks Piper when the girls sit back down. I turn my head to keep my smug-ass smirk to myself. I know where he's going with this. He likes her. It's so obvious the way he can't keep his eyes off her and hangs on her every word.

"Who, me?" Piper asks, setting her beer down by her chair.

"Yeah, we know all about Ms. Reed, but not much about you. Are you from New York?"

"Well, my family is from Connecticut. I moved to New York for college. That's where I met *Ms. Reed*," she says, smiling over at Dani. Dani just shakes her head and laughs. She's already grown accustom to Tucker's suave ways. "Dani and I became fast friends. It's pretty much been me and her against the world since."

"Until you left me," Dani teases. There's a smile on her lips, but I don't miss the flash of sadness in her eyes. She's truly been missing her best friend. On the phone the other night when she told me she felt alone, I knew I had to change that. I had to show her she has someone . . . *people* . . . in this world who care about her . . . *for* her. It's what made me jump in the car and head to the airport. I couldn't get to her fast enough.

"Oh, Dani," Piper says, reaching over and grabbing her hand. "You know I didn't want to leave you."

"I know. I'm just teasing." She shifts awkwardly in her seat, obviously not fond of all the eyes on her. "Besides, if you hadn't moved to Birmingham, I would have never had the chance to meet all of these awesome people," she says, waving her hand around the fire.

"And what a tragedy that would've been," Deacon pipes up from the other side of the fire pit.

"Right?" Cami says, chiming in. "I mean, how on earth would you have survived, Dani?" She laughs as Deacon pulls her over onto his lap.

"Well, I love you all, but I'm pooped. How about a big breakfast in the morning?" my mama asks, standing up from her chair.

She's answered with unanimous approval. Tucker even says he'll be back out, but I'm guessing it's for more than just breakfast.

"I'm hittin' the hay, too," my dad says. "Y'all be good. Make sure the fire is out before you turn in."

"Ten-four," I tell him, knowing I'll probably be the last one here.

"I think I'm going to have to call it a night, too," Cami says. "Carter is with my parents and it's way past his bedtime."

"Well, I rode with Cam, so I guess I'm out, too," Tucker says, standing and stretching his arms above his head. I catch a glimpse of Piper checking him out. Maybe the feeling is mutual. "But," he says, clapping his hands together, "I'll be back bright and early for breakfast!"

"I'm gonna walk them around to the front and then head to the house," Deacon adds. "I'll see y'all in the mornin'."

"I think I'm gonna go to bed," Piper says. "It's been a long day." She stands up and hugs Dani, and just like that, Dani and I are alone.

"I had fun today. Thank you." She's leaning back against the chair and I reach up to brush a stray hair from her face.

"I'm glad you had a fun day. You needed it."

"I could use a whole bunch of days like this."

I smile, liking the sound of that. "Wanna take a walk?"

"Sure."

I pour a bucket of water over the dying embers and take Dani's hand into mine. This isn't the first time I've held her hand, but it's the first time I've done it and felt like there's a real chance for more. I thread my fingers through hers, loving how they fit perfectly between mine, and we walk the short distance to the pond.

When we get there, we both sit on the edge of the dock and Dani slips her hand back into mine. "I like holding your hand," she says quietly when she notices me looking at her.

"Is that permission to hold your hand anytime I want to?"

"Yeah, I guess so." She twists her mouth into an adorable smile. I can't help but think back to the first time we took a walk out here and how badly I just wanted to touch her, but I'm eternally grateful I didn't. I'm sure I would've royally fucked up and we might not be sitting here now.

That whole patience talk from my mama is playing on a loop in the back of my mind.

"What about kissing you? Can I do that?" I ask, not wanting to take this a step further than she's willing to go, but wanting it so bad, I had to ask. My stomach is in knots at the thought of her lips pressed against mine. I haven't thought this much about a kiss since Cindy Maloney kissed me in the seventh grade. She was a ninth grader, and she kissed like a senior. I didn't know what to expect, and after it was over, I definitely didn't know what hit me. Pretty sure I barely remembered my name

Dani looks over at me, her smile falling. I'm afraid she's going to tell me no, but she swallows hard and leans a little closer. When her tongue darts out and wets her lips, I lean even closer. "Is that a yes?" I ask, feeling nervous yet hopeful.

She doesn't speak. She just nods her head, leaning until our lips are almost touching. "I've wanted to kiss you since the first day I met you, so you better make it good," she whispers. I can't help but smile before softly brushing my lips against hers. The movement is slow and gentle, but intense and heated—unlike any kiss I've ever experienced.

Reaching up, I place my hand on her jaw and pull her closer, deepening the kiss. She opens her mouth, inviting me in. She tastes so good and feels so right, I have to repeat my new mantra over and over in my head: *slow.*

Kissing a girl has never felt this good. I just found my new favorite pastime—kissing Sheridan Reed.

Twenty-Two

Sheridan

J'M AWAKE BEFORE THE SUN, lying in bed, letting my mind drift. My fingers go straight to my lips, brushing over them, remembering the kiss from last night. It was everything I dreamed it would be and more. There was a feeling that started in my head and went all the way down to my toes. It left me breathless, yet full of life—content, yet begging for more. I dreamed about it—his lips, his hand on my cheek, his breath on my skin—and more. So much more.

My alarm goes off way too early for my liking. I set it for six so I'll have plenty of time to pack my things back up and spend some time on the internet working out my itinerary for the next week. I'm planning on taking a laid-back approach. I mean, when in Rome, right?

The deadline for the article is two weeks from today. If I can get all of the photographs taken in the next week, I figure it would give me another week to compile my notes and write the copy portion of the article. All I really need to do is decide how many miles I want to travel in one day and find places to stay along the way. I'll probably just end up in roadside motels, so there aren't any reservations to be made.

I roll over and look out the window as the sun begins to make its debut. It has me itching to grab my camera and join it. There's nothing like watching a sunrise. It's the fresh start to a brand new day—a chance to start over or try something new.

I slip my feet into my flip flops and grab my camera. Quietly, I tip-toe down the hall, stopping for a second in front of the room Piper slept in last night. Inching the door open, I see she's still sleeping like a baby. Piper is a lot of things, but a morning person is not one of them. I close the door and continue my way downstairs.

Everything is so quiet. I've never been here when there aren't delicious smells coming from the kitchen or boisterous laughs and conversation filling the house. I love that, but I also love this—the quiet stillness.

Twisting the lock on the back door, I open it and the soft sounds of birds chirping fill the air. A rooster crows in the distance, and the dew of the morning wets my feet as I walk. When I step into the clearing at the back of the house, closer to the pond, I'm greeted with a beautiful orange sky fading up into a soft pink. The sun hasn't quite made it to the horizon, so I sit and watch . . . waiting patiently for the perfect moment.

I don't even realize I have company until a soft, "Beautiful, huh?" comes from beside me. Annie's hand brushes my hair back off my shoulder in such a tender, loving way. Something about the beauty of the moment makes tears come to my eyes. It's such a motherly gesture, and I've missed having that in my life so much. I want to melt into her touch.

She leaves briefly, coming back out a few moments later with two cups of coffee. "This is where I start every morning," she says, sitting next to me.

"I would too if I lived here."

"Best show of the day, and that's saying a lot around here." She winks and smiles.

I breathe deeply into my cup of coffee, instantly feeling more alert. The sun peeks over the horizon, so I set the cup down and begin shooting, searching for the perfect angle and lighting.

"Sometimes you've just got to be patient and wait for it to come into focus," I whisper, turning the lens. Holding my breath, I press the shutter button once . . . and then again. I adjust the light balance and press it again. "Someone once said life is like a camera. Just focus on what's important and capture the good times, develop from the negatives, and if things don't work out, take another shot."

"Sounds like wise advice," Annie says, wrapping both hands around her cup with a sly smile on her lips. I quickly turn the camera toward her before she swats her hand in the air toward me. "Not before I have my face on." She laughs. Micah's smile lights her face, and I suddenly miss him, even though I just saw him the night before. "Come on, sweet girl. Let's go get breakfast started before everyone wakes up."

I like cooking with Micah and Deacon, but it's nice having the kitchen to ourselves. Annie and I work side by side in perfect unison—beating eggs, frying bacon, kneading dough for my granny's cathead biscuits. I also share my recipe for sausage gravy, which is similar to Annie's. We tweak it, combining the two to make something new.

"Ahhh," Piper says, yawning and stretching on her way into the kitchen. "Something smells good. Am I getting Granny's gravy?" Her eyes light up, and I have to laugh. She looks like a kid in a candy store. "You have no idea how bad I've missed Granny's gravy. Gah, there were mornings I would sit and daydream about it. I tried this gravy at this restaurant that serves breakfast down by my work, but it just wasn't the same."

"Well, I think it's time someone learns the recipe. What do you think, Dani?" Annie asks, measuring out a cup of flour.

"Listen," I say, holding up my hands. "I've tried to teach her. Your patience is better than mine, though, so feel free to give it a shot."

Piper laughs. "I'm a horrible cook."

"Oh, nonsense. Everyone can cook. It just takes a little patience, like anything good in life." She winks at us. I continue with breakfast while Annie gives Piper a lesson in Gravy 101.

When the majority of breakfast is cooked and we're finished setting the table, we pour fresh cups of coffee and sit at the bar. "Now, Piper," Annie says, putting some cream and sugar into her coffee cup, "I'm gonna need a report when you get back home. You'll have to let me know how the gravy makin' goes. And next time you're down, we'll tackle biscuits."

"Okay, I'm gonna do it," Piper says with determination.

I love how Annie casually slips in "next time you're down" like it's a given. Once Annie Landry takes someone into her home—into her heart—you're there forever. She's everything a mother should be: accepting, loving, forgiving, caring. She knows just what to say to turn a bad day around. And she gives the best damn hugs. Well . . . second best.

"So, Dani, do you know where you're going on your road trip?" Piper asks.

"Yeah. I need to look up a few more things, but I pretty much know where I'm headed. And if I get lost, I'll just stop and ask for directions. I'm not in a big hurry."

"Where are you starting?" Annie asks.

"Here. Well, at Pockets," I tell her with a smile.

Annie nods. "Well, that'll make a couple men happy."

"Yeah. I mean, that's pretty much where the idea came from, so of course I have to start there."

"Man, those boys are gonna have some serious sucking up to do. You should start makin' out your Christmas list now."

We all laugh because Micah and Deacon are over the moon about their restaurant being featured in *Southern Style*.

"I have four stops in between and honestly, I could do more than one stop a day, but since I'm not really under a time constraint, I'm going to take my time. I'm even planning a side trip to Laurel. I want to go to my storage building and look for a few of my granny's old recipe boxes. I thought they'd be good inspiration for the cookbook I'm working on."

"Oh, Dani. That's great," Annie gushes, reaching over to grab my hand in hers. "I'm so happy you're taking a little time for yourself. Stopping in your hometown is just what you need. I bet Granny will have some hidden gems in there just for you." She smiles, and I nod, hoping she's right. I really miss my granny, but more than anything, I just want to feel close to her again.

Sometimes going back to the beginning is what you have to do when you've lost your direction.

"I wish you could come with me," I tell Piper. "One day isn't enough time for us to catch up."

"Gosh, I wish I could, too," Piper whines. "It sucks having to work sometimes." We all laugh, and Annie jumps up when the timer for the biscuits goes off.

"Time to ring the dinner bell," she says, and for a second, I think she's joking. "Go ring it, Dani. It'll get them boys here faster than anything."

"You mean that bell out back?"

"Of course. You didn't think that was just there for decoration, did ya?"

I laugh. "Actually, yes, I did."

"Well, maybe for some folks, but it comes in handy around here. Be careful. Jose and Johnny will be the first to show up. You better grab some leftovers from last night and put them on the back porch for them."

I shake my head and do as she says. Grabbing two bowls out of the refrigerator, I walk out back, set the bowls down, reach up to the rope, and ring the bell. Sure enough, the two big Labs run up the gravel path as fast as their four legs can carry them. They come to a screeching halt at my feet, immediately digging into the bowls in front of them.

After ringing the "dinner" bell, I run upstairs to shower. Once I'm dressed for the day, I toss the few things I haven't packed into my bag and look around the room for any lingering items. I'm planning on leaving right after breakfast. Piper has to leave to catch her flight and I need to get an early start. Even though I have my route mapped out, I don't know exactly where I'm going, so I want to allow plenty of time for pit stops and scenic routes. I'm not looking forward to saying goodbye to Piper; telling her goodbye always sucks. But, at least this time I have plans to see her again in a couple of weeks. Without a job to go back to and no boyfriend waiting for me, I feel free to roam . . . free to figure things out and stretch my wings a little. I haven't even bought a ticket for my return flight yet.

When I get downstairs, everyone is already gathered around the large table in the kitchen. The noise level is at an all-time high. Plates are being passed and people are reaching over each other to grab biscuits and bacon. It's perfect. I wish I'd grabbed my camera.

But, there's no Micah.

I glance through the big windows and see him walking up the gravel path. He has his boots on, an LSU t-shirt, shades down, and a large duffle bag thrown over his shoulder.

He's perfection.

The sight of him reminds me of how he looked the day he took me around the plantation. I had to fight so hard to keep my mind in check, constantly reminding myself I was here on business and had a boyfriend.

But I'm not here on business now. And I sure as hell don't have a boyfriend.

Those thoughts make me smile so big.

"Dani, come eat, honey. Once Micah gets in here, there won't be anything left," Sam says, sitting back in his chair with a newspaper and cup of coffee.

Micah walks in and sets his duffle bag down by the back door. He takes the sunglasses off and sticks them on the collar of his shirt. His eyes start at my face, slowly working their way down, causing tightness in my chest and heat to flood my body. When he makes it back up to my face, he smiles, and I have to wonder if he's thinking about the kiss from last night. I know I sure am.

"Come fix you a plate, Micah," Annie calls from the other end of the table.

"Were you gettin' your beauty rest?" Tucker asks. "'Cause damn, you need it!"

Micah shakes his head, laughing. He pushes Tucker practically out of his seat as he walks by and takes one of two empty seats at the table. I walk around and sit next to him.

"Good mornin'," he says, leaning over and pushing a strand of hair behind my ear.

"Good morning." My cheeks feel flush at his casual, yet intimate touch that no one else seems to notice but me.

"Coffee?" Piper asks, holding up a carafe.

"Uh, no. I think I'll have some orange juice." Anything to cool me down.

"What's with the bag?" Deacon asks, pointing to the duffle by the door. "You planning on staying the week in Red Stick?"

"Red Stick?" I ask, not knowing where that is.

"*Baton Rouge*," Micah says slowly. "Get it?"

"Um, no." I shake my head, feeling like I'm missing out on something. "Should I?"

"Well, not unless you know French," Annie says. "Baton Rouge means red stick in French."

"Ahh, gotcha," I say, nodding. "So, are you staying the week in Red Stick?" I ask, looking at Micah like I know what I'm talking about.

He laughs, shaking his head. "No, I thought I'd take a little road trip."

I put my fork down and cover my mouth with my napkin, coughing into it as my eyes go wide with surprise. *Did he say road trip?*

"Road trip?" I ask.

"Yeah, I thought I'd tag along, give you some company."

"Really?"

He nods. "Unless you don't want me to."

"No! No, I do." I nod my head and smile behind my napkin, trying not to show him how much I want him to. It never occurred to me to ask him to go with me. I just assumed he had to work.

"Well, I think that sounds like a wonderful idea," Annie says, clearing away a few plates from the table. "Don't you, honey?" she asks Sam.

Sam smiles behind his newspaper before saying, "Sounds like a fantastic idea." I watch him as he lowers the paper, making eye contact with me and then winking—just like Micah.

"I'M GOING TO MISS YOU," Piper says, squeezing me tightly.

"I'm going to miss you, too," I tell her, squeezing her back just as tight. "But at least we won't have to wait as long to see each other this time."

"Two weeks."

"Yeah, two weeks. And then, hopefully, I'll be able to visit more often."

"Uh huh," she says quietly, still holding on to me. "I'm thinking you're going to have several reasons to come down here more often."

"Stop."

"Just sayin'," she sings in my ear. "I love you."

"I love you, too. Be careful."

"Always." She jumps in her rental car and waves out the window on her way down the drive. I look over to see Tucker standing on the front porch with a wistful look in his eyes. I'm going to have to remember to ask her about him when she calls later.

"Ready to go, Chuck?" Micah asks, tossing our bags into the trunk of the rental car. We decided we'd take it since his truck is still at the airport in New Orleans. Deacon told him he and Cami were planning on going there for a "hot date" next weekend, so one of them is going to drive it back for him.

"Yep. I'm driving."

Twenty-Three

MICAH

*A*S SOON AS I PUT the car in park behind Pockets, my lips are on Dani's—my hands in her hair. I try to be gentle, but I haven't been able to think of anything else since we kissed last night at the pond. My incessant thoughts and the need I have for her make me desperate. Dani doesn't seem to object as she grabs my shirt to pull me closer. She moans softly just about the time my elbow accidentally jabs the car horn. It blares, making us both jump apart, ending the kiss too quickly.

"Wow." Dani's face is flushed, her eyes wide. Somehow, she looks more beautiful than she did just fifteen minutes ago. I feel like she gets more and more beautiful every day.

"Yeah, wow," I say, rubbing my thumb over her bottom lip. "You said I could kiss you whenever I want, so I'm gonna hold you to it."

"I said you could *hold my hand* whenever you wanted," she corrects me.

I trace her jaw with my fingertips and slide my hand to the back of her head before pulling her face close to mine. "Does that mean you don't want me to kiss you?"

"That's not what I said at all, but since we're on the subject, I guess it would be okay for you to kiss me on occasion."

She's so fucking cute.

"Well, then, I look forward to the next occasion." I place a gentle kiss on her mouth and pull away, knowing we have a full day ahead of us.

When we walk through the back door of the restaurant, we find ourselves in the middle of a very busy kitchen. It's almost time for our lunch rush, so everyone is running around making last-minute preparations.

Trying not to get in the way, I introduce Dani to as many people as possible, including Joe, our cook. Joe, Deacon, and I are doing an interview for the article, so I let him know to meet us at the bar when he gets a break.

Dani pulls her camera out of her bag and tells me she's going to take some pictures of the dining area, so I go to the office in search of my brother.

"Hey, Deke. You ready to head up to the bar?"

"Yeah, man. Just finishin' up some paperwork." Not many people see this serious, hardworking side of Deacon, but honestly, he's the reason Pockets and Grinders are so successful. He likes to take risks, but they're always calculated, and so far, they've worked out well for us.

I stroll up behind the bar and fix everyone a Coke. Dani immediately catches my eye and I watch her work, thoroughly enjoying the view.

I still can't believe she's giving me a chance to prove myself to her, and I pray to God I don't screw it up. If I mess this up, I know without a doubt it'll be unintentional. There's no way I could ever hurt her on purpose. The thought of losing her, even now, makes my heart hurt.

"Why the long face?"

Turning toward the voice, I see Dani and automatically smile. "No reason. Just thinkin' about things."

She leans over the bar to get closer to me. "Are you not wanting to go on the road with me? It's okay if you don't. I mean, I'd miss the company, but I'd understand."

"Nice try. You're not getting rid of me that easily, Chuck." I take her hand and lift it to my lips, watching as her eyes darken to a beautiful shade of forest green. I kiss her lips to see if they can get darker—until the sound of broken glass breaks us from our bubble. I turn around just in time to see Jamie's ponytail flying through the air, following her into the ladies' bathroom. The tray of drinks she was obviously carrying is now a sticky mess on the floor. Once she's inside, we hear a muffled scream of frustration.

"Is she . . ." Dani starts, quirking an eyebrow and pointing her finger toward the bathroom, "is she . . . another?"

Realization hits me, and I'm quick to answer. "No! Definitely not! I've never even come close to bein' with her."

"Okay, settle down," she says, laughing. "Well, she's obviously not happy about seeing us together."

"I know this is harsh, but I honestly don't give a shit. She's been nothin' but a pain in my ass since grade school. I gave her a job because I needed a waitress and she's really good with the customers."

Sighing, I push away from the bar and motion for a busboy to clean the mess while I pick up the tray and take it to the dishwasher. Good waitress or not, she might've just earned her ass a ticket out the door.

Deacon sees me from the office and walks to the bar with me, greeting Dani with a hug. Joe finally joins us and brings with him a plate with a pocket on it. He sets it down on the bar in front of Dani.

"Oh, good," she says, smiling. "I was going to ask you to plate a pocket so I can have one to photograph for the article."

"Well, this ain't your average pocket," Deacon says, sliding onto the barstool beside her.

"Oh, really?" She positions the plate just right under the light and brings her camera up to her eye. "What's so special about it?"

"You, my friend, are looking at the very new, very special, sweet and spicy chicken étouffée pocket. We call it 'The Dani'."

Dani quickly looks up at Deacon and then over to me. Her mouth drops. "Really? You named a pocket after me?"

"Well, we had to do something to show you how much we appreciate you featurin' Pockets in your article. This is big time for us, Chuck." I wink at her, enjoying her shock and awe.

"I'm flattered." She lets the camera hang from the strap around her neck and brings her hand up over her heart. "Seriously. This is the coolest thing ever."

"Well, maybe you should try it before you get too carried away," I tell her, inching the plate toward her.

Her eyes light up and she twists her lips into an adorable smile. "I can't believe you made a pocket named after me."

"You might hate it. Try it and see what you think," Deacon says. "We could always go back to the drawin' board if you don't like it."

"This is *so* going in the article."

"Try it!" Deacon and I both yell at the same time. Joe is standing over to the side with his arms folded across his chest, chuckling at the three of us. I can already tell he's just as smitten with her as we are.

"All right, all right! Geez, you don't have to get so testy." She rolls her eyes and picks up the fork on the plate. "You guys *really* didn't have to do this."

"Oh my God, woman. Just try the damn pocket!" I take the fork from her hand and cut off a bite. When I hold it up to her mouth, she smiles a devious smile. Wetting her lips with her tongue, she finally opens up and takes the bite, moaning shamelessly as she chews.

She knows exactly what she's doing to me, and I hate her for it.

"Mmm, *so* good!" she exclaims, slapping her hand down on the bar.

I clear my throat in an effort to get my head out of the gutter. "Can I get you something to drink with that?"

"Another Coke, I guess." She takes the fork from my hand and goes in for another bite. "A beer would be great with this, but since we're heading out on the road soon, I better not."

"Have a beer. I'll drive."

"Well, aren't you sweet? First, you offer to keep me company, and now you're going to be my chauffeur." She smiles, shaking her head. "A girl could get used to this kind of chivalry."

I roll my eyes. *If it's chivalry she wants, it's chivalry she'll get. I'd like to chival her right out of her pants.* "So, what's it gonna be? A Coke or a beer?"

"Coke. I try not to drink before five, except on days my boyfriend sleeps with the therapist."

"Ex."

"Yeah, ex." She pops another bite into her mouth to hide her smile before taking the pen out of her hair and jotting down a few notes in the journal she brought with her. Without the pen holding her hair up on her head, it slowly begins to cascade down her back.

Holy fuck. I clench my jaw and briefly close my eyes, willing my dick to stay in line. *This might've been a bad idea.* I'm not sure I can do slow with Sheridan Reed. I want to. I want to do everything right with her, but she might kill me in the process.

"I'll get you that Coke."

INSTEAD OF STICKING AROUND AND doing the interview Dani wanted at the restaurant, we decided we could finish that part while we're on the road. Dani's been grilling me for the past twenty miles. I think she's past her normal set of questions and is now asking things she just wants to know. Normally, I'd find a way out of a situation like this. I hate talking about myself, but I want to with her.

I want Dani to know me.

I want to know everything about her.

"Tell me about college," she says, pulling the visor down to keep the sun out of her eyes as we head east on Interstate 12.

"I went."

"Ha ha! Very funny. I want details," she says firmly, leaning her head against the seat. "What did you major in?"

"Business."

"That sounds too boring for someone like you."

I chuckle at her response. "Well, I knew early on I wanted to open a restaurant with Deacon. We'd been dreaming that up since we were kids. LSU didn't offer a Hotel and Restaurant Management degree, so I went with business."

"What about Deacon?"

"He majored in business, too."

"I'm sure there're other schools that offer Hotel and Restaurant Management degrees."

"Yeah, but none I wanted to go to. The only other thing I wanted to do was go to LSU."

"So, besides majoring in business, what else did you do in college?"

"Joined a fraternity, got into *just* the right amount of trouble, and managed to graduate on time . . . with honors."

"Really?" she asks, pushing her sunglasses down on her nose and looking at me over them. "Micah Landry, top of the class?" She pauses for a second, continuing to look at me. "I'm impressed."

I laugh, keeping my eyes on the road. Sometimes, when she looks at me so intently, it makes me nervous. I don't know why, but it does. And I like that it does. She makes me feel things no one else ever has.

"What about you?" I ask, wanting the focus off me for a minute, but also just wanting to know more about her.

"I went to NYU."

"And?"

"Oh, you want to know more?" She has her sunglasses pulled back up over her eyes and her head leaned back against the seat with a smirk on her lips. I love that she gives my shit right back to me.

"Yes, please." Which is code for: *I want to know everything.*

"Since you said please." She smiles before continuing. "There's not much to know, really. I knew I wanted to go somewhere with a good fine arts program, so I applied to a few schools, but NYU was my shot in the dark. When I was accepted, it was one of the happiest and saddest days of my life. Happy because it was a dream come true—one I hadn't even really allowed myself to dream yet. But sad because I knew I'd be leaving Laurel, leaving my granny." She sighs for a second, staring out the window. "Knowing what I know now—that I only had a few more years with her—I would've stayed closer to home."

"But she had to have been proud of you."

"Oh, she was. She was always my biggest supporter. It didn't matter what I was doing. If it made me happy, she was cheering me on. I remember the day my acceptance letter came in the mail. She made me smothered pork chops that night for dinner with her better-than-sex chocolate cake."

"Better than sex?" I laugh. "Are you kidding me?"

"No, that's what she called it. That's what all the ladies at the bingo hall called it."

"And was it?"

I notice the flush in her cheeks and the movement in her neck when she swallows hard.

"Yep, pretty damn good," she squeaks out.

"You have the recipe?"

"I don't, actually. I wish I did, though." She pauses for a second, biting her bottom lip. "Damn, I miss that cake . . . and sex," she mumbles so quietly, I almost miss it.

"What?" I ask on reflex. My mind and dick needing clarification on that last part. *Did she just say she misses sex? God, please let that be what she said. Actually, God, please let that* not *be what she said.* I feel my whole body stiffen. Dani missing sex could quite possibly switch this from slow to fast in record speed.

"Nothing," she mumbles, focusing on something out her window. Needing a minute to get myself in check, I'm secretly glad she doesn't want to elaborate.

"So, tell me about NYU," I say, clearing my throat and trying to change the subject.

"NYU was good. I really loved the school. It's what I always dreamed it would be. When I was younger, the only thing I wanted was to get out of Mississippi and live in a big city. NYU was all of that."

"Were you in a sorority? Did you live on campus?" I ask, knowing I'll have to prompt her to get more info.

"No sorority," she says, laughing. "That wasn't quite my scene."

"What was your scene?" I ask.

"I don't know," she sighs, shrugging.

"Did you get in any trouble?" I ask.

She laughs again, leaning her head against the seat and turning her gaze to me. "No. Well, at least not until I met Piper."

"I can see that."

"I was just a small fish in a big city, but when I met Piper, she would drag me out on the weekends, and we'd go explore a new section of New York. It was a lot of fun. She knew much more about New York than I did. Having grown up in Connecticut, she'd been there quite a bit."

"What did you major in? Photography?"

"No, I majored in journalism and minored in business, but I took a lot of photography classes."

"Well, you're brilliant at what you do. I think you're a natural. The way you see things is something that can't be taught. It's like you just know."

"Thank you." She looks back over at me. "Really. That means a lot."

"I speak nothing but the truth."

"So, what about after college?" she asks. The way she dodges questions lets me know she doesn't like talking about herself any more than I do.

"Deacon and I actually opened Grinders before I graduated college. We took out a business loan together and found a place downtown. It worked out great. We already had an apartment close by we were living in while going to school, so it made sense."

"Do you guys still have an apartment there?"

"Yeah, it's where we stay when we work late. It's better than making the forty-five minute drive home at three in the morning."

"That's really cool." She looks down and then shakes her head in disbelief.

"What?"

"Nothing. It's just . . . I feel like I know you so well. I mean, we've had a dozen sessions of twenty questions," she says, laughing. "But you still seem to surprise me . . . impress me."

"I'm not trying to impress you."

"I know. And that makes it even more impressive."

"Okay, you can stop with the compliments now," I tell him, feeling my cheeks heat up.

"There's nothing impressive about opening up a restaurant."

"No, but it's impressive to know what you want to do with your life and go after it. So many people sit around waiting for their dreams to come true and sometimes it never happens. They just waste their life away . . . waiting."

"Yeah, I'm not one of those people."

"No, you're not. You're not a waiter. You're a go-getter."

"Now you sound like my dad."

We sit in comfortable silence, listening to the playlist I put together for our trip. Jimmy Buffett has been singing about cheeseburgers in paradise for the last few miles.

"Speaking of cheeseburgers," Dani says, and I laugh. "Our next stop is a hamburger joint. Do you like hamburgers?"

"Who doesn't like hamburgers?"

"Vegetarians?"

"Deep down, I bet even vegetarians crave a big ol' juicy hamburger."

She laughs. "I couldn't be a vegetarian. I like bacon too much."

"Bacon is the gateway meat."

"The what?" she asks.

"Gateway meat. It's the one that sucks them in."

"Them, who?"

"Vegetarians. It's basically the marijuana of the meat world."

She laughs so hard, she claims she might pee her pants. It's adorable. If she's not being cute, she's being adorable, and if she's not being adorable, she's being sexy. There's seriously nothing she could do that wouldn't affect me.

The rest of the drive goes smoothly with random conversations that make me fall harder and harder for Sheridan Paige Reed.

She decided she wants to drive to Pensacola, Florida today, the farthest destination on our trip, and then slowly make our way back home.

The girl is a genius.

When we find the motel she saw on the internet, we pull into the drive. Both of us hop out, needing to stretch our legs after being in the car for a few hours. It's still a little early for dinner, so we decide to check into our rooms—*plural*. If we're going to take things slow, I can't sleep in the same room as her.

Great Southern Motel. I'm not sure how great it is, but at least it looks clean. I think I'll take over on the lodging for the rest of the trip.

"So, I guess we can take a nap or something until dinner time." She scrunches up her nose, squinting against the sun in her eyes.

"Sure." I'm not sleepy, though. I'm used to a lot longer, much more tiring days than this. Hanging out and riding in the car with Dani is hardly work. It's actually something I wouldn't mind doing every day.

"How about I meet you back out here at seven?"

"It's a date."

"A date?"

"Yeah." We haven't been on one of those and I want to. I wouldn't necessarily pick Jerry's Drive-In, but it'll work. "Maybe after we eat, we can drive down to the beach. It's been awhile since I've been here."

"It's a date," she says, a warm smile gracing her beautiful face.

I decide to kick my shoes off and lie back on the bed for a few minutes, but a few minutes turns into a forty-minute nap. When I wake up, it's darker in my room and quiet, except for the water running on the other side of the thin wall in Dani's room. I still have enough time to clean up before dinner, so I grab my toiletries and turn the shower on, trying not to think of a naked Sheridan Reed on the other side of the wall.

Fifteen minutes later, I'm showered, shaved, and in clean clothes. Looking around the room, I decide to steal the blanket off the bed and toss it in the car, just in case we want it later at the beach. For *sitting*, of course.

When I walk out of the room, Dani is closing her door behind her, and she looks gorgeous—rested, fresh-faced, her hair curled around her shoulders.

"Hey, good lookin'." That earns me another show-stopping smile. "You goin' my way?" I ask, pointing to the car.

"Actually, I think you're going *my* way."

I laugh, nodding. "That, I am." I can't help the ridiculous smile on my face. I don't think I've ever been happier about the direction I'm going.

"What's that?" she asks, pointing to the folded up blanket.

"For the beach later."

"Good thinking."

"Always gotta be prepared," I say, smiling as I toss it in the back seat before opening her door for her.

"Were you a Boy Scout?" she asks, sliding into her seat.

"Yes, I was. So you know you're in good hands."

I shut the door behind her and run around to the driver's side, ready to get this date started.

A few minutes later, we're at Jerry's Drive-In. From the name, I thought it would be one of those places where you park and order from your car, but when we pull into the drive, it looks more like a diner.

"This place has been here since like 1938," Dani says, grabbing her camera out of its bag. "I love old places like this."

"Well, let's go get our burger on," I say, jumping out of the car and running back around to open her door. She smiles at me when she gets out. Leaning over the door, she kisses me right on the lips.

"What was that for?" I'm not complaining, but it was sudden and unexpected. And it's the first time she's initiated a kiss.

"For being sweet and you. Also, thanks for coming with me. This wouldn't be nearly as fun by myself."

"Thanks for letting me tag along." I breathe her in and close my eyes, trying to commit everything about this moment to memory. "Is this an occasion?" I ask.

"It's our first date."

"Good, so it's okay if I do this." I reach up, cup her jaw, and pull her lips back to mine. She tilts her head to the side, inviting me to deepen the kiss, and I do, completely losing myself in her.

For a split second, I forget we're standing in the middle of a parking lot.

I forget we're taking it slow.

Dani's hands grip the front of my shirt right before she breaks the kiss, inhaling deeply. I look down to see her eyes closed and a small smile on her lips.

"That was . . ."

"The best one yet," she says.

I chuckle, wiping some of her lip-gloss off the side of my mouth. "We should go in," I tell her, before I give in to my urges, push her up against this car, and try to compete with the kiss we just had.

When we walk into the tiny restaurant, the waitress takes our drink orders and asks if we need a minute to decide what we want to eat.

"We'll have the double bacon cheeseburger," Dani says, handing the menus back without even looking at them. "Two of them. And two Cokes."

Kay, the waitress, smiles at us, telling us our order will be right out.

"What if I didn't want a bacon cheeseburger?"

"Too bad. I read all the reviews online and that's supposed to be the best thing here. I couldn't let you make a mistake by ordering something sub-par."

"Thank you for looking out for me."

"Always." She smiles as she looks around the restaurant. "While we're waiting on the food, I'm going to take a few indoor shots. I called ahead and talked to the owner. He's supposed to be around here somewhere so I can ask him a few questions. I figure we can drive back by tomorrow and I'll get my outside shots then, when the lighting is better."

I watch as Dani walks around the place taking pictures, loving the way she focuses in on something other people wouldn't even notice. After a few minutes, a guy in a white apron steps out of the back and introduces himself. Dani shakes his hand with confidence and sits down at the bar, pulling out her journal. They talk for a few minutes and he beams at her. I know he sees what I see—beauty, intelligence, wit. She's something special and watching her makes my chest tighten and my insides feel warm.

When she glances back at me and sees our waitress setting two plates down, she points to our food and shakes his hand again before joining me back at our booth.

"These look amazing," she gushes, sliding back into the booth. She snaps a few shots of the burger on her plate, glances at the screen on the camera, and tries again, until she gets the perfect shot.

I'm trying to figure out how I'm going to fit my mouth around this thing, but Dani doesn't hesitate. She just picks it up with two hands and dives in. As she bites down on the burger, the ketchup oozes out and clings to both sides of her mouth.

"You've got a little something . . ." I say, pointing to my own mouth.

"What?" she asks, still working on the mouthful of cheeseburger. "Here?" She points to her cheek, but not exactly where the ketchup is.

I shake my head. "No."

"Here?" she asks, pointing to the other side.

"Nope."

She shrugs and takes another huge bite.

This girl. I love her.

Whoa. What the fuck, Micah?

I choke on air and reach for my drink.

"You okay?" she asks, setting her burger back on her plate.

"Yeah," I say, rubbing the back of my neck, trying to get my shit together.

"You going to eat that burger, or are you just going to look at it?"

I laugh, shake my head, and pick it up with both hands. Mimicking Dani, I just go for it. All in.

"You got something right there," she teases, pointing to my face.

ONCE THE CAR IS PARKED near the beach entrance, I glance over to see Dani taking her shoes off.

"I want to feel the sand on my feet."

"Good idea." I push my seat back so I can reach my feet, pull my boots off, and stuff my socks down in them.

"Ready?" I ask after tossing them in the backseat and grabbing the blanket.

"Yep."

"When's the last time you were at a beach?" I ask, reaching over to hold her hand as we walk down the boardwalk.

"Years."

"Me too. Which is crazy since we live so close. Deacon and I used to meet some old college friends down here, but we've been busy the last few years running both restaurants."

"Yeah, Piper and I came down here for spring break our senior year of college, but that was like four years ago."

"How crazy would it be if we were here at the same time?" I ask, my mind running wild with what ifs.

She sighs, holding my hand a little tighter for balance as her foot slips in the sand. "I'm glad we weren't."

"Me too. Sometimes, it's all about the timing."

"Yeah, it is."

We walk along the beach, listening to the waves crash against the shore. The way the moon glistens off the water reminds me of the pond.

"Wanna sit for a while?" I ask, pointing to a spot in the sand. There's hardly anyone out tonight.

"Looks like a good spot to me."

I spread the blanket out and fall down on it. Dani pauses for a second, like she's trying to decide where to sit, before settling right between my legs.

Equally the best and worst decision she could've made.

I take deep breaths, forcing myself to remain as calm as possible, but her sweet and spicy scent isn't helping. "Uh, tell me something . . ." I say, trying to have something other than her extremely close proximity to focus on.

"What do you want me to tell you?" she asks, her voice calm and quiet.

"Anything. Tell me something I don't know about you."

"Haven't we talked about me enough today?"

"Not even."

Dani exhales deeply. "Okay, um . . ." She pauses while she thinks. "Well, this is embarrassing, but . . . I never learned how to ride a bike."

"Are you kidding me, Chuck?"

"Nope. And if you tease me about it, I'll slip Ex-Lax into your coffee."

"Holy shit. Are you sure you're not related to my brother?"

"No, and I'm glad I'm not because this would be weird. Even worse, I couldn't do this," she says, turning around and kissing me.

Twenty-Four

Sheridan

I LOVE MORNINGS AND THE feeling of a fresh start when I wake up. I especially love waking up happy. Lately, it seems like every morning I wake up, all I can think about is everything wrong in my life. It's not like there haven't been bright spots. I just haven't been able to see them for the clouds. Before this week, I honestly can't remember the last time I woke up truly happy. However, that's changed. Every morning since I flew back to Louisiana with Micah, I've woke up with a spring in my step and anticipation. The dread and weight is gone. I feel alive and free and like my life is going somewhere.

I know I owe a lot of this to my current project with *Southern Style,* but more than that, I owe it to Micah.

Micah.

I can only imagine how amazing mornings would be if I woke up next to him, and believe me, I've been imagining it . . . a lot. Sometimes, it's all I can think about—being with him. My body begins to flush—again—and I know that's my cue to hit the shower.

As the water heats up, I inspect my reflection in the bathroom mirror. I smile when I see my lips are still a little pink from all the kissing

Micah and I did last night. Technically, it's from all the kissing we've done this entire trip. It's been ages since I've acted this way—making out like a teenager without a care in the world—but that's what I feel like when I'm with Micah. Carefree. Alive. Maybe even *loved*.

I refuse to get ahead of myself or jump into anything too quickly, but I know my feelings for Micah are changing. How could they not? He's such an amazing man, and he's trying so hard to be good enough for me. His words, not mine. But, I do appreciate him trying to take things slow. He's more of a southern gentleman than he gives himself credit for.

After I shower and get ready for the day, I gather my things and head for the door. When Micah insisted on being in charge of picking our hotels, I grumbled at first. I may have also accused him of being spoiled, which he didn't deny. In all truthfulness, his hotels are much better than the one I got us in Florida, but I'm not ready to admit that to him just yet. I think I may be getting a little spoiled, too.

Just like every morning this week, Micah is waiting for me outside my room so we can check out and get breakfast. I don't even try to hide the way my eyes travel over him, appreciating the snug t-shirt and well-worn jeans covering his body perfectly. And he's doing the same to me. At first, it made me self-conscious when he looked at me this way, but now, I practically crave it.

"Mornin', sunshine." He steps forward and places a sweet kiss on my mouth before taking my suitcase out of my hand. There are times when the modern city girl in me wants to protest against his chivalry, but I know it makes him happy to do things for me, so I stay quiet. It really is sweet. I'm just not used to it.

Someday I will be, I bet.

After breakfast, we load up the car and start heading toward Hattiesburg, Mississippi. We spent all day yesterday in Mobile, Alabama, hanging out at the beach some more in between our visits to two local diners. We even stopped at their Carnival Museum. I was shocked to learn Mardi Gras actually originated in Mobile. Micah claims it took the people of Louisiana to turn Mardi Gras into the major party it is today. He also took that opportunity to invite me to experience Mardi Gras in

New Orleans with him, and it makes me wonder whether he realizes he's making plans for us *seven months* from now.

Of course, I accepted.

When we cross the Mississippi border, my stomach starts tensing in anticipation. Knowing we'll be in my hometown soon creates a blend of nervousness and excitement with a little bit of sadness thrown in. I'm sure it'll be a true test for Micah to see me like this, but I'm not going to hide my emotions from him. He'll either accept them or he won't.

Trying to distract myself, I ask Micah to tell me another story about him and Deacon growing up, and he easily obliges. I swear, we could write a book about their adventures and mishaps. It'd be like a modern-day Tom Sawyer story.

"One time, when Deacon was about fourteen and I was twelve, we rode out about ten miles away from the plantation. Deke was on a four-wheeler, I was on my dirt bike, and we were joy-ridin' around the swampland, just goofin' off for a few hours. After a while, my bike ran out of gas, and we didn't know how we were gonna get it back to the house. Of course, lookin' back, we should've driven the four-wheeler home, gotten some gas, and brought it back to the bike, but we were young and stupid, so that thought never crossed our minds."

"Oh, no. What did you do?"

"Well, Deacon had rope with him, so we tied the bike to the back of his four-wheeler and I rode the bike while he pulled it home. The problem was we tied the rope to only *one* side of the handlebars. I had to fight like hell to keep the bike straight."

Micah cracks up with laughter, and he's so adorable, I can't help but laugh with him.

"We were such dumbasses. It's a wonder my mama didn't get rid of us for the hell we put her through."

I love how his face lights up when he talks about Annie.

"So, we're movin' along and Deke's doin' a good job of goin' slow since we're still around swampland. But once we make it to the road leading back to the house, I guess he forgets he's towin' me because he takes off like a bat outta hell. I'm holdin' on to the bike as hard as I can while it's bein' dragged across the gravel. When he finally remembers

me, he looks back, and the bike is on its side, still tied to the four-wheeler, but I'm way back on the ground down the road 'cause I couldn't hold
on any longer. He was so freaked out. I can still remember the look of
panic on his face as he ran up to me."

"Were you hurt badly?"

"Nah, I had some scrapes and bruises, and the wind was knocked
outta me, but I was fine. The bike, though, looked like shit. Once Deacon
realized I was okay, he really got scared thinkin' about how we were gonna tell our parents what'd happened."

"Oh, shit. I bet Annie was pissed!"

"Hell, yeah, she was! So was my dad, but he just let Mama chew us
out while she doctored my wounds. Of course, we were grounded for a
few weeks, but that never stopped us from actin' up for too long."

Micah's story works like a charm, and soon, I'm relaxed in my seat.
My stomach is a little sore from all the laughing, but it's so worth it.

When I see the Jones County sign, I know we're close. Sensing my
anxiety, Micah reaches over and grabs my hand, saving me from biting the last of my nails off. A smile crosses my face and I reach down,
grabbing his phone from the cup holder. It's been playing a mix of Tab
Benoit, Micah's favorite, and Miranda Lambert, my favorite. The song I
find on YouTube starts filtering through the speakers and Micah loosen
his hold on my hand.

"NSYNC?" he asks, chuckling and shaking his head. "Really?"

I hold his hand tighter as I give him his first lesson of being in Laurel,
Mississippi.

"It's a rule. When you're in Laurel, you *must* listen to NSYNC."

"Is this a rule you and your friends came up when you were nine?
Some rules are meant to be broken, you know?"

"Don't hate, Micah. NSYNC is still great music. I mean, if nothing
else, that band gave us Justin Timberlake. But, if you must know, I'm
not the only one who has to listen to NSYNC when I drive into town."
I smile, looking over at him as we drive into the city limits. "This," I
say grandly, sweeping my arm out in front of us Vanna White style, "is
Laurel, Mississippi, the hometown of *the* Lance Bass."

"Really?" Micah asks, sounding surprised. "And here I thought the biggest thing to come out of Laurel was sitting right beside me."

"You don't have to kiss up. I already like you."

"Only speaking the truth."

I take in the sights, which aren't much, but they're home . . . or at least, where home once was. Technically, home was my granny, but this is as close as I can get to her and her memory. I glance over at Micah and see him mouthing the words to the song still playing.

"You like them," I tease.

"Shut up." He smiles widely. "If you make fun of me, I'll slip Ex-Lax into your coffee."

"Damn. You play dirty."

"Learned from the best," he says, pulling our joined hands up to his mouth and placing a kiss on mine. That simple kiss shoots throughout my entire body like electricity. "Where to? I have no idea where I'm going."

"I want to stop by my storage building first. There're a few things I need and it's been a while. I just need to make sure it's all still there." Peace of mind. That's another thing I'm after today. "Turn left at this next stop light."

"You need me in there?" Micah asks, pointing up to the storage unit in front of us.

"Uh, no. I think I'll be good."

"Well, I'm right here if you need me."

I nod and hop out of the car. After I try the combination on the lock a few times, it finally pops open. The combo is my granny's birthday, but I forgot I put the year first and the day and month last to switch things up. Not that anyone wants to break into this place. The items in here are only valuable to me. Besides, there aren't many people left on this planet who care enough. When the door of the unit rolls up, I'm hit with sensory overload. Her old rocker from the front porch is front and center, and the dresser I used to sit and play dress-up at is against the back wall. Something about this place smells like her. I don't even know how that is possible after all these years, and it might be my imagination, but it's like she was just here . . . like I just missed her.

I inhale deeply, closing my eyes, trying to make this moment last just a little longer.

"I've missed you so much," I whisper, walking over to the rocking chair and gently sitting down on it. There's a storage bin to my left labeled blankets, so I open it and find the last quilt she made right before she died. Taking it out, I shake it open and wrap myself in it.

It's a hot day in the middle of the summer in Laurel, Mississippi, but I don't care. Pulling my feet up into the chair, I kick off the floor and sit, rock, and remember.

When I open my eyes, a familiar box catches my attention. It was one she kept in her kitchen—the jackpot I've been thinking about. Quickly, I fold the blanket back up, put it back in the storage bin, snap the lid down, and set the bin outside the storage unit. It's coming with me.

Walking over to the stack of boxes against the wall, I take the top two off to get to the one I was hoping to find. Cracking the lid, just to make sure the recipes are still there, I see my granny's handwriting on top. But it's not a recipe. It's a letter.

How could I have missed this?

I know I was grieving the last time I was here, but I don't know how I could've missed something like this.

My Dearest Dani,

I'm saving this to give to you on your wedding day, but in case something happens to me between now and then, I'm writing this letter in hopes you'll find it when the time is right.

This book was given to me by my mother the day I married your grandfather. I think it saved our marriage, or at least saved us from eating burnt chicken every night. So I'm hoping it will bring you good luck as well.

Sweet girl, I want you to know you're the best thing that ever happened to me. Most people say that about their children, and your mother was my greatest accomplishment, but you saved me. If it hadn't been for you, losing your grandfather and then your mother would've been the death of me. But you gave me purpose and kept me from wallowing in my grief. I want you to know you were a blessing from the day you were created. There was never a doubt in my mind that you would go on to do amazing things. I'm so proud of you. I can say that without hesitation, regardless the occupation you choose or anything else you've done in life, because what's inside of you makes me proud.

You've not had the easiest road in life, but you've always shown great strength, even at a young age. Hold on to that strength, Dani, but also allow yourself to be vulnerable.

One thing I'd like to leave you with is this . . .

Let your heart be your compass.

Everything you need in life is right there inside you.

And last, but not least . . . you're never alone. I'll always be right here with you, even if I'm no longer on this earth.

All my love,

Granny

My sob echoes into the small space as I wipe the tears that have fallen to my cheeks with the back of my hand, hugging the letter to my chest. Under the letter is what looks like a cookbook from the 1950s. Its outdated cover is faded and the edges show years of kitchen use. There're a few splatters here and there. I open it and press my nose into the pages, hoping for a hint of her kitchen. Pulling it back, I quickly flip through the book. Beside each recipe are notes in her handwriting. In some of them, she's written how she changed them, made them her own. On one of the pages, she wrote: *Not Matthew's favorite*. I laugh through my tears, trying to picture her making dinner when she was my age, newly married.

I didn't know my grandfather, but I've seen so many pictures of him, I feel like I knew him. He was handsome—tall and slender. From what my granny told me, he was mild-mannered, never had a harsh word for anyone. She would laugh and shake her head, reminiscing on how he would leave the disciplining to her. He loved my mom more than anything. My granny always said it was a blessing he died before my mom, because if he hadn't, he would've died from a broken heart.

I came for recipes, but this is so much better. This is more than I ever could've dreamed of finding. When I put the letter and the cookbook safely back into the box and close it, I notice something else: a faded gold compass embossed into the worn green lid.

Let your heart be your compass.

"Thank you, Granny," I whisper, closing my eyes.

"Hey," Micah says, leaning against the side of the building. "You okay?"

"Yeah." I turn away from him, drying the tears from my cheeks one last time. "I'm good."

"Find what you're lookin' for?"

I look back over my shoulder feeling like my entire world has been righted . . . like everything just came into focus. "Yeah, I did."

"Are these all you're taking?" he asks, pointing to the small stack of boxes on the ground.

"For now." One of these days, I want all of this in my house. Not my apartment in New York, but wherever I put down my own roots. I want my granny with me.

"Ready?" Micah asks, shutting the trunk.

"Yep."

"Still wanna drive by your old house?"

"Yeah. I'm kinda scared, but I want to see it," I tell him, climbing into the car.

Micah closes the door behind me and walks around to his side. "What scares you?" he asks when he gets in.

"I'm worried it won't look the same," I admit.

"And that'll make you sad." He doesn't ask. He knows.

"Yeah," I whisper, looking out the window as we make our way back to the main road.

"Which way?"

I point left to the road that'll lead us out of town. It doesn't take long to get there, and I don't even have to tell Micah when we've arrived. He can tell by the way I grip the door handle and practically glue my face to the window as I stare out at the two-story yellow house. He parks on the side of the road and waits patiently as I try to process the different emotions surging through me.

"You sure you want to do this?" His voice is gentle, like he's worried he'll startle me and I'll run off.

I nod my head and take a deep breath. "Being here is surreal. It's exactly the same, but different. After I sold this place, I honestly never thought I'd come back, but it still means so much to me."

"Want me to see if anyone's home?"

"I'll do it, but I'd love some company."

His thumb caresses my cheek, and I can't help the smile that blossoms on my face. "You've got it."

As we walk to the front door, I automatically reach my hand out to him. He doesn't hesitate to take it and link our fingers. I don't know whether I'll ever be able to express how much it means to me to have him here with me, but I have a feeling he knows.

Micah gives my hand a squeeze to reassure me before I knock on the door. A few short moments later, I'm standing in the backyard of my childhood home.

"They kept the tire swing!" I rush over to what was one of my favorite pastimes and see the tire is the same, but it's held up by a newer, stronger rope. "I used to swing on this for hours, sometimes not stopping until I threw up."

Micah laughs. "What?"

I shrug my shoulders. "I get a little motion sick sometimes."

"Get on it. I'm sure the Millers won't mind."

"No way!" I'm sure the nice family I just met wouldn't care, but still, I'm too old for a tire swing, aren't I? "It's for kids. I'm too big for it."

"Bullshit. I'll help you up, and I promise not to push you too hard."

I can't believe I'm agreeing to this, but at the same time, I'm just as giddy as I used to be whenever I'd swing here. Maybe more so.

When I place my hands on Micah's shoulders, he grabs my waist and effortlessly lifts me up, placing me on top of the tire. Once I'm situated comfortably and holding on to the rope, his hands slide down and rest on my thighs.

"Don't let me fall," I say, jokingly, but when he answers, "Never", there's passion in his voice I wasn't expecting. It leaves me breathless.

There's a change in the air, and neither of us can deny the intensity enveloping us. Micah's eyes are a deep blue, and he's looking at me like he can see right through to my soul.

We're now the same height, so he has no problem pulling my mouth to his. The last couple of days, our kisses have been sweet and fun, exploring and teasing, but this kiss . . . this searing kiss is full of desire and unspoken promises. Warmth spreads throughout my body as I sink my fingers into his thick hair, and his deep moan only spurs me on. When we finally separate, we're both panting and dazed. If his hands weren't still on me, I'm sure I'd slide right off this tire.

"Maybe I should get down."

"That's probably a good idea."

Micah helps me down and my legs wobble, though I'm not sure whether it's from being on the swing for so long or the kiss we just shared. The cocky grin he gives me tells me what he thinks the cause is.

I pull my camera from the bag I brought with me and start taking pictures of the tire swing, the trees that used to hold my granny's hammock, and the old red barn sitting out in the field—pictures that are just for me. It's in front of the barn where I find myself locked in Micah's arms again, but this time, his embrace is full of support and concern as I allow a few tears to flow down my cheeks. I'm amazed by how he seems to know exactly what I need, sometimes before even *I* know.

For someone new at all of this—whatever *this* is—Micah Landry is a natural.

Twenty-Five

MICAH

*N*EVER IN MY LIFE DID I think I'd eat a peanut butter burger and like it. Scratch that. I loved that fucker. When Dani told me about Topher's Rock 'N Roll Grill, it sounded like a great place to stop for lunch, but I had no idea I'd be eating a burger literally slathered with peanut butter. Don't even get me started on the peanut butter and banana shake I had with it. So fucking good.

At least I waited until Dani fell asleep in the car to unbutton my jeans.

Standing in line to check in at the hotel, I'm blown away when Dani turns to me and asks if we can share a room. "It's been a long, emotional day. I don't want to be alone."

I'm not going to dwell on the fact that she said she doesn't want to be alone instead of saying she wants to be with *me*, in particular. I'll take what I can get. Besides, I can't say no to her, especially when she looks at me with those big green eyes.

Thankfully, they only have rooms with king beds left, so it looks like Dani and I will be snuggle buddies.

Once we're settled in our room, I start to feel a little nervous. I don't know what Dani expects of me. Our agreement to take things slow has stayed in place for most of the trip. There have been a few times when our kisses have turned heated, but we've been able to pull back. I know sex isn't a given just because we're sharing a bed tonight, but fuck me if I'm not dying to make love to her.

It doesn't escape me that I think of being with Dani as making love. This is the first time I've thought of sex in that way, but it's true. It's what I want to do with her; it's how I want to show her what I'm feeling. I've never felt this way before, and I have no idea what's going to happen once we're back in Louisiana.

Panic starts to pulse through my body at the thought of Dani going back to New York once our road trip is over. I want her to do whatever she needs to be happy, I just hope I get the chance to make her happy, too.

I need a distraction before I wear a bare spot in the carpet of the hotel room. Dani's so preoccupied with her treasures from the storage building, she isn't paying me any attention.

"Hey, I'm going to hop in the shower . . . unless you want to first?"

She looks up from her granny's cookbook and smiles. "I can wait. I'll take a bath when you're done."

Well, there goes my plan to rub one out in the shower. No way *am I doing that knowing she'll be sitting in the tub moments later.*

Instead of relieving stress my usual way, I simply stand with my back to the shower head, letting the hot water beat down on my shoulders.

I know what I need to do. I need to be honest with Dani and tell her how I feel, but the truth is, I'm too damn scared. I know she just broke up with Graham and she's focused on getting her career going in the right direction, so I don't know if she's even in a position to accept my feelings, much less return them.

I step out of the shower and dry off, resolved to keep my feelings to myself. Despite what my heart is telling me I should say, I don't want to pressure her or complicate things for her. She's having fun doing this article; I'm not about to mess that up.

Not thinking about what I'm doing, I open the bathroom door with only my towel wrapped around my waist.

"Want me to start your bath water?"

"Oh, um . . . yeah, sure. That'd be great," she murmurs. She doesn't even try to hide the fact that her eyes are taking in every inch of my chest and arms, and I realize this is the first time she's seen me without a shirt.

I clear my throat and she snaps out of whatever trance she was in.

"Oh, I'm sorry," she murmurs, dipping her head to hide the heat on her cheeks, but I see it anyway. "I, uh . . . I just didn't know you had tattoos." Her stammer is adorable and the way she looks back up through her lashes and checks them out makes my cock stir.

Letting out a low chuckle, I turn around and walk into the bathroom to start her bath. I need a distraction before I show her more than my tattoos.

When she walks into the bathroom a few seconds later, I watch as she bites her lip and hides her face with her hair, obviously embarrassed or feeling uneasy, so I grab her arm and make her face me.

"Hey, don't do that," I tell her, pulling her lip from her teeth with my thumb. "I like that you were looking at me, and it's okay if you don't like my tattoos. They're not for everyone."

"No, I like them very much." She blushes again, and I'm quickly reminded my arousal will be very obvious through this towel if I don't get out of this bathroom right the fuck now.

I release her arm and walk to the door, putting some distance between us. "Thank you," I tell her when I'm far enough away to keep from pulling her to me and never letting go. "Enjoy your bath." I smile teasingly and waggle my eyebrows at her before closing the bathroom door behind me.

After we're both cleaned up and dressed, we decide to take it easy for the night and hang out in the hotel bar for dinner. It ends up being a great decision because there's a live band playing, and they're actually really good.

"I'm still leery of liquor, so I think I'll stick with beer tonight."

"A beer sounds perfect right about now. Good call, Chuck."

I laugh as she rolls her eyes at my nickname for her. I can't help it. I've always given people nicknames. Maybe it's a southern thing, I don't know. I'm just glad she doesn't scowl anymore when I say it.

"How are you feelin' after the day you had?" I ask.

She's quiet, which makes me worry I've upset her. When she looks up at me and smiles, I'm able to breathe again.

"I'm good. I'm really good, actually."

I take her hand in mine and squeeze it. "I'm glad. You're such a strong woman, Dani. I hope you know that." I pause to keep myself from saying too much. "I think you're amazing."

She shakes her head like she doesn't believe me, but it's true and I feel better just getting it off my chest. She's incredible.

After we finish our meal and listen to the band for a while, I notice Dani trying to hide a couple yawns. I'm kinda tired myself. It's been a long day. So, I scoot my chair back and lean down until my mouth is at her ear. "Come on, sleepy head," I say loud enough she can hear me over the music. "Let's go to the room."

I reach for her hand and toss some cash on the table. She doesn't hesitate to take it, and I can't help but love how good it feels simply holding Dani's hand . . . just touching her.

It feels so good, in fact, I wrap my arm around her and pull her close to me in the elevator. Her arms fit perfectly around my waist, and she rests her head on my chest. I swear I hear her sniff my shirt, but I keep quiet.

Once we're in the room, we quietly get ready for bed. I'm dying to know what she's thinking—what she wants—but I'm following her lead tonight.

I'm already in bed with only my sleep pants on when she slips under the covers facing me. We simply lie there, staring at each other until she whispers, "Can I touch it?"

My mind goes straight to the gutter and by the look of horror on her face, hers does too, but she quickly corrects herself. "I meant your tattoo. Can I touch your tattoo?"

Not able to hold it in any longer, I throw my head back and laugh. We both do. We laugh so hard, we're crying. This moment is absolutely perfect.

When we finally settle down, I move closer so she can touch the ink on my chest. Her finger lightly traces the lines of the oak tree, leaving a trail of goose bumps in its path. When she gets to where the roots of the tree spell the word "family" right over my heart, she removes her finger and kisses my skin.

Never has such a simple act felt so intimate . . . so powerful.

I don't want to ruin this moment and break the spell we seem to be under, so I freeze and wait for her next move.

She places a soft kiss on my mouth before closing her eyes. I run my fingers through her hair, moving it away from her face, and whisper, "What do you want?"

Her eyes open, confusion shining bright. She twists her mouth and presses her lips together like she wants to say something or ask something, but she hesitates for a moment before finally asking me to hold her.

So I do.

When I wake the next morning, my arms are still wrapped around a sleeping Dani. Her head is on my chest, nestled under my chin. Her arm is loose around my waist. I've never felt so content. I don't want to move. I don't want to wake her. I just want to soak up as much of this moment as I can. The thought of her leaving and going back to New York has been plaguing me since yesterday. If this is the last time I get to do this for a while—or ever—I want to make the most of it. I want to memorize every soft breath, every freckle on her shoulder, the feel of her body against mine. When I look down at her, my chest feels tight. Watching her is pretty much the best thing in the entire universe. I feel so lucky to just know her, let alone get to be near her like this.

At least we have one more day, and I'm going to make the most of it.

The morning is quiet. It seems Dani is in quite the contemplative state as well. We move around each other like planets orbiting the sun—taking turns brushing our teeth, making sure the other doesn't forget things in the room, and I make her a cup of coffee, just like I have every other morning we've been together.

When we get in the car, she lets out a heavy sigh.

"Everything okay?" I ask, reaching over to take her hand. Touching her is becoming second nature. I don't even think before I do it. It's going to kill me when I can't do it on a regular basis.

"Yeah, just thinking."

We drive in silence until we're outside of Jackson's city limits headed south on Interstate 55 toward Baton Rouge. The drive is less than three hours, so if we don't make too many stops, we'll be there a little after noon. Since we're staying at my and Deacon's apartment for the night, we'll drop our bags off and freshen up before I take her to Grinders for dinner and show her a little bit of the city. I can't wait for her to see the place. It's something Deacon and I have put so much of ourselves into, I'm really proud of it.

The restaurant has kinda grown up with us. We started off small, taking out a small loan while I was still in college to buy an abandoned two-story building in the older part of downtown Baton Rouge. Most of the remodeling work we did ourselves or paid our buddies to do on the weekend, usually in beer and free food. Over time, it's developed into a well-known establishment, catering to the college crowd and tourists. We bring a band in on Friday and Saturday nights. It's a lot more citi-fied than Pockets. There're two levels, with the top level overlooking the small stage. A friend of Deacon's hooked us up with a class-act lighting package, and although the bands we bring in are local, they're fantastic. Almost as good as our food.

I look over at Dani and see she's chewing on her bottom lip, obviously still deep in thought. I think about letting her be and hoping she works out whatever's on her mind, but I can't keep myself from asking her. If there's something I can do to take the worry on her face away, I'll do it.

"Penny for your thoughts?"

She leans her head back against the seat and turns her gaze from the window over to me.

"I want to get a tattoo."

That wasn't really what I was expecting, and I don't think it's what she's been thinking about this whole time, but I'll take what I can get.

"You know what you want?" I ask.

"I know exactly what I want." Her eyes bore into mine, and I can't help but wonder if her words have a double meaning. I can't let myself get too hopeful.

"I can call my guy in Baton Rouge and see if he can work you in, if you're serious."

"That'd be great." She gives me her first real smile of the day and I give her one in return. If a tattoo is what will make her happy, then I'll make it happen. Besides, it'll be hot, no matter what she gets.

Dani seems to be more relaxed the rest of the drive to Baton Rouge, not as quiet. We do a couple rounds of twenty questions and fight over the songs we're going to play on the radio. Just normal shit.

Once we're at the apartment, I bring our bags in while Dani freshens up.

"You want somethin' to drink?" I ask her from the kitchen. When I don't get an answer, I decide to look for her.

Seeing Dani standing in my bedroom, looking at my bed, makes my heart squeeze and my stomach tighten. I can't resist walking up to her and wrapping my arms around her. She turns in my arms and lays her head against my chest.

"I wish you'd talk to me," I whisper into her hair, wanting to know what's bothering her and not caring if I sound desperate in the process.

She looks up at me before standing on her tiptoes and bringing her lips to mine. Her nails scratch at the scruff on my jaw as she kisses me gently. "We can talk about it later. Right now, I just want to enjoy this last day with you," she says, almost pleading.

I swallow the lump in my throat as my worst fear comes true. This is it for us. When we get back to French Settlement, it will literally be the end of the road for us. Dani will go back to New York and I'll go back to doing whatever it is I did before her. But I don't want to. I don't want that life. I want this one. The one where she's in my arms. Where I make her coffee every morning. Where she falls asleep against my chest every night. That's the life I want.

Pulling her face back to mine, I kiss her until we're both breathless—until resolve settles into my bones.

If today is the last day we have, then I'm going to make it perfect. It might not be the right time to tell her how I feel, saying those words now might seem rushed or like I'm saying them to get something in return, but I can show her. I want her to know how much I want her, and not just for tonight—more like forever.

The first thing we do is grab lunch to-go from T.J. Ribs and bring it to the campus of my alma mater. I want her to see this. This place was such a vital part of my life and making me who I am today. I want to share it with her. I take us to a spot in the grass that gives us a perfect view of the Indian Mounds of LSU.

"This is beautiful," Dani gushes as we sit on the blanket I've laid out for us.

"It's one of my favorite spots here."

"I can see why." She kicks her shoes off onto the blanket and twists her hair up on her head. I love it when she does that. This is my favorite version of Dani—relaxed, natural. It seems as though she's resolved to make the most of our time together, too. After our moment in the apartment earlier, it's been light and fun ever since. "Thanks for bringing me here."

"Thanks for wanting to come."

She nods at me and smiles. I hand her her barbeque from the bag and grab mine as well. "We better eat up. Frank said he'd open up earlier just for us, so we need to be there by three, which means we've only got about an hour."

"Should be enough time to eat this and kick back for a nap." She winks at me, taking a big bite of her barbeque. The sauce dripping down her chin reminds me of the first night of our trip when she had ketchup all over her face. This time, instead of telling her about it, I lean over and lick it off.

She stops mid-chew, looking over at me. "Did you just lick me?" she asks, narrowing her eyes. She's so damn cute.

"Yep." I nod and casually take a bite of my food. "You taste delicious."

The look on her face shifts from playful to something else—something like desire. I feel it, too. I've felt it mounting since the night we kissed at the pond. It's like small sparks under my skin, slowly building to a roaring blaze.

"I can't believe you licked me," she says, still a bit dazed from whatever is happening between us.

I smile at her, shake my head, and focus on my food. "You sure you want to get a tat?" I ask, switching gears. "You know it's permanent, right?"

"Yes, I know it's permanent, and yes, I'm sure."

"Do you know where you want it?"

"On my arm. I want to see it every day."

That answer makes me happy. I was afraid she'd say on her back or hip, which would require her to remove her clothes. I know it's crazy, and I know I haven't even seen them, but I'm not fond of another guy seeing the goods.

"Are you gonna get something?" she asks, setting her mostly empty food container back in the bag.

"I was thinking about it."

"Do you know what you'd want to get?"

"I always have something in mind, but I probably won't decide until I get there."

Once we finish eating, we lie back on the blanket, taking turns making out shapes in the clouds above us. There's one that floats by I swear looks just like the poop emoticon. When she laughs uncontrollably, with her head on my chest, I drink it in. "You're so gross," she says, slapping at me playfully. I grab her hand and quickly roll her over, hovering above her, my arms caging her in.

"I'll give you gross," I tease, sticking my tongue out and inching it closer to her face.

"No!" she squeals, struggling to get away from me, but I have her trapped. "Micah!"

Before long, we're a mess of twisted limbs, sweaty, laughing, and completely out of breath. I brush the hair off her face and cup her cheek. "You're so beautiful."

"So are you," she says, honesty in her eyes. No one's ever called me beautiful. It's kind of a girl term, but I like it coming from her.

I kiss her for a few minutes, being mindful that we're in public. Before things get too heated, I slowly pull back and take a good look at her, hoping when she goes back to New York and I'm missing her, I can close my eyes and remember her just like this.

"We better get going. Can't keep Frankie waiting. He's kind of a diva."

The tattoo shop isn't very far from Grinders, so I park in my usual spot behind our building and we walk over. Dani is full of questions about the area and the restaurant on our walk to the shop. I love that she's so interested and really seems to love it here. French Settlement is my home, but Baton Rouge is a close second.

When we make it to Third Street Ink, I see Frankie through the glass windows. He waves and runs over to unlock the door. "Micah," he says boisterously, "long time, no see!"

"Yeah, it's been a few weeks. How ya been?"

"Good. I did some new work for Deacon not long ago. He said you had some ideas for some new ink."

"I do, but I called today for my . . . uh," I hesitate, wishing I had some kind of claim to her, some way to show that she's mine. Since I don't, I settle for introducing them. "This is Sheridan Reed. Dani, this is Frankie."

"Nice to meet you." He smiles, shaking her hand. "So, do you know what you want?"

"Yeah, I do." Dani pulls out the old box from the storage unit and shows it to him, pointing to the compass on the lid. "I'd like this. Right here," she says, pointing to her forearm. "Except, where there's an 'N' for north, I'd like mine to have an 'S' for south."

Frankie smiles, nodding his head. "South, huh? I like it."

The two of them walk over to the counter as he begins to sketch out the tattoo. When they both agree on the design and size, he walks her over to his booth and places the transfer on her arm. "How's that?" he asks.

She holds it up, inspects it, and then looks at me. "What do you think?"

"I think it's perfect."

Without hesitation or reservation, she looks back at Frankie, and says, "Let's do this."

He works fast, and since the design isn't that complicated, he's done in no time. Dani winces a few times when he hits a sensitive spot, but for the most part, she takes it like a champ.

After he has her bandaged up, he looks at me. "So, you gettin' somethin'?"

"I have a few things in mind, but I think I'll stop back by some other time," I tell him, wanting to get over to Grinders before things get too busy. I really want to show Dani around and introduce her to the staff.

"Okay, I'll pencil you in for a few weeks out."

"Sounds good. Maybe for after I close one night. I could bring you second dinner."

"It's a date."

Dani laughs and thanks Frankie for doing her tat on such short notice. He tells her it was his pleasure. Frankie and I go way back. Deacon and I have been coming here since we were in college. Even when we're not getting any work done, we sometimes stop by and hang out after we close up shop.

"Does it hurt?" I ask, pointing to her bandaged arm.

"Nah. It's a little sore, but nothing too horrible."

"We'll get you some ointment for it later. Actually, I probably have some at the apartment."

She nods, looking down at her arm as we walk across the street.

"Are you having second thoughts?"

"No," she says, shaking her head and laughing.

"Want to tell me about it?"

"This?" she asks, holding up her arm.

"Yeah."

She shrugs her shoulders. "It's kinda hard to explain."

"Try me."

We stop just outside of Grinders and I motion her over to a bench nearby. I want to hear this. I want to know why she chose a compass and why she had him put an "S" in place of the "N". I'm trying hard not to read too much into it, but my mind has been theorizing ever since she sat down in that chair.

"I felt lost," she says, staring out at the cars passing by. "Have you ever felt lost?" Her eyes are sad as she looks over at me, and I'm not sure whether she's expecting me to answer, so I just nod.

She lets out a deep breath before continuing, directing her gaze back to the passersby. "When I lost my job, and then Graham pulled that shit with the solo vacation . . . I remember feeling so lost, like my compass was broken. I actually thought that. Like, I was standing in the middle of a big city and couldn't find my way. The things that had been guiding me were slowly slipping away and I couldn't tell which way was north."

She sits quietly for a second, gathering her thoughts, and I let her, giving her all the time she needs. "When I got the call from Piper to come down here and do the article, it was the first time in years I felt excited about life—about what I was doing and where I was. When I went back to New York, I realized it had a lot to do with the location, but even more to do with the people."

Her eyes close and she gently touches her arm. "I realized it wasn't north I was looking for, after all," she says, smiling up at me. "My granny confirmed that for me the other day. In that box was a letter . . . a letter I somehow missed all these years. In it, she told me my heart is my compass." She pauses for a second, reaching down to lace her fingers through mine. "Everything I was searching for, every question I felt like I didn't have an answer for," she says passionately, "it was right here," she places her hand over her heart, "I just needed a little help finding it."

I smile because she's smiling, but more importantly, I smile because I like what I'm hearing. Above everything else, I want Dani happy, and if there is a slight chance her being here . . . with me . . . could make her happy, I'd be the luckiest guy on the planet. I want to fall at her feet and tell her to stay . . . to let me make her happy . . . but I don't, because I don't want to jump the gun. Instead, I grab her hand tightly and pull her up, placing a kiss on her nose, her cheek, and then her lips. I want to take it further. I want to show her exactly how I feel about her, but there's one last thing I'd like to do before that happens.

"You wanna go check out Grinders?" I ask, motioning toward the front doors.

"Definitely."

Once inside, Dani is so enamored. Her face says it all—bright eyes, big smile. "I thought Pockets was great, but this place . . ." she looks around, taking in the brick walls and low lighting, "this place is fantastic."

"Thank you. We're pretty proud of it."

"I'm so glad you brought me here." She reaches up and kisses my cheek. "Show me more."

And I do. I introduce her to the kitchen and wait staff. Their sly smiles and raised eyebrows don't escape me. They've never seen me bring someone here, not like this. I mean, I've brought women here before. Shit, most of my dates in college took place here because Deacon and I worked so damn much. But I've never brought anyone here, introduced them like this, and shown them around, outside of my family. This is a first for me. I show Dani the office I share with Deacon and the first dollar we ever made eight years ago.

After the tour, we sit in a quiet booth up top and I order several of the house specialties for us to share. When we first opened this place, we sold nothing but grinders, hence the name. Everyone around here sells po' boys, which are basically the same idea, but we wanted to do something different. And to be honest, we felt like Grinders was a better name than Po' Boys. It fit the image we wanted to set. Since the beginning, we've expanded the menu, selling other things besides sandwiches, but the name stuck. One of our best sellers is shrimp and grits. We use our Grandma Landry's recipe, and it's a hit.

When the food arrives, Dani tastes a bit of everything, and with each bite, she moans her approval. And with each moan, I have to restrain myself from throwing her over my shoulder caveman-style and taking her back to the apartment to have my way with her.

Fuck slow.

I'm ready to show her how I feel . . . how she makes me feel. I know my mama said patience, but I don't want to have any regrets when Dani gets back on that plane to New York.

"You ready?" I ask, wiping my mouth on my napkin.

"I'm ready if you are."

"Let's go."

I wave to Crystal on our way out, telling her to let Larry know the food was delicious. Dani chimes in, sending her praise as well. Crystal waves back and winks at me behind Dani's back. "Have fun," she mouths.

I grin and nod. The need to get Dani back to the apartment is growing with each passing second. Every brush of her hand against mine, the way she tosses her head back and laughs, her sideways glances . . . all of it feels like foreplay—sweet, torturous foreplay.

When we get up to the apartment, Dani quietly goes to the bathroom, looking back at me over her shoulder, silently talking to me with her glance. We haven't said more than a few words to each other since we left the restaurant, but our touches have said plenty. They've said, *I'm ready. I need you. No more slow.*

I lock the front door behind me and walk into my bedroom, sitting on the edge of the bed. The bathroom door creaks open a few minutes later and Dani walks into the bedroom. Her hair is loose around her shoulders and she's only wearing a t-shirt, one of mine I loaned her in Alabama when we were at the beach. She leans against the doorframe and crosses one leg over the other, watching me.

My fingers ache to touch her, so I stand up and walk over to her, brushing my fingers lightly down her arm. The way her skin pebbles under my touch makes me want to do it more—touch her more. I don't know what she wants or how far she wants to take this, but I want it all. "Tell me to stop," I whisper, warning her with my words, giving her a chance to put the brakes on, but she doesn't. She shakes her head slowly and leans into my hand as I cup her cheek.

"I want this. I want *you*. Tell me you want this, too," I plead.

"I do," she says. "I want you, Micah."

That's all I need—her permission, telling me we're on the same page. My mouth is on hers and my hands move swiftly down her body, gripping her backside and picking her up, allowing her legs to wrap around my waist. I kiss her hard, pressing her into the wall, letting her feel just how much I want her. Her fingers twist in my hair, pulling me closer. I could take her here, up against this wall, but I want more than that. I want to look into her eyes. I want to memorize every inch of her. I want *making love*—not fucking.

I carry her over to the bed and lay her down, loving how her gorgeous red hair spreads out over my pale blue blanket. She's everything—my hopes, my dreams, my desires, all wrapped up in one amazing package.

"Off," she commands, tugging at the bottom of my shirt.

I reach back and tug it over my head, tossing it beside the bed. Her hands roam up my stomach to my chest, tracing the tree like she did last night. Our eyes lock and the intensity I'm met with matches what I'm feeling inside. She sees past who I've been, who other people see—she just sees me. I love seeing myself through her eyes.

I want her to feel as good as she makes me feel.

Pulling at the hem of her shirt, I inch it up her body, placing soft kisses along the way. Words are on the tip of my tongue, wanting to be said, but I'm still scared to utter them aloud. So, I let my lips and hands say the things I'm afraid to. I kiss every inch of her body, some parts more than once. When I make my way back to her mouth, she kisses me with fierceness and desperation. Her voice is sure when she whispers, "Make love to me."

Those words—*my* words—coming from her, make every emotion come to the surface. I feel raw and exposed, laid bare before her, but I'm not afraid. I want this kind of intimacy with Dani. I crave it.

When our remaining clothes are on the floor, I reach over to my nightstand, grab a condom, and quickly roll it on. Gazing down at her naked body, I tell her how beautiful she is and smile as I watch her skin blush, traveling from her cheeks down to her full breasts.

"Amazing," I say, lining myself up and slowly pushing inside. Once our hips are flush, I'm overwhelmed with how perfectly we fit together, how incredible she feels. I'm almost afraid to move. Afraid this moment will fade away.

My body tenses and my eyes close until Dani presses her hands to my face.

"Look at me," she demands. "I feel it, too. Please, don't stop."

Lacing my fingers through hers, I begin to move, and almost laugh at myself for doubting this couldn't feel better than a minute ago. With every thrust, touch, and kiss, the pleasure only intensifies until we're both crying out, finding our release together.

I have never felt this way, and I know, without a doubt, I'll never get my fill of her.

CHAPTER
Twenty-Six

Sheridan

I WAS RIGHT. WAKING UP with Micah *is* amazing . . . almost as amazing as sleeping with him. No, not sleeping with him—making love with him . . . *to* him. Because that's exactly what we did last night . . . no less than three times, mind you.

My body still tingles from the way he touched me just over an hour ago, but more than that, my heart is full. It's as if he's awakened a part of me—a part of my soul—I thought was gone forever . . . or maybe didn't exist at all. I feel light and sated at the same time. Content. Excited. Peaceful. Happy—so very happy.

"We're gonna have to get up at some point," a husky voice says softly in my ear.

"I wanna stay here," I complain, wishing that could happen. I wish there was a way to hold on to how I'm feeling right now, how he made me feel last night.

"We can come back any time you want."

"I'd like that."

"How about I make you coffee and we grab breakfast on our way out of town?" he suggests, kissing me softly before rolling away from me, taking the warmth and goodness with him. "I know this great donut shop we can stop at." I instantly miss the way his skin feels against mine. I want it back the second he slips out from under the blanket. But the view of him is exceptional. Taking a second to drink him in, I watch his muscles flex as he slips on his jeans from the floor beside the bed.

Seeing him like this—being with him like this—I knew it'd be good. I knew it'd be life changing. I just had no idea *how* good and *how* life changing.

When it comes to Micah, I've feared I'll allow myself to fall for him, to love him, and he won't return the fall or feelings. A few weeks ago, I wasn't sure he was capable of being in love, or being with one person. But by the way he's been this past week, the way he's tried so hard to prove his feelings to me, it's changed the way I see him. I don't see the playboy. I see someone who is good down to his core and honest to a fault. I see someone who works hard for what he wants and believes actions speak louder than words. I see someone who values his family over anything else in this world. And all of that has made me fall in love with him.

I'm *so* head-over-heels in love with Micah Paul Landry.

I also fear that if I tell him how serious I am about him and us—like, I want forever—he'll get spooked. I want to give him all the time he needs to get there on his own. Part of me thinks he might be there. The other part of me thinks he's afraid, too.

Why does love have to be so scary?

On the drive home, I can't quit staring at my arm. Micah doctored it for me before we left his apartment, so it's covered in ointment. I haven't had much of a chance to admire it, but the more I look at it and think about it, the more I love it. I told Micah a little about the reasoning behind it yesterday, but it's more than that. I didn't want to freak him out by telling him *he's* my south—he's what my heart wants.

"I really love it," he says, glancing over.

"I do, too. Thanks for taking me." I smile up at him, loving the way he looks at me. "Thanks for coming with me on this trip. You have no idea what it means to me."

"Don't think I came on this trip for completely unselfish reasons."

He winks and smirks before turning his eyes back to the road. "I came on this trip as much for me as I did for you. I couldn't stand knowing you were so close and not being able to be with you." Reaching over, he takes my hand in his, brings it to his lips, and kisses it—like he's done so many times. "If I hadn't come with you, I would've probably tracked you down like some stalker."

I laugh.

He laughs.

It's easy.

It's us.

I'm not ready for this to end.

I want this every day for the rest of my life.

The drive back to the plantation is a short one. Baton Rouge is less than an hour from French Settlement and before we know it, we're pulling off the dirt road onto the lane leading up to the house.

"Do you ever get used to this view?" I ask, still in awe every time I see it.

"After twenty-seven years, I still think about how beautiful it is when I pull down this drive, especially after I've been away for a few days."

"Good. I'm glad it's not just me."

"Looks like Mama has some company," Micah says, nodding to a car sitting in front of the house. He pulls my rental car up next to it and puts it into park. "Doesn't look familiar, though."

"You don't think Piper decided to surprise us and come back down this weekend, do you? I think she would've called first to make sure we'd be back."

"Yeah, Tucker didn't mention it when I talked to him the other day."

"I can't believe those two are talking." I shake my head and smile.

Micah laughs. "You're tellin' me."

When we walk through the front door, Annie is talking to someone in the kitchen.

"Mama," Micah calls out, "we're home."

Turning the corner to the kitchen, I expect Annie to greet me with one of her warm hugs—hugs I've missed in just the few days we've been gone. What I'm not expecting is Graham Harrison sitting on one of the stools at the kitchen bar, sipping a cup of coffee.

"What the hell are you doing here?"

Graham stands up, smiling ruefully, and walks over, wrapping his free arm around my shoulder. "I've missed you so much, baby," he whispers in my ear. "I'm so sorry. I just needed to talk to you . . . to make things right." I'm so shocked he's here, I don't even have time to reject his touch. I smile, painfully, over his shoulder at Annie.

Micah bristles at my side, slowly taking his hand from the small of my back. I hate this. I hate that Graham is here. I hate that I have to deal with this when I was feeling so happy and content only moments ago.

Annie looks at me apologetically. "Seems Mr. Harrison flew all the way down here to talk to you. Apparently, he didn't get a chance to say everything he wanted to say the last time y'all talked." The purse of her lips and arch of her eyebrow tells me she's not pleased to have him in her kitchen, but being the southern woman she is, it's in her DNA to be hospitable.

"I also have some very good news for you. I wanted to tell you in person."

"Let's go outside," I tell him, pulling away and heading for the front door. Whatever it is he has to say, I don't want it to be in front of Micah or Annie. I've been embarrassed enough because of him.

I wait for him by the front door with my hands on my hips. His leg is stronger now, but he's still moving a little slow, even with the cane he's using for support. Of course, he makes a show of walking with a limp in an attempt to gain some sympathy, but I don't think anyone here is falling for it.

As I wait for him to walk through the door, I hear Annie say, "Bless his heart", but I know she doesn't mean it in a nice way. I have to muffle my laughter as I follow him to the porch.

Graham carefully sits on the porch and I take him in, looking for a twinge of attraction, lingering love, any feeling connected to him, but I can honestly say I feel nothing. Nothing anywhere close to what I feel for Micah.

"What do you want, Graham?" I lean against the porch railing with my arms crossed. The faster we can get this over with, the better.

"Don't be like that." He gives me that look, the one he always gives me when he's done something he knows I'm upset about. That look used to be enough to make me cave, but not now—not anymore. "Sit by me. I've missed you."

"I'm fine where I am, thanks. Now, explain yourself. Why are you here?"

He blows out a frustrated breath, knowing his charms aren't working on me.

"I wanted to tell you some great news." He flashes me his million-watt smile. "I got you a job."

"You could've told me that over the phone. And I have a job. I've *been* working."

"I hardly call what you've been doing work." He snorts, his demeanor shifting from sickeningly sweet to asshole in two point one seconds. "I got you a *real* job." He stands and walks closer to me, reaching out to touch my arm, but I pull it away. "You have a position at *The Times* waiting for you back in New York. Isn't that great?" he asks, pleading with his eyes for me to get on board with what he's telling me, begging me to see how great this is. "I know it's what you've always wanted to do, Dani. *You want this.*"

When I still won't let him touch me, he huffs and sits down in a chair a few feet from me. "I know you want this, which is why I had to rush down here to this shithole and tell you in person. You should be happy."

I gape at him, speechless. So many things run through my brain, I can't put an entire sentence together.

Graham laughs at me. "See?" he says, his arms stretched wide. "That's more like it. I knew you'd be speechless! Now, we just need to get your things and get the hell out of here." He stands and reaches for my hand, but before he can touch me, I move to the side.

"Come on, Dani. Enough is enough. You played hard-to-get, and you won. It's time to grow up, say thank you, and be happy, dammit!"

"I *am* happy."

"Good. Now, let's go." He takes a few steps back toward the door, but stops when he realizes I'm not following. "Where are your things?

Are they still in your rental car?"

I shake my head. "I'm not going with you."

"You just said you're happy."

"I am . . . I'm happy *here*," I say, pointing down to my feet. "I don't want a job at *The Times*. *You* want me to have a job at *The Times*. That's you. It's not me."

"You can't be serious. Any reputable photojournalist would *kill* for a job like this! I can't believe you're acting like this after I came all the way down here . . . just for you."

"You should've been thinking about me before you fucked your therapist."

Graham groans, rolling his eyes and letting his head fall back in frustration. "Are we going to do this again?"

"Again?" I ask, raising my voice. "Are you serious? Am I just supposed to forget that happened?"

"It was a mistake, Dani. I told you that. It wasn't what it looked like."

"I'm not stupid, Graham. It was exactly what it looked like. It was *you* not caring about us or our commitment to each other. I thought you loved me, and I was trying to make things work, but you have to admit we'd been drifting apart for months . . . maybe longer. Cheating on me was the final straw."

"I thought you were more forgiving than that."

"I am," I say, slapping a stray tear off my cheek, pissed that I'm letting him get to me like this again. "I forgive you. There. Is that what you want to hear?"

"If you forgive me, then come back home with me."

"That's not my home."

"Oh, really? Have you moved since the last time I saw you?" I want to slap that mocking smile off his face.

"No, but it's not home." I glance down at the fresh ink on my arm and then look back up at him with a surge of confidence. His smile slips as mine grows. "It's not where I belong."

Chapter Twenty-Seven

MICAH

"MAMA, WHY WAS THAT ASSHOLE in this house?" I'm pacing the kitchen floor, trying not to freak the fuck out while Dani is outside talking to Graham.

"I told you. He said he needed to talk to Dani."

"He could've waited in the damn car. I don't like him bein' here."

"Micah, I'm sorry. I didn't even realize who he was at first. He just introduced himself as bein' a friend of Dani's. I didn't know how long y'all would be, so I invited him in. He's only been here about thirty minutes."

"No, Mama. I'm sorry. I shouldn't snap at you. I just wish he'd leave us . . . leave *Dani* . . . alone." I wrap my arms around her and she crushes me to her in a protective hug.

"I take it things are going well with you and Dani?" she asks softly.

I pull away and run my fingers through my hair. "Yeah, things are great . . . at least; they were before that dickhead got here."

"Listen to me, son. I'm forgiving your language because I know you're upset, but if you think for one second Sheridan Reed is going to fall for that man's bullshit, you might not know her as well as you think."

Fuck.

She's right. I know she's right, but I can't help but worry I might've waited too long to tell Dani how I feel about her. I tried to show her during our trip, especially last night, but what if it wasn't enough?

I can't lose her.

I *won't* lose her.

Please, God, don't let her choose Graham.

I don't know how long they've been outside talking, but it's been fucking long enough. I storm through the kitchen and foyer, preparing to fight for my girl, but stop short when I hear raised voices coming from the porch.

"I forgive you. There. Is that what you want to hear?"

Dani, no.

I hold my breath, willing my heart not to break. I love her, and I want what's best for her. She has to make the decision for herself, and whatever it is, I have to accept that.

"No, but it's not home. It's not where I belong."

"Where exactly do you think you belong?"

Fucking Graham.

"Here. I belong here."

Hell yeah! That's my girl!

Graham laughs. "I tried to show you a better life . . . something other than being a hillbilly. I spoiled you, helped you with your career, and now you're throwing it back in my face? I should've known you were a lost cause."

That's fucking it!

I practically rip the front door off its hinges when I open it to see Dani and Graham squaring off on the porch. My blood is boiling, but I put a calm smile on my face. I like to catch my enemies off guard. The surprise tactic is where it's at. "Time to scoot, buddy. I think the lady's made it perfectly clear how she feels."

"Oh, I see how it is. You're slumming it, huh, Dani? My dad was right about you. You're a waste of my time."

"Just leave, Graham!" Dani yells.

I never thought I'd hit someone using a cane, but there's a first time for everything. I clench my fists, ready to attack, but Graham finally uses his brain and starts walking toward his car. As a last insult, he spits on the ground before getting in and driving off.

I look over at Dani and try to gauge how she's feeling. She doesn't look sad. She looks pissed. I just hope she's not pissed at me.

"Dani? Baby, are you okay?" I step closer to her, wanting to touch her, but not wanting to push too much.

As soon as her eyes find mine, her fierce expression cools and she gives me a confused smile.

"Of course I am. Why?"

I chuckle, relieved, wondering why I'm so surprised by her response. I shouldn't be. She's incredible.

"You didn't think I was going to leave with Graham, did you?"

"I hoped not. I even prayed you wouldn't, but I had to let you make up your own mind."

"Micah, my mind was made up a long time ago."

"I was afraid I'd missed my chance."

"Your chance at what?"

I take a deep breath, preparing myself for the nerves I'm sure are about to come, but they don't. All I feel is peace and contentment. Looking down into her deep green eyes, I just know. I know I love her. I know I want to spend every second of every day with her. "Telling you how much I love you."

Her eyes light up and a hopeful smile plays on her lips. "Well, here's your chance."

I place my hands on her hips and gently pull her to me. "Sheridan Paige Reed, I love you so much. I should've told you sooner, but I was scared. You think you might love me back?"

She wraps her arms around my neck and stands on her toes, barely touching her mouth to mine.

"Yeah, I think I just might."

The thought that she feels the same way has my heart practically beating out of my chest. Relief floods my veins as she looks up at me. I see it in her eyes.

"I need to hear you say it."

"I love you, Micah Landry. You're my south." She takes my face between her hands and presses her lips to mine, planting herself even more firmly into my heart and soul. When she pulls back, she looks deep into my eyes with so much warmth and contentment. "You're where I belong."

Epilogue

Sheridan

IT TOOK ME TWENTY-FIVE YEARS, but I can honestly say I finally know where I'm going in life. I've found my focus—my sweet spot, if you will. It wasn't an easy road getting here, but the journey is what makes the destination so sweet. Had I not been through the challenges I've faced these past few months, I might not have realized how amazing this feels. The truth is, had I not lost my job and then my boyfriend, *I might still be lost.*

That old saying that hindsight is 20/20 is so true. If I'd known then what I know now, I'd never have lost a moment's sleep or cried a single tear over Graham Harrison. In fact, I'd have followed my heart a lot sooner and allowed it to lead me back home.

But, timing is everything, and I'd go through a dozen heartbreaks if I knew Micah Landry was waiting for me at the end of it all.

After Graham made his last-ditch effort to win me back, if that's what you can even call it—*such a pretentious prick*—Micah and I holed up at the cottage for a couple weeks. It was blissful. I was able to finish my article and turn it in ahead of schedule. Piper was pleased. The editor-in-chief was pleased. The article comes out in two weeks and I can't wait to see it in print. I even snuck a picture of Micah in there. He doesn't know it yet, and he'll probably shoot me, but he was better than any model I could've paid to be in the shot. And when you catch someone truly enjoying something, rather than staging it, the feeling translates over to the picture.

Piper seems pretty confident she'll be able to keep me busy with freelance work for the magazine, but I've also sent my résumé and portfolio over to a few other magazines. Freelance is what I should've been doing all along. It allows me to be creative and totally immerse myself in a project. Plus, I can pretty much live anywhere, which is the biggest benefit. It's the reason why I'm currently standing in the middle of an empty apartment.

I've packed up everything I want to take and given away all of my furniture, including that disgusting bed I never slept in again after walking in on Graham and Kaitlyn. The only thing not in a box is my suitcase full of a few days' worth of clothes, my toiletries, and the air mattress I found in the top of my closet.

It's kind of weird knowing I'm only going to be in New York for two more nights, but I'm not sad. I'll miss my Chinese Restaurant and Central Park, but that's about it.

Well . . . and maybe the Brooklyn Bridge.

And Rockefeller Center.

But, other than that, everything else I want is in Louisiana.

Fortunately, I have plenty of pictures, and New York is only a three-hour plane ride away. I won't be a stranger. I'll be back.

When my phone rings, I grab it without looking to see who it is. I already know.

"Hello," I say seductively.

"Is that how you answer the phone for all the guys who call?"

"No, just you," I sigh. "Besides, you're the only guy who calls. The only guy I want to call."

"I like that. Let's keep it that way."

"I was planning on it."

"Good," Micah says. The growl in his voice goes straight to my stomach, causing it to tie into a tight knot, and a warmth spreads through my body.

"God, I miss you," I tell him, lying down on the hardwood floor, wishing he were here.

"I miss you so much, baby. You have no idea."

"Oh, I think I do." My voice takes a bit of a sad turn. I can't help it. When he calls me, I'm reminded of just how much I miss him and that I'm here alone when I want to be with him . . . and Annie, and Sam, and Deacon . . . and Cami and Carter . . . even Tucker . . . and closer to Piper. I sigh heavily into the phone.

"You okay?"

"Just feeling lonely and sorry for myself."

"It's not gonna be much longer. Then you'll never have to be lonely again."

I close my eyes and a smile breaks across my face. "You always know just what to say."

"I wish I was there so I could *do* something rather than say something. I'm a lot fonder of actions."

"You're really good with actions."

"That's right, and don't you forget it."

"Well," I tease, "it has been a few weeks."

He growls into the phone again, letting me hear his frustration. "Seems as though I need to remind you."

"That's what I was hoping for."

He chuckles and I can imagine him running a hand through his hair, a smirk placed firmly on his lips. "Tell me something good."

"I'm going to see you in two days."

"What else?"

"You're never going to have to go back to New York again," he says, pausing. "Unless you want to. And hopefully, I'll be with you."

"I want you with me always."

"And I'll be able to kiss you any time I want."

"Oh, do you plan on living in Baton Rouge?"

"No, but it's only forty minutes away. If I need a kiss bad enough, it's a short drive to get my fix."

I laugh into the phone, rolling onto my side. "I love you."

"I love you so much it hurts." He pauses, and then says, "Tell me something good." In the background, I hear a door shut and some shuffling. It sounds like he just got into his truck.

"I have my entire apartment packed and the movers will be here tomorrow."

"Look at you, you little worker bee."

"Hey, when I set my mind to something, I get shit done."

"I love that about you."

"I love everything about you."

"Even my stinky feet?"

"Those, I tolerate, but everything else? Yeah, pretty much."

There's a knock at my door and I'm not sure who it could be. I'm not expecting anyone until the moving company tomorrow.

"Hey, someone's at the door. Can I call you back later?"

"Yeah, sure," he says.

"Okay, love you."

"Love you, too." I'm just getting ready to push end when I hear him say, "Oh, and, Dani?"

"Yeah?"

"I can't wait to kiss you."

I smile, loving his random thoughts. "The feeling is mutual, Micah Landry."

I end the call and pull myself up off the ground, groaning at my sore back, legs, arms—everything is sore from packing and moving boxes around.

When I unlock the door and pull it open, I can't contain myself. I squeal like a child and drop my phone to the ground, launching myself at the best damn thing I've seen in two weeks.

"Micah!"

He picks me up and puts his lips anywhere he can find exposed skin, kissing my lips, cheeks, forehead . . . down my neck, inhaling deeply along the way. "God, you're a sight for sore eyes. I love you so much."

"I love you," I breathe, kissing him as he stumbles into the apartment and slams the door behind us with his foot. "What are you doing here?" I ask between kisses.

"I thought you could use some help."

"You're crazy," I say, laughing and kissing him some more. My heart is so happy, it feels like it may burst.

"I also thought we should do these last couple of nights in New York properly." His lips are on my neck, taking away all coherent thought. The feel of his hands on my ass and his body pressed against me causes a fire to ignite deep within my belly and my head starts to spin.

If I had to take a field sobriety test right now, I'd fail miserably.

Micah takes a second to look around the apartment. "Holy shit, you really did get everything emptied out of here."

I nod, smiling. "Yep."

"Where the hell were you planning on sleeping the next two nights?"

Pointing to the air mattress still in its box, I say, "There".

"Oh, hell no. Uh uh." He shakes his head and slowly lets my feet slide to the ground. "That's not gonna work for what I had in mind." He pulls his phone out of his back pocket and begins pecking away at the screen. A minute later, he puts it to his ear. "Yes, I was wondering if you have a room available for tonight and tomorrow night?"

There's a pause, and he looks over at me, his eyes blazing with what I know now is want and desire. He wets his bottom lip with his tongue, reaches out for me, and grabs my waist, pulling me to him. "That's perfect," he says into the phone, but it sounds like a double entendre. Leaning forward, he brushes his nose along my jaw, nipping at the skin as he goes. His days' worth of stubble deliciously stings my skin, making every nerve in my body feel like a livewire. "Micah Landry," he says. "That's right. Thank you."

He slides the phone back into his pocket. Cupping my face, he pulls me to him, devouring my mouth with his—slow, then fast. Hard, then soft. His teeth graze my bottom lip, biting down gently, conveying how desperately he wants this—me. I grip his shoulders, pulling myself closer, holding on for dear life.

"I want you," I mutter. "So damn bad." My breaths come heavy and quick. "I've missed you so much. I didn't even know I could miss someone so badly."

Micah pulls back and looks at me. His piercing look goes straight to my soul. "I couldn't stand being away from you another day," he confesses. "That's really why I'm here." He smiles, and it lights up the room, painting the walls with sunshine. "See? Selfish."

Tears well in my eyes, unexplainably.

"What's wrong?" he asks, kissing the first tear that slides down my cheek. "Are you sad about leaving?"

"No," I say, letting the tears fall, because I'm not sad. The smile on my face contradicts that idea. "It's like a sunshower," I tell him.

He smiles again, looking at me like I've hung the moon. "Like a sunshower, huh?"

"Yeah, you know when everything is sunshine and happiness, and the rain comes, but it doesn't bring with it all the bad stuff, just rainbows?"

"God, I love you, Sheridan Reed."

He does. He loves me. And he doesn't just tell me, he shows me.

About the Author

FIRST THINGS FIRST, WE'RE THE realest.

Oh, wait. Iggy already used that one.

Well, let's see . . .

What some people don't know is there are two of us and we're both Jennifers. How lucky are we? The most common name from the 70's! Our parents were so original.

We found each other through Twilight and tornadoes. Sounds like a crazy combination, but it's true. We were roaming around in the same groups of people on social media, but we hadn't really became friends. But that all changed on a stormy Oklahoma night when we noticed that we were both experiencing the same tornado warnings.

We met a week later for lunch and the rest is history. We already knew we had the whole Twilight thing in common, but what we learned that day is that we both loved music and traveling. Together, we've been everywhere. Well, not everywhere, but a lot of places . . . Seattle, Forks, LA, New York, Chicago, Philly, Nashville, and New Orleans, where our hearts reside.

About six months after we met, we also realized we both had a passion for writing. When we started outlining our first story, we thought that would be it. One story and done. So, we dumped everything we loved into those 100,000 words. If you're familiar with the term "crack fic", that was kind of what it was for us. We had fun with it and let ourselves live on those pages.

But it was like Lays potato chips.

We couldn't write just one.

So, twenty stories later, here we are—publishing our first novel. And how crazy is it that we went back to the beginning.

Finding Focus was originally a Twilight Fan Fic titled *Southern Comfort*.

CONNECT WITH US

www.jiffykate.com

OR FIND US ON

Facebook
Instagram
Twitter

Acknowledgements

WHAT A JOURNEY THIS HAS been; and as with any journey, there are so many people who have helped us along the way. So, we thought we'd start at the beginning.

We'd like to thank our Fic Sensei, Michelle Hager, and our long-time love, Charity Harrington. They were our first readers and we love them. We'd also like to thank Nic, The Ficwhisperer, for for seeing something in our little story and putting us up on The Lemonade Stand.

To Debra Anastasia and S. L. Scott, we say thank you for being so supportive from the very beginning. Your professional advice and hand-holding has been invaluable.

To Team Jiffy Kate, thank you doesn't seem like enough. Christine Viox, Rachel Pooler, and Pamela Stephenson your corrections, comments, and suggestions are what kept us going through the re-write. Lynette Nichols, Katie Boberg, Amy Viar, and Amanda Daniel thank you for being awesome pre-readers. Without all of your sparkly red pens and insightful reviews, this story wouldn't be what it is today.

Sitting back and reflecting over the past four years, we get a little teary-eyed. We realize that so many people played a part in getting us to this point and we couldn't be any more grateful. There's no way we'd ever be able to list all of you by name, but you know who you are.

We also have to thank Stephenie Meyer. If it weren't for her and her books about vampires, we'd never found each other, let alone all of our amazing friends and our passion for writing. Twilight Forever.

We'd also like to thank our professional team: Indie Solutions by Murphy Rae for our editing and proofreading, and Jada D'Lee Designs for our beautiful cover. Heather Maven, you are a force to be reckoned with and you have the best connections. Thank you for taking pity on two newbies and being so helpful! Christine at Perfectly Publishable, you are amazing. Your professional touches are just what we needed. We can't say thank you enough! Lori Wilt, the way you stepped in and helped us promote our book has been nothing short of a God-send. Thank you.

These acknowledgements and dedications wouldn't be complete without us thanking our amazing families for their support. We also thank God for blessing us with creative minds and the drive to follow our dreams.

And all of you, our wonderful readers, thank you. Thank you for your support and friendship. We love and appreciate y'all so much.